NORTH

of

HERE

OTHER TITLES BY LAUREL SAVILLE

Unraveling Anne

Henry and Rachel

NORTH

of

HERE

LAUREL SAVILLE

LAKE UNION PUBLISHING

Published by Lake Union Publishing, Seattle
www.apub.com

Amazon, the Amazon logo, and Lake Union Publishing are trademarks of Amazon.com, Inc., or its affiliates.

ISBN-13: 9781503951242 (hardcover)
ISBN-10: 1503951243 (hardcover)
ISBN-13: 9781503949980 (paperback)
ISBN-10: 1503949982 (paperback)

Cover design by Shasti O'Leary-Soudant / SOS CREATIVE LLC

Printed in the United States of America

First edition

MIRANDA AND DIX

As Miranda moved through the house, putting away a load of laundry, picking up the glass her mother left in the living room the previous night, straightening the magazines on the coffee table, removing a few dead flowers from a vase, she found herself glancing out of each window, her view of him coming and going, her perspective on him a bit different from each vantage point. He was like a man inside a kaleidoscope to her, fractured bits and pieces coming together and moving apart and then coming together again in a slightly different form.

There he was again, hoisting an ax overhead, then crashing it down on a bucked-up piece of wood with a force so fluid, so skillful, the log seemed to split willingly, happily, obediently.

Then he was on his back in the gravel driveway, his body half buried underneath the tractor her father kept for other men to use, his long, lanky legs sticking out as if they were another part of the machine itself.

Later he was up on a ladder, reattaching something to the ridge of the barn, something that had been making a gentle flapping noise in the night. It was a sound that drove her mother crazy, but which Miranda knew she'd miss once it was gone because otherwise the nights were filled with a quiet so deep, so pervasive, she sometimes felt compelled to walk out into it, to see if there was substance or feeling in it, as if it were a dark lake in which she might be contented to drown.

She paused by a window that framed his figure on the ladder. She counted the rungs partially obscured by his body. One, two, three, four for his legs alone. His stiff Carhartts—for that's what they called them up here, not just canvas pants; no, they were a particular type of work pants that deserved the respect of a proper name—gave shape and form to his legs, which accounted for so much of his height. His hair, obviously long not by decision but by simple inattention, sprang out from under the ball cap that shaded his eyes, already framed by wrinkles earned by years of working outdoors, even though she knew he was just thirty. She wasn't sure how she knew that. Something she had overheard. Her father pressing him about his future plans or something. A challenge Dix would have dealt with as he did most things, with the hint of a smile, a few words, and then the taking up of a tool of some sort.

"Marshall!"

Her father's voice leaped in the open window, making Miranda flinch. The man on the ladder kept at his methodical, precise hammering.

"Marshall!"

This time a bark. Then her father came into view, reading glasses in one hand, drinking glass in the other. Miranda reflexively checked the clock. 4:19. Part of the unwritten WASP rulebook: Drinking could commence anytime after four. Any earlier would be unseemly. Unless, of course, there was a barbecue. Then beer could be consumed with impunity. After all, that didn't really count as alcohol. Especially if it came from a can. Her father was wearing boat shoes and wide wale corduroys, a button-down shirt, sleeves rolled up. He was dark blue on the bottom, light pink on top, a green web belt delineating his middle. He was broad in the shoulders and all the way down to his hips. A square block of a man. Not fat, expansive. Steely wisps of hair rose and fell on the top of his mottled head in the early summer breeze as he strode across the lawn that the man he was yelling at had mown for him earlier in the day. He reached the foot of the ladder and tried again.

"Marshall!"

When even this did not elicit a response, Miranda's father banged the flat of his hand against the ladder. The hammering stopped and the shaggy head up by the roof inclined itself downward.

He'll never learn, Miranda thought.

Everyone called the man on the ladder Dix. Like the term *Carhartt,* the single name and the way it was said had certain implications for the people in the valley. No further explanation was required. Dix. Local, competent, someone to be trusted. Someone who could take care of himself. And you. Without making you feel as if you could not take care of yourself. If only you had more time and less money. Which of course was untrue, but never stated. Because then men like Miranda's father would try to prove you wrong. Which would lead to you being out of work and to men like Miranda's father being injured.

Miranda could not hear what was being said but saw her father pull a piece of paper out of his pocket. A list of chores. Their first few weeks here in the summer always went like this, with Dix pointing out all the things he had done over the winter to keep the place sound and her father pointing out all the projects he wanted done to make the place look better. The items on their lists never overlapped. As a teenager, Miranda had never noticed any of the various and divergent things that either man cared about. She had barely even noticed either of the men. But things were different now.

She had been out of college for a year. She hadn't figured out what to do next. A degree in anthropology with a minor in environmental studies didn't give her a lot of options. Her summers had been spent with volunteer work, AmeriCorps, Habitat for Humanity, a trip overseas to interview African women about their children, how they cared for them. The only thing she felt she knew was that she wanted to help people. She wanted to help heal what was wrong in the world. But the problems seemed so big and overwhelming. So numerous and various. She had spent months removing invasive species from a conservation area and replanting native shrubs and trees. But instead of feeling accomplishment, she had felt discouraged by the knowledge that just over the next ridge, the invasives were setting seeds and sending out runners, ready to recolonize any bare patch of land. The low-income house she had helped build was given to one family on a list of dozens who were waiting and waiting. Miranda had a difficult time focusing on what had been done instead of what there was left to do. She found herself sighing a lot. Her mother hated the sound of her sighing.

Her parents had suggested she take the past year off. As if there were something concrete in front of her that she was merely postponing instead of just the empty road of an unknown future. They had told her to enjoy herself, suggested she have some fun. She wasn't sure what that meant. She knew they thought she took herself—not the world around her, but herself—far too seriously.

The unstated subtext within this mild criticism was that she should be more like her brother. At least, that's what the implication used to be, until his insistence on fun had resulted in such devastating consequences. Miranda had spent some time visiting a few friends, looking for ideas and inspiration as much as company, but most of them had jobs—many in the firms of their fathers or their fathers' friends or their friends' fathers. They were busy and she was not. She had volunteered at a women's correctional facility and had been dumbfounded by the inmates' casual acceptance of a stint in jail as a kind of respite from the outside world and by their sense of entitlement about all they were "due" while incarcerated. She thought they'd be appreciative of her sincere desire to help them improve themselves and had been shocked to find they were neither thankful nor interested. She looked on job-listing websites that catered to nonprofits, sent out a few résumés, but never heard back from anyone. Time drifted by—an endless, uninterrupted horizon of loosely structured days.

In the middle of winter, Miranda had moved from her family's two-hundred-year-old, white-clad-and-green-shuttered Colonial on a leafy cul-de-sac in Connecticut where she had grown up to their imposing, traditionally built log "cabin" in the densely wooded mountains of the Adirondacks. She had wanted to get away from watching her mother fill her days with small tasks that accomplished little more than taking up time, like getting a mani-pedi, fluffing the pillows on the sofa in the rarely used living room, flipping through a catalog and folding down corners on pages with pictures of things she'd never get around to ordering, writing thank-you notes to hostesses of cocktail parties and fund-raisers, or standing over the gardener as he kneeled in the dirt, pointing out weeds that needed to be plucked or flowers that needed to be dead-headed.

Once in the mountains, Miranda put in a few hours here and there trading work for next season's produce at a mostly fallow, local, small-scale, organic farm and tutored middle-school kids at the library two afternoons a week. She found herself astonished at their ignorance not just of grammar but of things like checkbooks, mangoes, the location or relevance of a particular European city. So many of these children lived in a moment-by-moment world with little room for what Miranda was slowly starting to realize were luxuries: curiosity, ambition, and reflection. They came in with dirt-caked fingernails, amid a swirl of acrid barn smells, reminding her of the Pigpen character in the *Peanuts* comic. They casually spiced their everyday speech with the harsh pepper of swear words. They saw their time with her as a kind of punishment, not an opportunity for enrichment. Which is exactly how their teachers had presented it to them—remediation for poor performance. In between, when the weather was decent—which it rarely was, being more commonly either too cold and too snowy, or, later in the year, too buggy and too hot—she took long hikes through the thick woods, enjoying the comfort of being hemmed in on all sides by dense walls of trees.

During the colder months, Miranda's parents came up only one weekend a month. If that. Miranda soaked up the solitude in between their visits and avoided making any decisions.

Then her brother died.

Her mother couldn't stand to be in the house that reminded her so much of him, so she fled Connecticut for the mountains. In the aftermath of his death and her mother's arrival, Miranda gave up the tutoring. She had meant to go back to it, but she began to watch her mother instead. How long she lingered in the big bed made of logs, to match the house. How long she sat in the birch rocker, staring out the window, her hands trembling ever so slightly in her lap. How little tonic she mixed with her gin when she poured it into the glass with the moose printed on the side.

Then her father started coming around more often and staying longer. When spring hit with the full force of greenery pushing its way past the thick curtain of winter's gray, instead of his usual Friday-evening-to-Monday-morning, every-other-weekend routine, he'd increasingly show up Thursday afternoons and extend his trip until Tuesday mornings. He, like Miranda, watched his wife as if she were a pot set carefully on a low simmer but that still might miraculously boil over. Miranda never saw her father cry about her brother. The only thing that changed about him was a certain lopsided set to his mouth. It had always been there but was made more manifest by grief, like a listing building that had sunk deeper in the muck.

In the weeks following her brother's death, when the air was thick with sadness and empty of activity, Miranda watched how her parents drifted by each other without touching or making eye contact, two magnets with opposite polarities. She noticed the liver spots and raised veins on her father's hands as he poured coffee or shook out a paper. The way his eyebrows furrowed together when he looked at his wife, and the way his cheeks sagged when he looked at a photo of his son. She noticed the way her father waddled, stiff in the hips, swinging rather than lifting his legs. She found herself tallying how many times her father cleared his throat with irritation as her mother poured herself another drink.

When Dix was around, he provided a welcome counterpoint to these observations. She'd note the way he strode forward, bent slightly in the middle as if he were trying to get ahead of himself, how many apples he ate along with his sandwich and thermos of coffee in the middle of the day. She'd register whether he'd washed his pants or whether they still held yesterday's dirt. She began to admire the calluses and scarred digits on his hands when he passed her a cardboard box with a dozen irregular, multicolored eggs from his neighbor's chickens.

The days after her brother's death were unusually hot and dry for early summer. Her parents, who were often testy with each other in even the best of circumstances, were as brittle and crackling as the weather itself. Normally, her brother would be here to break the tension between them with a joke, a tease, or simply with the sudden influx of coltish energy that surrounded him when he arrived for the weekend with several of his pals, cases of beer, and a cooler of lobsters. His friends were a blur of boat shoes and web belts, button-downs and mops of hair. More than boys, but not quite men. They all introduced themselves with hearty handshakes and names that could be first or last—Tucker, Parker, Brooks, Hunter, Graham—but these were rarely used. Nicknames coded to some past misadventure that hinted of involvement with a drink or a girl were more common. These friends of her brother were three, four, and five years older—an eternity to a teenage girl—and seemed to regard her with friendly indulgence, as if she were the family dog. They'd whack a birdie or croquet ball her way as an invitation, a challenge, really, to come join them at whatever lawn game they were up to.

As Miranda recalled these weekends of summers past, so different from those of the summer in front of her, one of her brother's friends came to her memory whole and apart, not merely another in the usual crowd of tumbling testosterone. The man's name was David. She remembered because it was so plain. That particular weekend, she was still in the shower when everyone arrived, so had missed the introductions. She had put on freshly laundered jeans and a floral shirt made of corduroy to offset its otherwise obvious femininity. She had given her lashes a light coating of mascara. She had not wanted to appear as if she had dressed for them or because of them but wanted deeply, almost desperately, to be thought well of, to be seen as pretty by her brother's friends and by her brother himself, thinking, hoping this would make him proud of her. She had so little else to offer. She had wandered out to the deck, wanting to enter the party already in progress on the lawn from an oblique angle where she could observe them for a few moments without being seen herself. She was surprised to find a young man already there, sitting on the deck she had expected to be unoccupied. The sight of him startled her, and she bumped into a lounge chair. He looked up and stared at her, unblinking. She stared back, questioning. He gestured with his chin toward his foot, encased in a soft cast she hadn't noticed.

"Small mishap," he said, grinning. "Took a bit of a spill on my way out of one of Gotham's finest drinking establishments."

Miranda had just read *The Great Gatsby* in school. The young man seemed to have stepped right from the pages of that book.

"My name is David. You must be Miranda, the adorable younger sister I've heard so much about. Come," he said, indicating a chair. "Keep me company and help me cheer on the competitors at their noble sport."

She sat where he had pointed. David offered a comical and inflated commentary on their badminton game. He seemed to be entertaining himself as much as, if not more than, her. Miranda had little experience with flirtation. She was caught off guard, and then simply caught, by his manner. Most of his jokes were lost on her, but that didn't seem to matter. He occasionally broke through the performance with a direct question. What was her favorite subject? Earth science. How old was she? Seventeen. Was she planning on college? A consenting shrug. Did she have a boyfriend? An embarrassed head shake. Did she still play with dolls? She froze on this question, suspecting she was being made fun of. He stared at her, his icy blue eyes challenging her to parry. She remained silent, and a shout from the players over a bold return on a smash eventually drew his unsettling gaze back to the game.

Looking back, it seemed he was there only that one time. When Miranda met him again years later, it took her some time to place him, to remember the few moments they'd had in the summer sunshine on her parents' deck. Of course by then he had a different name, a different look, and she encountered him in a totally different context. It would take another teasing remark, that same smirking expression in his eyes, the similar seductive pull, for her to remember where she'd first met him.

Her brother took David away from her that day, off to town for a beer and game of pool. Her brother. Steven Prescott Steward. She always thought of him that way because that was how he introduced himself. But call me Scott, he'd always add, one hand out to shake, the other reaching forward to clap a shoulder, his teeth brilliant white against his peach lips, his eyes the shade of a spring sky, his hair streaked with the tones of honey and maple syrup, a heavy fringe forever falling in his face, enough years older than she was—a senior when she was a freshman, always on his way out when she was on her way in—to be tantalizingly close to a peer, but still just beyond reach. He was one who pumped hands, slapped men on the back, threw children in the air, squeezed women to his side, and told old ladies they were beautiful. He was a fantasy son come true. It wasn't until after his sudden death, the image of that mangled car branded in her mind, that Miranda wondered if he really was a perfect son, or if it had all been role-play; and if so, had he ever tired of the performance? She began to suspect that following the script of how to be the ideal firstborn probably made everything easier, because then you knew just what to do to be what others wanted you to be. And you were always guaranteed a positive reaction.

Miranda felt as if she was the complete opposite, fumbling through life, all thumbs. She was no good at cocktail-party chatter. She was best in a sincere one-on-one conversation. Or even better, alone with a book in her hand or surrounded by woods. She had none of Scott's charms, nor did she wish for them. But she missed them. She missed how his presence in a room allowed her to relax because he took up all the air, space, attention. He was supposed to be here, still. He was supposed to be getting ready to return to law school. He was supposed to lend balance: a father and a mother, a boy and a girl. Without him, everything was off-kilter. Without his smooth and slick veneer, the raw rot at the core of their family was exposed.

She went back to her job at the CSA farm as an excuse to get away from the desiccated feeling in the house. There were more hours to be had there in the summer season. Kneeling on the dry ground, clods of dirt in her hands and under her fingernails, salty sweat dripping from her brow, helped settle something in her that fluttered constantly and erratically when she was at home. Her father started to go golfing again, but Miranda suspected he really just went and hung out at the club. Her mother did not start anything again.

Miranda watched what was and was not happening around her and wondered what to do. She tried looking forward but saw only a dark road with a sharp curve that obscured her view of what might be coming. So she waited for something to happen, for something to break the spell they were all under.

Her mother said, "Leave it alone, Chick."

Her father said, "Shut up, Bunny."

Her mother set her teeth, silently pushed herself up from the sofa, and moved to the sideboard. She began very methodically using silver tongs to pick up ice cubes from the matching silver bucket and drop them into her just-emptied glass. How many times had Miranda's mother told her the bucket and tongs had been passed down from her grandmother? She didn't even bother with that, anymore. Miranda winced at each small clatter of ice against glass. Her father was at the back door, sitting on a bench, jamming his feet into tall Bean boots. Strong gusts of wind rattled the windows. Rain pelted down so hard it sounded like someone was throwing fistfuls of rocks at the house.

"Let Dix take care of it tomorrow, Chick," her mother said as she unscrewed the cap from the gin bottle.

"Shut up, Bunny," her father repeated. "Have another drink and let me take care of this."

He snugged his laces tight with a savage tug.

Miranda stood at the kitchen counter, her heart squirreling around in her chest, looking from one parent to the other. Her father stood, shoved his arms through the sleeves of his jacket, and clamped a hat on his head. He yanked the door open. Rain blew in. Miranda watched the drops sparkle as the lamplight touched them for a moment before they were absorbed into the worn area of wood by the back door.

Dix was going to fix that spot, she thought.

He was coming by next week to revarnish the mudroom floor. Then the drops would just sit there, waiting to evaporate or be wiped way.

The door slammed. It was late August. Heat, humidity, and thunderstorms had filled the month. Her mother opened a bottle of tonic water. It hissed in the quiet her father had left behind. The two women looked at each other, and her mother nodded, once, silently agreeing to an unspoken solution. The usual solution. The only solution. Miranda stepped to the phone and tapped in the numbers. It always took him a long, reluctant time to answer.

"'Lo," he said.

"Hi. It's Miranda. Sorry to call in the storm. It's late, I know. Such a crazy storm," she chattered nervously. "There's a tree out there, the big one by the garage, making a bad sound. I don't know, some kind of a groan, and Dad's gone out to give it a look. Afraid it's going to come down on the roof, damage something."

"If it comes down, it comes down," Dix said, his voice a low, comforting rumble. "Not much he can do about it right now. Nothing I can do about it, either. "

"Other than talk some sense into him," Miranda said. "Mother's afraid he'll get hurt."

Dix didn't respond.

"You know how he is, Dix," Miranda said quietly.

"I was on my way out anyway," Dix replied.

Miranda doubted this was true but appreciated the lie.

"Gotta go check on the Rawlings' place. I'll swing by."

"Thank you, Dix. Thank you so much."

Miranda and her mother sat side by side on the sofa, in silence, listening to the storm. It sounded like a madman trying to break into the house. Her mother sipped. Miranda fidgeted, picking at a hangnail. She imagined her father glaring at the offending tree, as if his stare alone could bring it into compliance. She hoped he'd just gone out to the workshop. He had a lounge chair out there. A few books and magazines. A bottle of bourbon. Sometimes he used the excuse of some sort of an outdoors project to get out of the house and went there instead. Miranda was afraid to go look, to check up on him. That would make him mad. So she and her mother waited for Dix to come and fix things. That was what he did. That was what they, and many others, counted on him for.

The gusts and slaps of wind were punctuated by cracks of thunder and flashes of lightning. The distance between light and sound shortened. Miranda counted the seconds. She got to three and then, thankfully, the interval began to lengthen again. There was a lull in the nerve-racking noise. Miranda held her breath. A new sound began. A low moan at first, it rose into a violent crescendo of pops and tears, which ended with a shuddering crash that shook the ground beneath the house. This was followed by a vacuum of silence. The sounds of the storm filtered in again, much more distant, the gaps between thunder and lightning greater and greater as the chaos moved away.

Miranda and her mother stared straight ahead and waited. Before long, there was the crunch of truck tires on gravel. They relaxed. Soon enough, they knew the door would open and the men would come in, stamping off the rain and discussing the next day's projects. Which would now include cutting up the fallen tree or branch or whatever it was that had broken free. Her father would insist Dix stay for a cup of coffee. Dix would politely decline, saying he had to get over to some other house, some other project, some other problem. But his presence, however brief, would restore her father's mood; he was not fond of the company of women.

They both counted the minutes. In fewer than expected, the door swung open, banging rudely against the wall. Stamp, stamp. Two boots. No voices. Miranda stood. Dix strode into the room and met her eyes.

"Call 911," he said.

It seemed that Dix never left after that day. Of course he had, Miranda knew it, looking back over the year that followed her father's sudden and instant death as he'd stood, looking up, blinded by sheets of rain, deafened by thunder, into an ancient tree full of invisible interior decay that allowed a waterlogged branch to split from the trunk and fall onto his head. Dix had other clients, other homes, that needed attending. He went home to shower, to eat. When the season came, he went hunting. But he found some reason to show up at least a few times a week. Mow the lawn. Put equipment away for the fall. Repair a stuck door. Take down the window screens. Miranda frequently offered him coffee. As her father would have done. He always demurred. Then, once, he accepted. They sat at the kitchen table together and said nothing. There was no tension or discomfort in the silence. When his cup was empty, he stood, squeezed her shoulder, and let himself out.

Miranda's mother's depression thickened into a cloak she pulled tighter and tighter around herself. Miranda found herself spending a large part of every day urging her mother to eat, to get outdoors, to call a friend. Eventually she even had to urge her to brush her teeth, take a shower, get out of bed. Her mother resisted with almost unyielding stubbornness. Sometimes she sighed. She often wept. For several months after her husband's death, she'd rouse herself once in a while, take two hours to shower, dress, dry her hair, carefully apply lipstick, and drive off to replenish her stock of gin. That errand took her a while. Sometimes hours. As she came back into the house one day, carrying a bag with two half-gallons of cheap gin instead of her usual top-shelf brand, Miranda asked her where she'd gone. Her mother had shrugged, grunted out the phrase, "For a drive." Miranda suspected she had started going several towns away, maybe as far as Plattsburgh, to buy booze. She probably didn't want anyone in town to know how much she drank. In spite of everything, she was still trying to keep up appearances. But as the snows came on in earnest and driving got hazardous, Miranda's mother dropped that pretense. The bags she carried into the house, bottles clinking against one another, bore the name of the nearest liquor store. Eventually, she didn't even bother going out at all. She began working her way through everything else in the well-stocked liquor cabinet. Then she went through the cases of wine in the cellar. Then the cases of beer. Her husband's stash in the shop. When all that was gone, she stopped drinking altogether. That was when Miranda got really worried.

Miranda had nothing to do with her own worry, sadness, and discomfort. It hung around her like a smell she could not locate or disperse. She did the small tasks of life—making coffee and toast, doing a load of laundry, washing a few dishes, sweeping the floor. She wandered slowly from room to room, only to find herself sitting on the sofa, staring out the window, not knowing how or when the scene outside had moved from the brilliant sunshine of the day to the inky darkness of night. When she heard her mother rouse herself from bed to use the toilet, she was always startled, forgetting that she was not alone. The days shortened. The gloom of winter outdoors matched the dark mood inside.

Miranda stared out the windows and found herself wanting to trudge through the snow, even if only on some fabricated errand to the barn, just to get away from the oppressive atmosphere of the house. But it was bitter out there. The deep cold in those mountains was the sort that immediately announced its ability to kill you. No matter how Miranda layered herself in scarves and hats, gloves and coats, which collected in the mudroom, the air seared her cheeks and assaulted her nose. The evergreens that rimmed the property and staggered up the steep hillsides all around—the trees she had always loved—began to resemble sinister beings to her, their feathery branches waving in the wind like malevolent arms trying to reach out and grab her. Miranda gave up on her attempted forays and stayed indoors, sipping cup after cup of tea and staring out at the endlessly swirling storms of white flakes and the mounds of snow that Dix piled high when he plowed the almost-never-used driveway. She spent hours in her brother's room, fingering the clothes that still hung in his closet, slowly turning the pages of his high school yearbooks and photo albums, drowning herself in deep pools of the past. She carried one of her father's pipes in her pocket, pulling it out from time to time and inhaling the fading aroma. When she ate, she consoled herself with chicken noodle soup, grilled cheese sandwiches, and chocolate pudding. The foods of her childhood.

Dix's arrivals and departures were the only break in the spell of her dazed mood, the only reminder that there was a world beyond the thick walls of logs that surrounded her. Seeing his truck come up the drive, spraying snow in front of it, seeing him make purposeful movements around the house as he beat back the accumulations of winter gave her a vague sort of hope. Then suddenly the snows stopped and were replaced by mud and muck and dark puddles. There was nothing more to plow. It was just wet and cold, the threat of winter still in the air. The lonely month of March passed. Then April, with its teasingly warm days and cautiously cool nights.

May arrived and, with it, the sound of truck tires on the gravel again. He was back. She watched as he dropped the tailgate and came around to the front of the house with a flat of annuals balanced on one arm and a bag of soil clenched in the other fist. This was once a task her mother had loved. The visit to the local nursery, where she'd wander among the bright flowers under the first hint of warm sun moderated by a still-cool breeze. Then back home, where she'd sift through the airy, salt-and-pepper potting soil, tuck in the plant pods, step back and admire how the pink, purple, and yellow blooms filling the various planters around the house stood out against the ruddy logs.

For the first time, Dix was doing what was not his to do.

Seeing Dix on his knees in front of the green planters with black dirt and bright annuals arrayed around him broke something loose in Miranda. She stood and shook herself as if she were a wet dog. She went into the bathroom, splashed water on her face, slapped color into her cheeks, and dragged a brush through her hair. She thought of her father and brother, and for the first time, instead of a blurry sadness, she was filled with the clarity of anger. She saw their deaths not as tragedies but as foolishness. Both killed in stupid, preventable, ego-fueled accidents of their own making. They hadn't been taken from her and her mother; they'd abandoned her and her mother. Dix had not. Miranda pulled on a pair of jeans and cinched them over her diminished frame. She went outdoors into the tentative sunshine of spring, knelt beside Dix, and wordlessly got to work. He smiled and made room for her at his side.

In the following weeks, the energy that had been dormant in Miranda all winter came forth like a bright yellow daffodil from a bulb buried for months in the frozen ground. She found a bucket, filled it with soapy water, and began wiping down surfaces around the house.

She stripped the beds, working around her mother when she would not rise, simply pushing her from side to side as she freed the sheets, leaving her sprawled across the bare mattress. She washed windows, threw out rancid food, got her hair trimmed, plucked her eyebrows, and asked Dix to make her a few raised beds where she could grow vegetables. Her head cleared. Her frame filled out. The house sparkled.

Then, one day, the phone rang. A voice full of cigarettes, whiskey, and the past said her name.

"Miranda, it's Richard Stone."

She recalled wispy hair, pouchy cheeks, chino pants with boats embroidered on them, and alcohol-scented breath. Her father's friend from Yale. A lawyer. The man who took care of her father's affairs. She fought the urge to call him Mr. Stone, as she had when she was a child. She'd seen him briefly at her father's funeral. She recalled how he had gripped her small hand in both of his large ones as he wept.

"Hello, Richard," Miranda said, her voice a question.

"I've been trying to reach your mother," he said, his voice also a question.

"Yes, she's been . . ." Miranda searched for the right word. "Struggling."

"Miranda, there are things that need attending to. Things we should discuss. I'm sorry to have to bring these things up with you, but, well, there is no one else."

Miranda had never thought about her isolation this way before. But it was true. There was no one else. Both sets of grandparents were long dead. Her father was an only child. Her mother had a brother somewhere in the Midwest, but their only contact was the annual exchange of a formal, impersonal holiday card, invariably signed without even a brief note or family update. Miranda had never wondered at the strangeness of this ritual, had never thought to ask herself why they bothered. She had accepted, unquestioningly, the notion that some things, many things, were just the way things were done. At least among a certain class of people. Her mother's class of people.

"Yes," she acknowledged to the man on the phone. "I suppose that's true."

"I think it best that we do this in person," Richard Stone said, his voice suffused with warning.

An image of the Connecticut house swam in front of Miranda's eyes. Like a picture on one of those Christmas cards, it appeared to her as perfect, stately, and fake. She'd thought to keep the cleaning lady on, asking her to keep an eye on the house. Other than that, she'd forgotten about the place. She realized that she had been quietly, blindly, hoping her mother would rouse herself and return to the house. To life. Soon. Any day. Hoped even that somehow, on the sly, when Miranda was out in the garden or at the store, her mother had gotten to her desk, made a few calls, taken care of some correspondence. Acted like an adult. A parent.

Miranda now knew, with painful clarity, that she couldn't wait any longer. For her mother. Or for her own life. The situation was ridiculous and untenable. She made a date to meet the lawyer in New York. She pushed it out two weeks. She didn't know why. She just knew she wasn't ready. She felt sure there was something, perhaps many things, she should do to prepare. She started to speak to her mother about it several times. But faced with her mother's blank stare, the words Miranda might have said became marbles in her mouth. Finally she did the only thing she knew how to do when confronted by a problem she didn't understand. The only thing that had ever resulted in a solution that worked. She called Dix.

"I have to go back home, Dix," she said. "I mean, back to Connecticut. I have to check up on things. Talk to my dad's lawyer. Take care of . . . of . . . of stuff."

"Yes," he said. "I imagine a lot of that has piled up down there by now."

His voice, his steadiness, was such a comfort to her. Something she felt she could actually lean into.

"I don't know how long it will all take. I'm worried about . . ."

He broke in, relieving her of the need to finish. "I understand," he said. "I'll come by the house every few days. I'll check up on your mom."

"Oh, Dix," she breathed, relief that he had answered the question she didn't even know how to ask flooding her voice. "Thank you so much."

Miranda started crying then. She didn't know how to end the tears or the conversation, but Dix didn't seem to mind. He just stayed on the phone with her. She listened to his strong, steady breaths in her ear and slowed her own breathing until it matched his. Only then did she feel ready to face what was ahead.

Miranda had referred to the extensively restored and renovated Colonial home set on three acres of manicured grounds as "home" for all of her life. Yet, when she pulled into the curved driveway lined with mature maple trees and stopped in front of the white clapboard edifice on a hot summer afternoon, it felt like she was visiting someplace she hardly knew. As if she were once again being dragged along to another cocktail party with her parents. She sat in her car and counted the months since she'd been there. It had been more than a year. Her twenty-third birthday had come and gone in that time, unnoticed, unmarked by herself or her mother. As she gazed out her windshield at the imposing structure in front of her, she realized that she'd expected it to look haunted and decayed, with broken windows and pieces of siding hanging off. Like she felt. But it looked only a little empty, a bit tired. Also like she felt. The housekeeper and groundskeeper had done their jobs. She wondered if, like her, they'd half expected her father to magically return, roaring orders. Or at least for her mother to appear, issuing directions.

Miranda got out of the car. The door clicked into the silence of the neighborhood. She unlocked the house, smelled potpourri and clean-ing fluids. But even those false, sweet scents couldn't completely cover the musty note of disuse. The housekeeper was thorough. The house was immaculate. All the food had been discarded other than spices and canned goods. The beds made taut. The bathrooms tidy and imper-sonal. No dust anywhere. The curtains hung stiffly. It felt like a hotel.

Miranda wandered through the still house and into her bedroom. One stuffed animal, a bear her father had given her, sat propped up against the pillows on her bed. Her bookshelf held a toy horse, a few yearbooks, a couple of photo albums, and some books typical of teen-age girls—Sylvia Plath, *Lady Chatterley's Lover*, Virginia Woolf, her first sociology textbook. A few out-of-date clothes hung in the closet. She hadn't realized just how long she'd been away. Exeter Academy and then Vassar College. Summer programs and internships. The house in the mountains. Her childhood mementoes had been long packed away and stored in the attic. Most of her clothes were at the log home. She was not much of a collector. A few pieces of inexpensive jewelry were all she typically brought back from her travels. Everything she saw in her bedroom belonged to a much younger version of herself, a self she could barely remember.

She walked down the hall to her brother's room. It held even fewer remnants of him. A lacrosse stick from his years at Lawrenceville. A few sport jackets. Some Harvard memorabilia. A similar collection of yearbooks, high school novels, and a few CDs.

Was this all she had to show for her life so far? Was this all he had left to show for his?

Their bedrooms were like movie sets, she thought. His death had been like a movie set, too. The car a shiny silver Audi, a gift from her parents for getting into NYU Law, twisted and entangled with the shiny silver guardrail on the Merritt Parkway. Scott and his friend Danny twisted and entangled with the car, inside. Both drunk from partying too hard in Danny's family's private box at a Bruce Springsteen concert in Madison Square Garden. Both dead instantly, no one else involved—at least there was that to be thankful for. Maybe Scott had swerved to avoid a deer or raccoon or something. Or maybe he had simply fallen asleep at the wheel. Maybe they were just blasting the stereo too loud, still rocking out to The Boss. But Scott had been driving, he had been drinking, and he had killed himself and one of his best friends. Danny's parents had been friends, too. Or at least they had mingled in the same circle. That didn't last. Thankfully, as she'd heard her father say under his breath a few times, they didn't bring a lawsuit. They were a big family of Irish Catholics, her mother had pointed out several times, as if this explained something. They had a couple of other sons, she'd said, as if this lessened their suffering. Or at least made it less intense than hers.

Which maybe it did, Miranda thought. *If only I had another brother. Or even better, a sister. A couple of sisters. Someone, anyone, to share this with. Someone to help me with all of this. Someone I didn't have to pay to help me.*

Miranda turned away from her brother's room and stood in the doorway of her parents' bedroom. It was a space she was, always had been, reluctant to enter. Not sacred so much as taboo. The expansive bed with the matching bedside tables. Her mother's robe hanging off the back of the door to the bathroom. She'd spent a lot of nights alone here, Miranda knew. Miranda's father tended to stay at their apartment in the city during the week. He'd come back for a kid's event or adult party, but otherwise complained about the commute, an hour on the best of days, often longer. He would tell his wife to come in for dinner and a show instead. Miranda recalled her mother getting dressed up from time to time for a trip to New York, and the relative novelty of getting to eat dinner in front of the TV with her brother and the babysitter. Then, several years ago, her father gave up the apartment. Looking back, it seemed sudden. For the first time Miranda wondered if her father had lovers—a mistress, a girlfriend. If that's why her mother drank. Or if her father took a mistress because her mother drank. Or if they both just used each other's bad habits as excuses to indulge their own.

These kinds of thoughts, she noted, were new to her. Seeing her parents not just as parents but as people with complex, messy, inexplicable lives of their own, full of errors of judgment and will. She sighed. She realized her childhood was not only over but nowhere to be found.

She moved to the study, a tidy space downstairs between the kitchen and living room, decorated in the masculine tropes of dark woods and leather furniture. There she found several boxes of mail. Mazie, the housekeeper, had kept up with the household bills. That had always been part of her job. She'd also often gone grocery shopping, picked up the dry cleaning, done other small errands. Miranda didn't know why her mother never seemed to have time for these little chores herself, but years ago there had been committees and boards and volunteer work. Then it became habit. Why take on what Mazie did so well?

Mazie had organized everything into four boxes. Magazines in one. *Town and Country. Vanity Fair.* The *New Yorker.* The magazines were her mother's. Things she flipped through over her first drink of the day and then fanned out on the coffee table. Miranda picked up one, ran her fingers over the cool, slick pages, and let it slip from her hand. These would all stop soon enough because there was no one to renew the subscriptions. Another box held letters, mostly the square envelopes of cards and personal notes. She plucked a few at random and slid her finger under the seals on the thick flaps of expensive paper. A condolence card from someone whose name she didn't recognize. An invitation to a garden club event. A request for a donation for a new arts center. A solicitation from a cable company. A notice from the school board. A form letter from a doctor's office notifying her mother that it was time to schedule a mammogram. Miranda wondered why Mazie hadn't forwarded all this stuff to them. Her mother must have told her not to, that she'd be down to take care of it. Mazie had learned over the years to do as she was told, to not ask twice. She would not have taken initiative on her own. There was also a box of junk mail. Of course, Mazie wouldn't be so presumptuous as to throw even this stuff away.

The last box was larger, full of oversize manila envelopes. In the upper left corner, each envelope had a unique combination of three or four last names printed in some conservative typeface above a New York, New York, return address. Miranda's throat tightened around the question of what those dozen envelopes might portend. Finance. Legal stuff. Business. Her father's business. Things that needed attending to. The stuff Richard Stone was referring to. Things far beyond her interest or experience. She'd need her mother's help understanding it all. She was afraid she wouldn't get it. She knew she wouldn't get it. Even the earlier version of her mother would probably not have been able to help her. She had managed their domestic and social lives. Miranda's father managed the rest. As Miranda had heard him say at many cocktail parties as he clapped his wife a little too hard on the back, sloshing her drink, barking out a practiced guffaw, oblivious to her wince: "I make the money. She spends it."

It was late afternoon. Long shadows came in the kitchen windows. Miranda's stomach growled. She was suddenly overpowered with the desire to leave. To flee. This was no longer home. Maybe it never had been. She had planned to stay at least two weeks, to head into the city to see Richard Stone at his offices. Maybe make a few such trips. Maybe even look up an old friend. Instead, she left the magazines and junk behind, put the other two boxes into the backseat of her car, turned the hallway light on, locked the door, and drove back the way she'd come.

Darkness was descending as she left the highway more than three hours later and headed onto the twisted two-lane road. It was a darkness made of more than just the absence of the sun; it seemed to emanate from the surroundings themselves. The densely branched, heavily needled evergreens, steep slides of charcoal rocks, inky shadows, and tree-clad mountainsides came right down to the edges of the pavement. A vague glow illuminated a closed gas station with rusted pumps. She caught a glimpse of a heathered sign for an attraction that had gone out of business decades ago. A tar-shingled house with dimly lit windows had a thin stream of smoke coming from the chimney, even though it was summer. A spotlight showed a yard filled with junk advertised as antiques. A farmhouse-turned-bar had a few people smoking on the porch, the embers of their cigarettes heating up to red as they inhaled. Miranda knew there was a frame out in front of that place, filled with firewood. She'd seen a man there, bent over a pile of bucked-up logs alongside the building, slowly splitting the wood into manageable sizes. Manageable for tourists. Three dollars a bundle. A fistful of small bills for a long day's hard work. Miranda wondered why her father ever thought to buy a house here.

"Just four hours from home. Easy highway drive. Stunning mountains. Great hiking. Wonderful fly-fishing. Good deer hunting," she'd overheard him tell people.

Only he didn't do those things. Had never done those things. He had hiking boots that he wore around the property and into town, not into the mountains. Took a fly-fishing lesson once, then left the rod in the garage. They ate venison and trout, but these were bought from others, not acquired by his own hook or gun. He had camping gear, which her brother had used a few times with friends, but just on their own property, down by the river so they could smoke pot away from her parents. Alcohol was approved; marijuana was not. As far as Miranda could tell, mostly what her father had done when he was in the mountains was golf, read the paper, work at spreadsheets on his computer, and sip bourbon. The same things he did back in Connecticut.

As she drove, Miranda remembered coming to these mountains for the first time when she was in grade school. Back then it was for summer camp, her memories a blur of other children, endless mostly competitive activities, and the overarching wish that she could just be alone. When she tried, wandering away from the hoots and howls, bathing suits and archery, campfires and cabins, into the cool woods nearby, she got in trouble and a counselor would yank her back with a firm grip on her arm as if she was about to fall off the edge of something. Then, after she stopped going to camp, sometime in her middle school years, her father bought land and began the protracted process of building their own "cabin." The project ballooned into a three-thousand-square-foot, traditionally built log home with every modern convenience and significant nods to the great camp style. Real logs. Hand hewn. Notched. Chinked with old-fashioned oakum.

Her father got no pleasure from the process, she recalled, continually damning the architect, the contractor, the site, the blackflies and mosquitoes, the schedule, the delays, the very land itself. But he stubbornly persevered, apparently determined to win against them all. Then, finally, it was done, their grand camp miraculously rising in stately fashion from two acres of cleared land hemmed in by the forest, with a garage and workshop adjacent and a path to a traditional lean-to down by the stream.

For Miranda, the house was a kind of living, intimidating thing. She would place her palms on the logs, feel the warmth emanating from them, and imagine they had somehow stored the heat of the men's hands who had worked on them. She appreciated that the home was handmade, but she did not like its imposition into a landscape she was falling in love with. She began to spend hours hiking whatever sloppy, root-riddled path she could find. She never tired of the deep comfort of the black mud and dark trees. She loved the subtle surprise of a clump of bright mushrooms, a patch of dogtooth violets, the scramble of a deer fleeing, the grock of a raven, or the wail of a distant loon. She marveled at the quantity of hidden ponds and quiet streams, the salamanders and frogs that reemerged from the silent winter into the damp spring, the gift of an unexpected vantage point at the crest of a tree-crowded hillside suddenly unveiling a new vista. She even admired the blackflies because, she reasoned, they kept other people away. Well, they kept summer people, tourists, people from the tristate area away. The locals and year-round residents just swatted at the bugs and waited for the clouds of irritants to dissipate.

Even though she had been on these roads many times, Miranda drove carefully. She knew the dangers: sharp turns, leaping deer, drunk teenagers. She came into the small town nearest what she now thought of as her true home. Passed the Fishing Hole diner. The golf course and club. The outfitter and guide shop. The craft store that sold delicate watercolor landscapes set in rugged frames and rough furniture finely crafted from birch trees. The gift shop that sold linens and trinkets printed and shaped in the guise of moose and bears but made in China. She found her own driveway in the deepening dark and listened as her tires rolled up the half mile of gravel—a driveway that would be impossible without Dix, or someone like him, to handle the winter plowing and the spring repair. It occurred to Miranda that the driveway had been the most important part of the property to her father. He valued it because it created privacy. Privacy from exactly what he never said. Privacy was simply a thing in and of itself to be coveted. Like success.

Whatever that was, she thought, with a bitterness that was new to her.

The house glowed gently from a lamp lit somewhere deep within the rooms. She grabbed the boxes of mail, closed the car door with her hip, and tiptoed to the back door—she didn't want to wake her mother. She fumbled with the door, her arms overladen, and managed to squeeze in without dropping anything. She flinched as the screen door banged behind her. She slipped into the kitchen, where the light above the stove was on—as she'd left it. She set the boxes on the counter and listened. Nothing. She figured her mother must be asleep. Miranda went back to the car two more times to get her things, each time quieter and more careful than the last. She listened again. Still silent. She flicked on a light and filled a kettle with water. She returned to the counter. Something different, out of place, in the living room beyond caught her eye. What she saw took her breath away.

There was a person on the sofa, at once strange and familiar. Her expression was blank and ghostly; her hair was sticking out in all directions like an unpruned shrub; her cheeks were hollow in the dim light. She was wearing a faded robe that hung limply from wasted shoulders, slippers broken down in the heels on her feet. It was her mother. Yes, just her mother. Terrifying in that moment of unrecognition.

My God, Miranda thought. *Has it gotten this bad? Has she gotten this bad?*

"Mummy?" she said, trying to keep the fear from her voice. "Are you OK?"

Her mother's eyes shifted in Miranda's direction but remained empty. Slowly, dim recognition began to fill them. Her mouth turned up in an expression that might be a smile but appeared more as a grimace.

"Miranda," she whispered. As if the young woman in front of her were an alien or a marvel, not simply her daughter.

"Mummy, I was in Connecticut. I was at our house. Remember? Remember our house in Connecticut?"

Her mother nodded, slowly, almost imperceptibly.

"I brought back some things. Some important things."

Her mother's head continued to bob. Encouraged, Miranda brought a stack of letters and cards over to the sofa and set them in her lap.

"Look. Cards and letters from friends, Mummy. From your friends. Remember all the friends you used to have? Down in Connecticut?"

Her mother looked from the mail to her daughter, her expression blank.

"Mum, there's a bunch of other stuff here, too. Stuff we need to go through. Stuff we need to figure out. Financial stuff. Legal stuff. I'm going to need your help."

Miranda was desperate to connect with the woman at her side. She scanned her face for comprehension of any kind. Her mother stared at Miranda for a few moments, then stood and allowed the envelopes to fall from her lap like dead leaves from a tree. She clutched her robe under her chin with one hand and shuffled away, back to her bedroom, without a word. The kettle screamed from the stove.

The next morning, Miranda called Richard Stone and left a noncommittal message with his secretary, saying she wouldn't be able to make their meeting, but she'd be in touch. Then she began to open the large manila envelopes she'd left on the table the previous night, prying open the flaps cautiously, as if there was danger inside. She found statements with long columns of numbers, various investment accounts, letters from lawyers about actions and cases and depositions, requests for signatures, direction, next steps. She had no idea what to do with any of it, about any of it. She tried calling a few of the numbers on the cover letters. She got voice mailboxes. She stumbled out some staccato story about trying to take care of her deceased father's affairs. She finally reached a woman who told her they could only speak to the surviving spouse. Miranda looked out the window as the woman spoke and saw the surviving spouse in question. In a sudden frenzy of ill-advised activity, still in her bathrobe, holding a mug of coffee in one hand and a pruning shears in the other, the surviving spouse was ineffectively hacking at a shrub, her face screwed up in frustration, tears glistening on her cheeks. Miranda hung up the phone and started crying, too.

Then, into the frame of Miranda's watery vision walked Dix. He took the tool from her mother's hand and gently, carefully, showed her what branches to clip. Miranda watched as he pulled at a twig, pointed to the exact spot to snip, used a finger to demonstrate the angle, and then handed the clippers back to her mother. She seemed to be paying close attention, but the burst of effort must have worn her out. She snipped a few twigs, then dropped the shears where she stood and wandered away. Dix followed her, keeping a respectful and watchful distance. Like a well-trained sheepdog, he herded her gently toward the house, through the front door, and in the direction of the hallway that led to her room.

As he returned, Miranda cleared her throat. Dix came and stood over her shoulder. He made a quick survey of the piles of paperwork spread across the dining room table. Miranda wiped her cheeks with the back of her hand.

"Looks like you need a lawyer," he said.

"It seems I already have several of them," Miranda replied.

"Well, your father had quite a few, that's clear," Dix said. "But I think you need a lawyer to help you with all his lawyers."

Miranda nodded. Dix took up a pen, wrote a name and number on the back of one of the manila envelopes, and then, before leaving her side, let his large, gnarled hand rest over her small, delicate one for just a moment. The feeling—a rough, comforting towel against shower-softened skin—lingered long after he was gone.

Warren Bessette had always lived within, and rarely ventured out of, the heavily treed and sparsely inhabited six-million-acre Adirondack Park, defined by a light-blue outline on maps of New York State. He'd been to Vermont several times. Blurry events to him now—a relative of his wife's got married, a client wanted to show him some land he intended to purchase, a friend took him fishing. There were also the few days he and Celine had spent wandering around Burlington's bricked-in streets and driving the nearby back roads between desultory and inconclusive appointments with specialists. All these exposures left a bad taste in his mouth that he couldn't quite source but suspected had something to do with the stiff superiority so many of the residents of Vermont expressed toward their own state and its inhabitants. He had also spent time in Albany, the capital, first for law school and then much later, when the doctors there finally diagnosed and tried to treat Celine's rare cancer. He liked Albany—its unapologetic scruffiness, architectural mash-ups, tree-and-row-house-lined neighborhoods nestled up against one another, and the rowdy political chatter of its pubs and coffee shops. He even forgave the place his memories of watching his wife waste away at the hospital because he remembered how carefully and gracefully they had cared for her.

He and Celine were both forty-one when she died, and he had never remarried. He had no desire for companionship other than hers. For a while, various women tried chatting him up at the post office or grocery store, a few came into the office to discuss legal matters and quickly tried to turn the conversation to more personal, social topics, but the grave coolness of his demeanor gave them no toeholds for intimate exchanges. He had grown up with Celine. They didn't become a couple until their last year of high school, even though her long black hair; pale, freckled skin; and thin red lips that readily broke into a sly smile had always been an indelible presence a couple of rows back in algebra class, a few tables over in the cafeteria, or passing him as she strolled up the aisle in the school bus, her stop two before his. Her slender silhouette stayed by his side as they graduated high school, went through college together at Plattsburgh State, and lived for the years of law school on a busy Albany street, in a tiny apartment that smelled of garlic and basil from the Italian restaurant below. They then returned to the mountains, where he opened his practice. Her lithesome grace was so soothing to him, even in memory, that all the doors to intimacy she had nudged open were available only to her. He had enough closeness with her—he felt the residues would last him the rest of his life.

Warren's law practice focused on the passages of life. Home purchases, divorces, custody issues, wills. It often troubled him that his services were called upon for far too many unhappy occasions. Somehow he had not considered that when he decided to become a "country lawyer," as the slicker, noisier, more ambitious classmates in law school had called his sort of practice in light mockery. Most of his clients were locals, and he was sometimes paid for his services with a hind of venison or a season of snowplowing, remuneration he valued as much if not more than money, as his needs for cash were few. Sometimes summer people came to him for work on real estate transactions or for local grievances with a neighbor, and on occasion, for work on things they didn't want their lawyer back home to know about.

Charles "Chick" Steward had requested Warren's services a few times. First, to buy his land, then to try to buy some adjacent land a neighbor didn't want to sell, and then to get advice on a dispute with the Adirondack Park Agency. They got along fine during the first transaction, but Chick had not liked the answers Warren had given him on the other matters. He wanted Warren to be more aggressive, to represent him more forcefully, to find a way around laws that were intended to protect the park and respect its "Forever Wild" statute. Chick Steward had always expressed disgust with what he called "that damn blue line." Warren did not share Chick's opinions. He was respectful and reverent toward what he felt was an admirable, flexible, progressive, and unique process of managing and preserving public lands while allowing for a range of private enterprise and ownership. He once pointed out that they were fortunate to live in the largest park, protected area, and National Historic Landmark in the continental United States. When Chick responded with a dismissive wave of his hand, Warren stopped engaging him in any sort of personal or professional conversation. After that, the two men were cordial when they ran into each other but didn't strain for politeness. This was no burden, as they didn't travel in the same circles. Warren didn't golf, preferring a glass of warm milk with a splash of maple syrup and a convoluted mystery or dense history book to the greens. Warren also had no interest in representing men who were accustomed to using money to get their way. He had heard rumors of Chick's shady real estate transactions, his unethical and risky business dealings. Most people had. It was a small valley. Gossip traveled on every gust of wind. Most people also just shrugged it off. They'd come to understand that was the way things were done "downstate," and in "the city." Warren had met Bunny Steward once or twice. She was a slender, brittle woman who seemed to be under an invisible and yet constant strain. He couldn't imagine it was easy being Chick Steward's wife.

When Dix brought Miranda in to see him, Warren was surprised to find that Chick and Bunny had produced such a lovely, diffident daughter. Miranda seemed so callow, as if she'd never heard a harsh word or suffered a disappointment, even though he knew the last year or so had been full of tragedy. Her hair was honey colored, her eyes faded-denim blue, her build slight but not insubstantial. She was almost beautiful—all that kept her from it was a sense that her features didn't seem quite reconciled—and she had a gossamer quality to her demeanor that was striking. Warren recognized her as someone who immediately, unknowingly, unintentionally, tapped into a man's protective instinct.

He was aware that her father had died when a tree branch had fallen on him in a storm. He could imagine the bluster and bravado that had sent the man on his stupid, ignorant errand to stand under and look up into a groaning, decayed tree while the wind and rain whipped around him. He had heard of the brother's death in a car accident almost a year before the father's. He imagined the mother and daughter must be fumbling in grief. There was a washed-out, worn-thin, translucent quality to the young woman's skin.

After Dix led Miranda into the office, he started to leave. Miranda looked up at him in alarm, so he sat down next to her instead. Warren waited for them to explain their business. Miranda remained quiet. Dix looked at the empty, expectant face beside him and then took up a thread of brief, simple introductions. Miranda's father had left a lot of what appeared to be unfinished business behind, Dix explained. There were no other relatives. Miranda's mother was . . . he paused before settling on the phrase "not well." Miranda could use some help sorting through things.

"Dix says my father respected you," Miranda told Warren in an unsteady voice. "I am a bit overwhelmed. I don't know what exactly I'm supposed to do."

If her father had respected him, this was news to Warren. Not that it mattered. Miranda was just being polite. She had those highly honed, formally polished, and deeply ingrained manners that kept other people at a slightly uncomfortable distance. Warren knew she was not aware of this; it was just something natural to her sort of people. He also had had enough dealings with her father to suspect the man had left quite a mess behind, and that Miranda might need much more help than she could possibly imagine. He was glad she had a friend in Dix. There was also no way this inexperienced, indulged young woman could suspect what an asset Dix could be to her. Warren knew that he was one of a very few people—or perhaps the only person—who knew just how many subtle, sophisticated, and largely hidden skills and assets Dix possessed.

Miranda placed a box of envelopes on Warren's desk. He skimmed the return addresses. All New York City. All a lot of trouble.

"I will be happy to help you," Warren told Miranda in a voice he had long practice at keeping neutral. "I appreciate your trust."

Miranda nodded.

"This may take a bit of time," he said.

It was a warning to her, but a subtle one. He didn't want to scare her. Just prepare her. He met Dix's eyes briefly. In that moment, he knew that Dix suspected just what a large and twisted mess they had to untangle.

Marshall Dixon Macomb was, by nature and experience, a solitary man. He was an only child of parents who were comfortable enough with each other's company that they rarely sought any other. They transferred this serene self-containment to him, and he grew up with trees and hillsides, dogs and horses as his companions. Having nature and animals as his ever-present, endlessly interesting, and yet soothingly neutral best friends left him regularly unsure how best to relate to humans. He found people were forever explaining in excruciating and, to him, irrelevant detail what they had done or said or what someone else had done or said. He could never quite understand what all this retelling of things already done and over was all about. Sometimes people would try and plaster some sort of larger meaning onto their stories, but it all seemed like so much regurgitation and a waste of time to him.

This urge to tell, or "share," as it was commonly called, often layered with griping about things beyond one's control, was an impulse he lacked. The sun always came up, but sometimes it was obscured by clouds; a grand tree fell down in a storm and became a nurse log for other trees; a deer died in a hard winter, giving lots of other small animals an important source of protein; cute baby birds also sometimes pushed their siblings out of the nest; foxes hunted both vermin and new chicks; mothers took care of their young simply because hormones compelled them to. He had little philosophy in him other than a dogged desire to do quality work, to be kind and helpful when called upon, to leave things better than he found them, even if that meant simply picking up a discarded can or candy wrapper on a trail. He never considered how rare and decent these qualities made him.

But others did. Some, anyway. Dix was a man who was either relied upon by people who valued what he offered or underestimated by those who did not. There were a few people, like Miranda's father, who did both. Dix didn't mind. He liked caring for things, even if those things belonged to other people. Even if those other people didn't properly appreciate the things he was caring for.

Dix had always seen Miranda as someone who belonged to other people. She was from away. She was a little sister in a wealthy family. Dix was dimly aware that her parents, like most summer people, assumed a man like Dix made his way through the world with his hands and had little in his head and less in his pockets. They assumed he was uneducated, unambitious, quaint, like an old farmhouse they admired as they drove by but would never want to live in. Ambition was a quality they defined in a very specific way, having to do with the quantity of financial resources available, square footage of houses owned, brand names of automobiles driven, stature of job titles held. These people never considered that ambition could be directed toward a quieter life, a life that took far less of a toll on a person and a place.

Dix first met Miranda when she was in high school and he was back home after college and a couple of years working for a land stewardship organization in Albany. He had started mowing lawns and doing odd jobs while he looked for work in the field. Little conservation work was forthcoming, but the handyman, carpentry, and caretaking work was plentiful—the summer people responded favorably to Dix's reliability, rugged looks that seemed to fit the mountain environment, and ability to speak in accurate grammar and to produce professional paperwork such as estimates and invoices. They never considered where he might have gotten these skills, just saw them as a welcome fluke, like an errant balmy and sun-filled day in the middle of March.

To Dix, Miranda was a distant thing. It was not so much that he found her unattainable as that he had no desire for her. She was quite simply something not useful in his world. Like her father's Mercedes-Benz, she was from and for a different sort of place. He noticed how she grew into her looks, how her various features caught up with one another and created a pleasant tableau. Like so many of these summer people, she was attractive but indistinct, well bred but lacking a certain crossbred vigor. Which could also be said of her demeanor.

However, during the last two years, he'd begun to notice a change emerge in Miranda. It wasn't just maturation. A serious and assessing expression had entered her face. The automatic adoration that had been there when she looked at her father evaporated. The automatic annoyance that had been in there when she looked at her mother also disappeared. She occasionally came over to Dix while he worked and asked if she could watch while he cut down a dead tree, sharpened the mower blades, or prepped the beds with compost and peat moss for her mother. She took an interest in the garden and asked Dix's advice on what varieties of tomatoes he'd suggest she get at the nursery. Sometimes she brought him a cup of coffee if he was there in the morning, a glass of lemonade if it was the afternoon. She started working at the local CSA farm and got sunburned cheeks and shoulders, bug-bit arms, chapped lips, and blonde streaks in her hair. She wore these rougher edges well.

After her brother was killed, he noticed that she became more solemn; after her father died, she seemed bruised in some deeper part of herself. Dix watched her search unsuccessfully for the source of her pain, a dog after a distant scent. When her mother started to decay, he watched Miranda become fragile, a thing in danger of being broken. Given as he was to fixing things, he had an almost continual impulse to step in to her, take her in hand, patch her up. He resisted, reminding himself that emotions were not things his toolbox could address. So he fixed things around her instead. He wanted to give her fewer things to worry about, even though he knew she would not notice, much less fret about, the things his eye leaped to: a loose gutter, a dull blade, a leaning trellis.

Then she started asking for his help. Not just with the things around the house, but with her mother, with her finances. He knew she had nowhere else to turn, but still he was touched that she reached out to him. He was surprised by the raw tenderness beneath her needs, that the things she asked for required neither his hands nor his tools but his common sense, cool head, and stalwart ways. Slowly, called upon in this way, his heart, which had been for him a mere functional thing, began to make its other uses known.

Miranda tried to find some way to talk to her mother about their "affairs." She had almost given up on conversation with her entirely but began slowly wading back in, first with just small observations about the weather, a bird she saw, what she was harvesting at the CSA farm. Her mother began to respond with a mumble or a nod. A small phrase, "That's nice, dear," or "Good for you." One sunny morning, Miranda tried to lure her mother to sit with her at the kitchen table.

"I got some of those peach preserves you love, Mum. Come," Miranda said, patting the cushion on a chair. "Come sit and have breakfast with me."

Her mother tottered over, wary, sensing a trap. She rubbed her forehead, raked her fingers through her hair. Miranda remembered that for most of her life, her mother wouldn't even leave her bedroom until her hair, makeup, and clothing had been carefully arranged. Everything always subtle, tasteful, nothing to attract attention, tightly controlled. Miranda watched as the disheveled woman at the table took a sip of coffee, carefully chewed a piece of toast. Spread the rest with jam and took another bite. This was progress. Her mother swallowed with effort. Washed everything down with more coffee. Miranda poured her some juice. She drank it down. She looked somewhat restored. Her eyes were less cloudy.

"Mum," Miranda said tentatively, "we have some things we need to discuss. We have some things we need to take care of."

Her mother looked up at her, wide-eyed and childlike.

At least it was eye contact, Miranda thought.

"We've got to think about the Connecticut house," Miranda said slowly, enunciating each word as if her mother were hard of hearing instead of broken down. "I don't know if you want to keep it."

She looked significantly at her mother; the other woman's expression did not change.

"We've got to figure out Dad's affairs. We've got to sort out our finances."

She waited a beat, wondering if any of this was getting through. There was no way to know, but it had to be done, so she plunged ahead.

"A whole bunch of correspondence came in. Stuff from lawyers, finance people. Things I can't figure out. I took it all to a lawyer in town. I'm trying to get us some help."

At this, her mother nodded. Almost imperceptible, just a dip with her chin. But enough to give Miranda courage to continue.

"I can't do this by myself, Mummy. I need you. It's just the two of us now. We have to figure this out. We have to work together."

Light began to emerge from her mother's eyes. Her hand was steadier on her coffee cup. She chewed with more vigor. She nodded steadily.

"Mum? Mummy, do you understand what I'm talking about? We have . . . there's a lot to do. Things I don't understand. Grown-up things."

Her voice cracked and her eyes dampened. Her mother stared at her and her expression began to come to life. Mild concern crossed her face. She reached out and touched Miranda's cheek with her fingertips.

"You're right," she said, her voice hoarse and distant from disuse. "I need to snap out of it."

Miranda was startled by this sudden expression of feeling and conviction. She watched in disbelief as her mother stood, tried to square her shoulders, took a step backward to steady herself, and left the room. Miranda listened to doors and drawers opening and closing behind her mother's bedroom door, water running in the shower and sink. There was something deeply unsettling about the sudden flurry of overly ambitious activity. Miranda didn't know what to hope for, what to look out for. So she waited to see what would happen. Her mother emerged an hour later, dressed, showered. Her shirt had been buttoned out of alignment, her lipstick was smeared a bit over one lip, and the gray roots of her black hair showed through from a severe part, but it was pulled back neatly into a barrette. She had a small purse on her forearm.

"Where are the car keys?" she asked.

"What are you doing?" Miranda asked.

"Going into town to get my hair done."

"They're in the drawer in the kitchen, right where you always put them," Miranda answered automatically.

She watched her mother fumble through the wrong drawer for a moment and began to regret what she had said. "Wait. Mom. Wait. Let me take you. Let me drive."

"No." Her mother's voice was firm. She found the keys and held them up, triumphant, a clownlike smile spreading across her face. "I've been a burden long enough."

Then she was gone, leaving Miranda frozen in place. When Bunny hadn't returned by lunch, Miranda told herself that this was all wonderful: a big, new step that her mother had taken back toward the world. When two o'clock came and went, Miranda tried imagining where she might have gone, then remembered the clothing store that she used to love. Maybe she'd gone shopping there or had stopped at the garden center, she told herself. By three o'clock, Miranda's self-imposed fake cheer began to wear thin. She called her mother's cell phone and was deeply discouraged when she heard it ring in the bedroom. By four o'clock, Miranda was in her own car, driving to the beauty salon. They told her her mother had come in; gotten a cut, color, manicure, and pedicure; but left by around midday. They said she was cheerful and that they were so glad to see her; it had been so long. Miranda left and drove around town, looking for her mother's dark-blue Volvo. It was nowhere to be found. She drove up to the club and circled the parking lot, but her mother's car was not there, either. Miranda parked, and racked her brain. Did her mother go up to Plattsburgh for some reason? Could she have taken herself to a restaurant? Was there a friend she might have gone to visit? There had been one friend. There had been a book group. Her mother had gone a few times. Then she gave up because she said they were choosing books that were more Oprah than *New Yorker*. Miranda had a general idea where the hostess's house was. For lack of a better idea, she went in that direction.

She drove for an hour down a series of roads that went from pavement to dirt and then back to pavement again. She knew the house was in a remote location. Her mother had commented about how hard it was to find. But everything around here was hard to find. Once Miranda found herself back on the paved road, she realized she'd simply driven in a large circle. She plunged forward again, this time looking for the small bed-and-breakfast her mother had mentioned as a marker. The light was fading. But finally Miranda saw the small ROOMS FOR RENT sign in front of a multicolored house. She turned there. The pavement had seen better days. She dodged potholes that the flat, early-evening light made difficult to see. Then her car bumped across something more substantial in the road. Miranda pulled over to see what she'd crossed or maybe hit. She got out of the car and saw she had merely driven over some long-unused railroad tracks embedded in the pitted and patched asphalt. Just railroad tracks, she told herself. Nothing sinister. Nothing damaged.

She wasn't ready to get back in the car. She felt stiff and sore from sitting so long with so much tension in her body. She pressed her hands into her lower back and stretched. She took a few deep breaths to calm herself and looked around, hoping the fresh scent of the woods would soothe her. The lowering sun glinted off something across the road. Miranda tilted her head back and forth, trying to discern what it was.

A car. A car partially jammed into the weeds and shrubbery, as if someone had stopped unexpectedly. She couldn't tell if the car was simply parked or had hit a tree—the vegetation was too dense. Maybe a deer had jumped out in front of it. Or the driver had found something he or she had been looking for. Miranda took baby steps across the street. She might be the only person passing by this spot for hours. Even days. She had to see if someone needed help.

She peered around the trampled scrub. A dark-blue car. A Volvo. The light was low enough that it was difficult to see in the windows. Miranda stepped closer. There was no one in the driver's seat. Or the passenger seat. Or the backseat. But there was a purse there, in the footwell on the passenger side. Not hidden. Easy for someone to steal. It took her a moment. The dark, smooth leather. The two rounded handles. The large gold clasp. They'd bought it together. Her mother had thought the hardware made it too showy. Miranda had encouraged her. Told her she deserved something nice like this, especially since she'd use it every day. Miranda had called it classy. Her mother had laughed. It had all happened such a long time ago. She couldn't remember the last time she'd heard her mother laugh. Bunny had been happy making that purchase. Once she was back home, she'd carefully filled the "pocketbook," as she called it, with her red lipstick and travel tissues in one pocket, a comb and small bottles of hairspray and lotion in the other, a wallet and notebook in the main compartment. Which stood open now, a gaping mouth hollering at Miranda from inside the empty car.

What the hell? Miranda thought.

She started yelling, trying not to panic, calling her mother over and over, switching to "Mum," and then "Barbara," and then "Bunny," and then back again. The silent woods seemed to mock her hysteria. She ran up and down the road, but there were no houses or driveways, no trails into the woods. Just the empty, weed-infested railroad bed.

Wait. Not so empty. There was someone lying on the tracks.

Miranda ran, tripping and stumbling over railroad ties that were skewed by decades of disuse and severe weather. She found her mother prone, arms folded neatly across her chest, newly manicured fingernails interlaced, her freshly darkened and blown-dry hair spread out over the blackened gravel around her head, with grass sticking up around her legs and feet. She did not open her eyes as her daughter approached.

"Mummy?"

Miranda slowed and kneeled in the dirt. Her mother was breathing. She seemed asleep. Deeply, quietly asleep.

Was this her plan? Miranda's thoughts raced. *When she left this morning, was this what she had wanted to do—get primped for death? Or was this a spontaneous action, an inspiration that had come upon her when she bumped over the tracks?*

Miranda had been so hopeful about her mother's focus that morning, hoped it was the result of a desire to return to life, not leave it. Yet here she was, waiting for a train on tracks that hadn't seen one in thirty years.

"Mum? Please. Mummy. Please don't leave me. Not like this. Not this way," Miranda pleaded.

And then she thought, *How sad. So sad. She can't even get her own suicide right.*

Miranda stroked her mother's cheek. Her eyes opened. Her expression was full of dull surprise, like she'd forgotten where she was and how she'd gotten there. She slowly sat up and rubbed her forehead with the back of her fist. In Miranda's tear-filled vision, her mother looked far away and watery, as if she were at the bottom of a pool. Miranda blinked to clear her eyes. It didn't help. There was something wrong with her mother's face. One side of her mouth drooped and her cheek sagged, a wet tea bag. Her mother tried to speak, but only one half of her mouth moved. A thread of drool slid out of the slack side. Her brow furrowed in confusion. She tried to speak again, but her lips would not cooperate in the forming of words.

A stroke, Miranda thought. *She's had a stroke. And neither that train that isn't coming nor the stroke will take her where she wants to go. Which is away from here, away from all this agonizing pain.*

Miranda screamed for help, but her voice merely drifted upward into the darkening sky. She left her mother, crawled and stumbled, got to her car, found her phone, thanked the God she didn't believe in that she had the merest of signals, and called for an ambulance. Then she went back to the tracks and held her mother, a rag doll, in her arms.

The next time Warren saw Miranda, she was much changed. She came in alone this time—there were delicate matters to be discussed—and he saw how the skin around her eyes was darker and their rims were reddened, her hair was twisted into a sloppy knot, her lips were tight and her gaze was clouded. Her eyes skittered over things, and she looked everywhere except at him. She slumped into a chair. Warren cleared his throat. He wished Dix was there, privacy be damned. He wondered if he should postpone. But there was nothing to be gained by delay. The quicker he got to the issues, the quicker they could be resolved. Things had been pushed off far too long as it was.

"I'm afraid I don't have good news for you, Miranda," Warren said.

He tended toward bluntness. This preamble was the best he could do to ease her into what he had to say. He watched as she tried to arrange her features into a simulacrum of strength. He was relieved that she didn't start to cry. He was no good with women and tears. He glanced at a box of tissues on his credenza. Miranda finally looked directly at him. He took this as evidence that he could continue.

"How much do you know about your father's financial and professional affairs?" he asked.

He was stalling a bit. For her and himself. He knew the answer would be zero. Miranda bit her lip, shrugged, and shook her head.

She's too young, too protected, for all this, Warren thought. *Her mother should be here.*

"Normally, I'd want to talk to your mother about all this," he said.

Miranda bit down harder on her lip, but this didn't stop the tears. He reached for the tissues and set them down in front of her. She tore one free and daubed at her eyes.

"Sorry," she said, referring not to his question but to her own crying. "It's been . . . um, she's . . . well, she's in the hospital." Miranda choked a little on a sob. "She's had a stroke. We thought, well, I thought, that she was depressed. She's been so depressed. For so long." Miranda tore the tissue into little pieces and crumpled them into a damp ball. "The doctors think she might have had a few strokes. A bunch of small ones. Kind of masked by her depression. And her drinking. Which of course contributed. And then this last one. Bigger. Impossible not to notice this time."

Warren had to look away. He was not turning from her tears, but to calm his own anger. Anger at the unfairness of life, the inability of money and class to protect someone from hurt, the many evils brought on by alcohol, the selfishness and arrogance of men like Miranda's father. Miranda began talking again, her words tumbling along.

"I should have known. I didn't know. I should have known. I should have done more. Gotten help. Should have made her get help. Right after my brother died. Shouldn't have waited so long. Shouldn't have waited until I found her on the train tracks. She's down in Albany. Have to wait and see what the doctor says. So far, he won't say much. Which makes me think it's bad. Real bad." She swallowed hard and wiped her cheeks. "So, no," she said, attempting to strengthen her voice. "We won't be able to get help from my mother. I'll need to deal with everything myself." Now she looked firmly at him, her eyes glistening. "I'm ready. I have to be," she said.

"Miranda, I am very sorry. You have had too much to deal with this past year or so. It doesn't seem fair."

Miranda shrugged again.

False bravado. As if there's any other kind, Warren thought.

"Sometimes, I'm afraid, life is like that," he continued. "One bad thing seems to lead to, to even cause, another bad thing."

Miranda looked away, out the window.

"I want you to know something right now and before we go on," Warren said. "I will help you. I will be here for you every step of the way."

Miranda nodded slowly, whispered, "Thank you," and started crying again, more quietly this time.

"Let me give you a minute," he said, standing up and stepping toward the door.

He left her alone so she had some space to collect herself, but also to ask his secretary to make a call for him. Miranda seemed more composed when he returned with a glass of water for her.

"OK," he said as he resettled himself behind his desk. "Let's get to work. Are you ready?"

Miranda took a deep breath, blew out her cheeks, and said she was.

"It all seems to have started," Warren began, "with the logs for your house."

Warren began telling her a long, convoluted story, which he had pieced together from documents Miranda had provided and conversations he'd initiated with various men around town. Warren had also had a long talk with Richard Stone over the phone one evening. Warren had noted the not-so-faint slur in the other man's voice, had heard the sound of ice cubes hitting a glass, had registered the unusual volubility as Stone warmed to the more sordid details of Chick Steward's story. So he was unsurprised that he received much more information than he would have expected to from a more discreet lawyer. Or one discussing the affairs of a living man. Or one who had not drunk quite so much.

Chick Steward had wanted a certain kind of look for his mountain home, and that took a certain kind of logs—the kind of logs that couldn't readily be bought around the Adirondacks anymore, the kind of logs that reputable contractors didn't have easy access to. He had found what he wanted in Canada and had them shipped down. He may not have been aware when he bought them, but the logs were far too good of a deal, Warren told Miranda, even though he suspected her father knew and enjoyed what he had done, putting one over on those who had tried to stand in his way.

Miranda frowned in confusion.

They'd been harvested illegally, Warren explained. People kept track of this sort of thing.

Then there was his contractor. He had done some things he shouldn't have. Maybe he did them on his own without telling Chick the ramifications, or maybe he did them at his client's direction. There was no way to know now. But the house was much bigger than had been officially permitted. The septic, well, and driveway were not to code. These things would be serious issues anywhere, but especially in the Adirondack Park. Somehow, all this illegal work had been signed off on by the building inspector. Hard to say whether he was dumb and lazy or had been paid off. Even if he hadn't noticed the violations, the neighbors had. Two had sued her father. One because the septic was leaching near his property; another because her father had dug out part of the stream to create that swimming hole and thereby disturbed prime fish habitat, and because an outbuilding her father had constructed was never permitted.

Meanwhile, the contractor had gone bankrupt and sued her father for incomplete payment. Chick had claimed shoddy workmanship. There was no way to know what really transpired between them. The contractor had since left the area. The building inspector who had signed off on the illegal work had retired on disability he claimed came from falling while on the job. People had seen him golfing. Not so disabled. The new inspector had been nosing around and didn't like what he was seeing. The former building inspector had had a large garage built but could not document paying for it. He had made other home improvements as well. The now-bankrupt contractor had done the work but never issued a bill. It was not clear who paid for it.

Warren paused in his story. Sighed. Then explained that there were suspicions Miranda's father had paid for the work at the inspector's home and rolled the charges into the work for their log home, in order to get the inspector to ignore the obvious infringements. Then he may have stiffed the contractor, who couldn't exactly sue for payment of illegal work.

Miranda listened in silence. In shock, Warren feared.

Finally she whispered, "I had no idea."

"Of course not," Warren said.

"But it sort of makes sense," she said. "I mean, I remember some things."

Warren decided now was not the time to discuss the risky investments Chick Steward had made, many of which had gone sour, or the soon-to-come cutoff of his employer-supplied health insurance.

"What do I do?" Miranda whispered.

"What do we do," Warren said. "I am here to help you. You will not, cannot, do this alone."

Had he lived, Warren explained, her father might have been able to extricate himself from the mess, but without him here, it seemed the best strategy was to help her find a way to cut the losses, staunch the bleeding, and try to get a fresh start and a clean slate. An unburdened future, Warren added.

Miranda blinked at him and nodded.

Warren told her what he needed right away was for her to get some paperwork signed by her mother—perhaps by her mother's doctors, if she was truly incapacitated—so Miranda could get power of attorney. Then he could act on her behalf. Something he assured her he wouldn't do without consulting her. He promised complete transparency.

"For now," he said, sighing with relief at the sound of a door opening and closing in the outer office and the footfall of boots on the rug, "go home and get some rest."

"I feel a bit shaky," Miranda said.

"I can imagine," he said, taking her elbow. "I called Dix. He's here now. He'll take you home."

Miranda went home and sat alone in the house her father had built. Flashes of memory exploded around her. Her father complaining about the neighbors to her mother. Her mother begging him to not dig out the river. Her father screaming on the phone. Throwing tools at a pickup truck as it blew gravel out behind its back tires and raced down the drive. Whispered conversations with men who were not friends and who did not come indoors but stayed close to their vehicles in the driveway.

Miranda was fearful. She had no idea how she would sort through all of this. She was afraid of the financial reality that she might be facing. She'd always had an allowance. Her credit card was connected to her father's accounts. She'd never even balanced her checkbook. She always knew she'd have to face the fiscal facts of her own life someday, but that day had been so easy to keep pushing off. Yet, as sobering as this news was, she felt sure that Warren's solicitude as she sat in his office was a sign that he was doling out the bad news a bit at a time. She felt sure there was plenty more to come.

Which it did. She learned bit by bit of her father's financial misdeeds and the mess he left behind. She looked at the numbers Warren showed her—the amounts wasted and lost left her breathless and dizzy. She cried so much over the ensuing six months that she felt desiccated, like something left in the desert. But in between the tears, she made things happen. She did what needed to be done. Guided by Warren, aided by Dix, she rose to the demands life—and death—required of her. Her mother was not going to recover, the log home was not going to be brought up to code, she was not going to inherit enough money to keep them both comfortable for the rest of their lives, as they both had expected.

Barbara Steward was installed in a small assisted-living community. She had often talked of going to a retirement community in the past, on days that she found the management of two large homes overwhelming. She said she'd play bridge, learn to paint watercolors, and never have to cook again. Miranda had seen the "senior living" brochures her mother had once collected, their slick pages filled with photos of vibrant, lightly wrinkled, silver-haired and smiling people biking, painting, listening to a concert, driving a convertible. Bunny hadn't done any of those things when she was well and would certainly not be doing them in her "retirement." The only wish of hers that would come true was never having to cook again. Instead, she was fed soft foods in her room by a cast of laconic, leathery women because she refused to eat in the dining rooms with the other residents. One afternoon when Miranda was visiting her dazed, confused, and silent mother in her beige room in the one-story complex up near Plattsburgh, she watched as a brusque woman briskly and efficiently tightened the sheets and comforter of the bed without disturbing their occupant, wiped her mother's face, brushed her hair, and tidied the food tray, all in a few economical moves. Miranda found herself envying the other woman's uninflected competence.

Maybe, Miranda thought, *I could learn to be that good at something. Maybe I could get into some sort of helping profession.* Miranda looked at the woman's nametag. TIFFANY. *How incongruous,* she thought.

"Thank you, Tiffany," she said, "for all your help with my mother."

The other woman murmured something and shrugged.

"Do you mind if I ask how you got into this line of work?" Miranda persevered.

In a few staccato sentences, Tiffany told her she'd gotten training as a health-care aide after her abusive husband burned down their trailer, mistakenly thinking she and their three kids were in it. Miranda brought her fingers to her mouth. Fortunately, Tiffany explained, without emotion, she'd left just that morning and was holed up in a battered women's shelter with the kids. It was too bad that the dog, two cats, and a parakeet had died in the fire, she added, but thankfully the bastard shot himself in his truck in the driveway while the trailer burned.

"The one thing he did right in his whole life," Tiffany said as she grabbed a tray and left the room.

Miranda got a real estate agent and put the Connecticut house on the market. It sold quickly, above the asking price, but her father had taken out a large second mortgage on the place and invested the resulting proceeds poorly, so after the taxes and Realtor's fees, Miranda was left with a sum that seemed to be missing a couple of zeroes at the end of it. Between these funds, the proceeds from a life insurance policy, the much-reduced assets in her father's once-hefty investment portfolio, and his Social Security due to her mother, Miranda and Warren were able to pay off some back debts, settle a couple of lawsuits, provide her mother adequate care, and put $75,000 into an account for herself. She accurately saw this as a sum that would merely buy her a bit of time to get settled, and then provide a buffer as she found her way into some sort of a modest job and new life. When she tried to imagine what that new life might look like, she could conjure only the image of an empty blackboard, smudged with the recent erasure of whatever guidance might have recently been scribbled there. She told herself, and Warren told her, too, to just focus on the tasks at hand. The rest would sort itself out soon enough.

The log home seemed beyond salvage. The expenses to get it up to code would be too great. It could no longer be lived in, but it likely would not sell with all its encumbrances. There were plenty of other places in the area rich people could buy that were just as pretty and a lot less burdened. Fortunately, since a bank would never have loaned money for a property like that, her father had paid cash. It was debt free. Miranda could just walk away from it. Dix helped her close it up. He drained water lines, sold the mower, tractor, and her father's lightly used tools. They took a few truckloads of furniture, clothes, books, and other items to Goodwill. Anything of value went into a storage unit while Miranda "sorted herself out."

When the day came for the final walkthrough, Miranda watched Dix survey the grounds, check doors, locks, and faucets, sweep the garage and barn. She didn't cry. She had no tears left. She knew Dix was also watching her, careful and gentle with his gaze, and she felt swaddled by the snug pressure of his attention. She reached over and squeezed his arm. His limb felt to her like a young tree with the bark stripped off. She knew he was concerned for her. She didn't allow herself to take it too personally. She knew he always cared for things that were broken, and she accepted that she fell into this category.

"I'll be OK," she said, trying for a smile.

"Where will you live?" he asked.

"I'm renting a little place in town."

"The Lewises' house?"

"Yes."

She had gotten used to Dix knowing things. She had stopped wondering how he knew so much and yet told so little. They stood in the yard in the late-afternoon stillness. A raven croaked from somewhere overhead, a desolate sound that somehow became companionable when another answered. A chipmunk ran under the porch. Miranda noticed that light was low. The days were short. Summer had come and gone without her noticing. The leaves had bloomed with color, faded to brown, and fallen to the ground. Snowflakes blew through the air. She shivered. Dix removed his coat and placed it over her shoulders. She shrugged herself into it gratefully.

"It's like a graveyard," Miranda said.

"Yes," Dix answered. "A peaceful place full of memories."

"Funny, that's not how I think of a graveyard. More like a place filled with ghosts."

Dix nodded slowly.

"I got some good news from Warren," she said, scuffing a toe in the dirt.

Dix lifted his eyebrows in question.

"Looks like someone may be interested in buying. Warren wouldn't tell me much. Someone he knows personally. Someone who wants to remain anonymous. He said he thinks whoever it is just wants the land and doesn't care about living here or the problems with the house. Wants to protect the land. Keep it wild."

Dix nodded again, a little more slowly this time.

"Must be nice," Miranda said.

"What must be nice?" Dix asked.

"To be able to do something like that. To be able to be generous. To have that abundance and instead of holding on to it, to share it. Quietly. Without drawing attention."

"Well, maybe the new owner won't post the land and you can still visit," Dix said hopefully.

"No, too many bad memories," she said. "I have to move on and get my own life started. Time to smash the rearview mirror." Her mouth twisted a bit. "Besides, they'll have to post, Warren says. Liability issues. Can't have someone coming up here, breaking into the house, getting hurt and suing."

"You've had quite the legal education lately," Dix said.

"Yes." Miranda thought briefly of the legal education her brother was supposed to have had. She sighed. "This place has had enough lawsuits for several lifetimes."

They were quiet together for a few minutes. Then Dix rolled his shoulders back and crossed his arms. He cleared his throat and rubbed his forehead. Miranda glanced at him. He was not a man given to unnecessary movement.

"I thought the Lewis place wasn't available for a bit," he finally said. "All rented out with summer people who were keeping it through the holidays."

Miranda sighed. Was there anything of import to her life that this man did not know?

"That's true. I'm going to stay at a little hotel near Mum until it's ready. I'll be able to check in on her. Look for a job. Probably need to take some classes. Not much in the way of employment for someone with my skill set, such as it is." She shook her head. "Weeding and harvesting vegetables is not much to start a career with. Neither, apparently, is a liberal arts degree."

Dix repeated his forehead rubbing.

"I . . ."

Miranda had never heard him hesitate, stammer like that. He seemed to be someone who did not speak unless he knew what was going to come out of his mouth. She looked up at him. He was a full head and shoulder taller than she. He stared resolutely ahead and she stared at the stubble, a cut cornfield, on the hard line of his jaw.

"I have a guest cabin," he finally said, his voice so quiet she had to lean toward him to hear.

She waited for more. She had no idea why he was telling her this. He was not someone who spoke about himself or his own life very much. At all, really. He didn't continue.

"Yes?" Miranda finally said. "A guest cabin?"

"It's a small outbuilding," he repeated, starting over, trying again. "At my house. Off in a corner of the property. Private. Tucked beneath some big pines."

Miranda felt her pulse tick up with hope. She was ready to be rescued. She imagined a cabin from a child's picture book with lightly frayed, white-lace curtains and a musty handmade quilt on a big bed built from logs. A rocker made from birch twigs on the porch and an old traveling chest that had been turned into a coffee table in the center of the room. But she pushed the image away and tamped her hopes down. A cabin like that, where she could find refuge under Dix's watchful eye? It was too good to be true, too much to wish for.

"It's not been used in years," he continued. "Not since my mother died and some of her people came up to pay respects."

Her people. Miranda had never heard relatives referred to in that way. She'd also never heard Dix refer to his family at all. She wasn't even clear where he lived. She'd asked him once. He'd responded with a single word: "North." Then, when she had looked at him quizzically, had elaborated. "North of here." Then, had nodded to indicate direction. As if this narrowed down the possible location of his home in any meaningful way. His voice moved on now, slowly, carefully, like someone crossing a river by stepping from stone to slippery stone.

"She used to invite people up from time to time. My mother, that is. She was from Virginia. My dad was from here. She had it fixed up real nice. No kitchen. But you—her people, friends, I mean, visitors—they used the main house for that."

Miranda clung to the word *you*. She felt the soft warmth of his kindness spread through her insides, push gently into the coldness that had settled there. She was afraid to speak, almost to breathe, in fear of breaking the fragile thing hope had become to her.

"I don't cook much," he said, sidling slightly off topic.

Miranda thought of the sandwiches he ate, which were made on big slabs of bread she knew he had kneaded and baked himself. The stews and soups that filled his thermos she knew were made from vegetables he grew, venison he hunted. She couldn't recall where she got this information from, but she knew it was true.

"It's empty," he said. "The cabin. Might as well put it to use."

Miranda stood, desire and fear competing for her attention. She took a breath.

"Dix, are you offering me . . . like, is this, would you be open to renting . . . ?" Miranda murmured, allowing herself to be enchanted with the image of a mossy cabin in the woods, a place for gnomes and fairies—or orphaned children.

"Oh, you don't need to pay me," Dix interjected, his voice suddenly in a hurry. "I wouldn't take any money for it. You could use it, just, you know, for as long as you need it. So you don't have to stay in a hotel. 'Course, you'd have to come see it. See if you'd be comfortable there. No TV. Sketchy cell service."

Miranda sighed. She nestled into her own fantasy of the place. "It sounds wonderful," she said. "I'd love to come see it."

They settled into quiet, each chewing silently on the decision they'd somehow just made together, the barrier they'd just crossed. A barrier they'd been getting closer to these past few months. Even though Miranda had insisted on paying him for as many of his services as she could, there were so many things he did for her that were impossible to quantify. The counsel and advice. The long talks. The ride to Plattsburgh when her car broke down and the trip to Albany to collect her mother. He was not a hired hand any longer. He was a friend. The only one she had. This kindness, this generous offer, she would accept. This she would take for free. Because it was for herself. It was a gift that had nothing to do with her parents or the past or the relationship of employer and employee Dix had had with her father. This was something between them alone. Miranda touched Dix's arm again. Let her hand rest there a moment this time.

"Thank you," she said, her voice a released breath.

Dix dipped his head. And for just a moment, the edges of his mouth turned up.

Dix gave Miranda careful directions, but his place was still hard to find, and there were few signposts along the way. She had asked him what color his mailbox was, but he said he didn't have one, as he picked up his mail at the post office. The first two turns were marked by street signs, but then she had to watch her odometer and count the tenths of a mile off one dirt road and then another, look for a falling-down barn and an abandoned farmhouse, try to find a bridge obscured by scrub growth, and then, if he hadn't been standing there like he had been set down by aliens, she still would have missed his driveway.

"You startled me," she said as she rolled down her car window.

"I thought I better come down and wave you in," he said.

"Good thing. I almost missed it."

He seemed nervous, something expressed only by an obliqueness in his gaze.

"Better let me in," he said. "It's a long driveway."

He climbed into the passenger seat of her Subaru, where he looked like a grown man on a tricycle, all knees and elbows in the compact space. Miranda stared straight ahead. She wondered if this was a mistake. She wondered if he was wondering the same thing. A man didn't live in a place this hard to find if he wasn't someone who valued solitude. Or if he liked the company of other people. She wondered why she'd been invited in.

Did he like her or feel sorry for her? Was he lonely or generous?

She'd known him for years, yet she knew him not at all. He was a collection of adjectives—reliable, capable, trustworthy, hardworking, skilled, private—but these words did not add up to a full person. Not yet. She wondered if that would change. If the man behind the list of admirable qualities would emerge.

The driveway took a turn and suddenly the view opened up. She saw a small glade among tall pines. At the center was a single-story home that took her breath away with its simplicity and elegance. There was a central square to the building, with two wings set at forty-five-degree angles flowing away from it. Large overhanging eaves protected its face while the arching branches of some deciduous trees she'd never seen before caressed the corners. The overlapping shakes were a lightly weathered brown, like bark. Several low walls and walks made of muted grayish-blue stones gave dimension to the yard. Mosses and creeping plants cascaded and merged together among the rocks. The home had the appearance of something that had sprouted up naturally. There were a few similarly subtle outbuildings scattered nearby, like leaves fallen from a tree. Everything was dusted with the first light snow of the season. Miranda turned off the car and sat, intimidated into silence by the serenity of the setting.

"It's not at all what I expected," she eventually whispered.

"No," Dix said. "I imagine not. Bet you thought I'd live in an old trailer or something."

Miranda flinched at the slight rebuke in his voice. Then conceded to herself that it was fair and due.

"Not that, exactly," she replied. As she spoke, what she had pictured, without really knowing it, came to mind. "I guess I expected a little old farmhouse with a big barn and a couple of dogs on the porch, chickens scratching in the yard. Something that maybe your grandmother once owned."

Dix sniffed his amusement. "My father designed this house. He was an architect," he said, then waited a beat, as if he knew that information would be unexpected, would need time to sink in. "My mother was a landscape architect."

Miranda's mouth fell open in surprise and embarrassment. She realized suddenly that she had admired Dix but also made assumptions about him as a "local." She had figured he had a poverty of experience and exposure, that his competencies had come more by hard-won experience than sought-after education. She had never considered him as a professional person because, in what she now realized was her own limited experience, serious careers were available in cities and in offices, not in the out-of-doors. Then she realized that almost everyone mistook him. Maybe that was OK with him. Maybe it was more than OK. Perhaps it was a willful and welcome protective mechanism.

She turned to say something to him, to apologize for herself, but he was already unfolding his body from the seat and the moment was lost. He stood in the drive and waved her out of the car. She got out and took a few steps in the direction of the main house, drawn there, intent on seeing how its sophistication played out on the inside, but Dix was heading in a different direction. She turned and followed him along a faint path that had yellowed the lawn to a far corner of the cleared part of the property. A giant beech tree shaded a small building. Spent nut casings—husks peeled back like miniature brown, bristled tulips—littered the mossy ground. She'd expected a cabin, something modeled after a traditional log lean-to. But this was a cottage. The style was Craftsman, not Adirondack. When they went inside, she found the bed was iron, not wood; the cover chenille, not quilted; the walls whitewashed bead board, not peeled logs; the curtains linen, not lace; the rocker on the little porch simple Shaker, not birch twig. It was a spare, unfussy hideaway. Miranda imagined that the woman who created it, Dix's mother, had been someone full of art, ideas, good taste, and the confidence and skill that allowed her to express restraint. And also a woman who must have remembered and called upon the daydreams of the girl she once had been.

Miranda did not want to leave. There was so much comfort to be had here. She turned to Dix and smiled. He nodded. The deal had been struck, accepted, wordlessly. He left her alone in the cottage, closing the door quietly behind him. Miranda listened to his few footfalls on the porch. Then, they were lost in the grass beyond. A raven gurgled and was answered. Ducks quacked at each other as they flew somewhere overhead. She sat in an upholstered chair in the corner of the room and levered off her shoes. Silence settled. She closed her eyes. This was a place where she could heal. She felt that. And at the same moment, she was overwhelmed with the realization of just how much healing there was for her to do.

DARIUS AND SALLY

His given name was David, but he called himself Darius. It was not a nickname. It was a name he had chosen for himself. He liked that both his names shared the same first letter, but the new name had a not-easy-to-place exoticism to it that thrilled him. He'd always felt the name his parents had chosen for him was generic and bland. He'd known too many others with that name, and they were all boring, he'd decided. He'd been named after a grandfather he didn't like much, someone who had started life in a small town in rural Pennsylvania, built a chain of hardware stores, and, while he made tons of money, stuck to frugal, simple ways. *Unsophisticated,* Darius thought. *Antiquated. Vaguely embarrassing.* His grandfather was someone who smelled of dust.

Darius's father had taken the hardware-store money to Wall Street, where he grew it exponentially. In contrast, he created a lifestyle that expressed his wealth in the subtle ways that were visible to other wealthy people: the Harvard MBA; the blonde, sincere but insubstantial wife who served on cultural groups' boards; the leather briefcases; the shoes and belts with discreetly placed logos that identified high-end brands; the monogrammed shirts; the summer house—not in the Hamptons, where one might have to mix with crass celebrities—but in an older-money enclave in Rhode Island.

Darius had first heard his new name when he was in high school. He had been playing a video game and drinking pilfered gin and tonics in the basement of a friend's house while an adult cocktail party carried on overhead. A heroic warrior character in the game was named Darius. Then, after dropping out of college and while driving across country, the name came back to him, and David decided to become Darius. The new name was part of his effort to describe, and maybe even begin to release, a man he was sure was lurking somewhere deep within himself, someone more grand than he yet was, someone destined for greatness, who needed only naming to become flesh and blood.

He had left college during his senior year without telling his parents. He had no plan. He had simply joined a friend on a skiing trip to Jackson Hole over winter break and then never returned to the University of Vermont. When the friend went back to college, he told Darius—then still David—that he could stay in his parents' condo because they were skiing in Europe over the winter. Darius and the friend had filled their days on the mountain slopes and their nights with an easy après-ski social life, but once his friend left he wasn't sure what to do with himself. Returning to college seemed retrograde.

He started bartending—his sparkling blue eyes, aquiline nose, eraser-pink lips, and chestnut hair that rode in soft waves over his forehead made for good tips. He also bought a few grams of coke with the intention of cutting it and selling it, but instead blew it with the waitresses, who took furtive snorts from the fake fingernails they dipped into his plastic bag while they stood shivering on the back porch during a smoke break. Then his college friend called and said his parents were on their way to the condo to do some fly-fishing, so he'd better clear out and make sure he got rid of any evidence he'd been there. He spent two days doing laundry and cleaning but got his friend in trouble anyway over a pair of women's lace underwear that had gotten kicked under the bed, a burn mark on the sofa from a dropped joint, and a grimy grill he'd forgotten to scrub.

Darius didn't know where to go next, so he spent a few weeks camped out on the lumpy sofa of a lifty he'd met. He went to the bank one day to get some beer money and found his account had been frozen. Apparently, parents had told parents. There was a serious phone call with his father where words like *responsibility*, *accountability*, and *appreciation* were used. Darius promised all of the above, as well as a return to UVM in the fall, with summer classes at a community college to catch up so he could graduate within the year. His account was reinstated and his monthly allowance reinstalled.

But it was a balmy, brilliant April and summer sessions were not starting for a bit. So he loaded up his Saab and, instead of heading east, turned his car toward the setting sun. He thought he'd try Southern California, maybe score a modeling gig so he could distance himself from financial reliance on his parents, learn to surf, get a tan. Classes could wait. However, after just a few weeks of squinting in the sunshine and wiping sand from his feet, he had become disillusioned. He was surprised to find California inchoate and inhospitable. There were so many other handsome, young, unemployed men around that no one took any notice of him. His charms were too East Coast, preppy, snarky, and filled with lingo and code that carried no weight in the airy, sunny, dry atmosphere. Surfing was also much more difficult and physically demanding than he had anticipated. Instead of showing off easy grace, he continually slipped and fell. He left the water dazed and bruised, his lungs burning with inhaled salt water. The sun was harsher than he'd expected, and he freckled, burned, and peeled instead of bronzing. He couldn't find the glassy, modern apartment on the beach he had imagined himself in, because his allowance wouldn't cover the rent even if he shared with several others, so after a month or so camped out in a friend's pool house, lying to his father during their occasional and uncomfortable phone calls, he repacked his car and headed back East.

Thinking there was little to do or see in the middle of the country, he got on the highway and drove and drove, stopping at rest areas to snatch a few hours of sleep when he needed it, filling the passenger-side floor of the car with crumpled wrappers from his fast-food meals. As the blacktop whizzed by beneath his tires, he resigned himself to a return to Burlington, Vermont, where he figured he'd reconnect with some pals, see if there was a late-summer class at the community college he could take to rack up a few credits, apologize sincerely to his parents for his six months of truancy, and try to make his words and deeds begin to match each other.

About an hour before he was to hit the dock of the ferry that would take him across Lake Champlain and back into the life he'd abandoned, he stopped. He'd left the highway hours earlier and had been driving along twisted two-lane roads lined with dense greenery, in-need-of-upkeep houses, and the gone-to-seed small towns of upstate New York. He was hungry. He passed a few restaurants with names like the Dew Drop Inn, but they all had pickup trucks in their parking lots and men with well-worn ball caps and dirt-caked boots coming and going through their front doors. He told himself these were not his sorts of places, that they were undoubtedly grimy and greasy. In truth, he was intimidated by the blatant demonstrations of rural masculinity. Finally, he found himself on a stretch of road with a gift shop that had hanging baskets out front, a store that advertised expensive and brand-name hiking and camping gear, signs pointing to a golf course. He slowed at a sign for the Fishing Hole diner and took note of a few lean folks emerging who were wearing pants with zip-off legs, high-tech sweat-wicking shirts, and web sandals with wool socks. He stopped. Just for a sandwich. Which, somehow, led to a life. Of a sort.

If pressed, Darius would not be able to say why, after lunch, instead of continuing to the ferry, he stopped at a multicolored farmhouse on the main road that had a ROOMS FOR RENT sign out front. And why, when the middle-aged, retired-from-schoolteaching-in-New-Jersey husband and wife who owned the B&B asked how long he wanted to stay, he said, "A week." He would not be able to tell you why, later that evening, back at the Fishing Hole diner, he picked up the local paper and turned immediately to the "For Rent" section. He was not self-aware enough or given to self-reflection enough to consider that he was once again simply avoiding college and his parents and the obligations they represented. He did, however, recognize something dark and protective in the landscape that surrounded him. There was also something vaguely familiar about the area that nagged at him. It took him several weeks before he remembered a visit here—or somewhere near here, somewhere like this—over a weekend in his last year of high school. A friend already two years into college had invited him to come along with a group. He didn't really jibe with the other boys, almost young men. They seemed to all be old-money WASPs, self-satisfied and jocular, where he was newer-money, brooding, uncomfortable with the assumptions and entitlements of the crowd. He felt slightly off balance with everyone. He got their jokes a moment too late and then not completely. There had been a sprawling log house where they stayed. Just before the trip, he had broken a bone in his foot when he took an awkward step off a curb after a night of drinking. A stupid accident that required a cast and kept him from the other boys' lawn games. There had been a younger sister. Shy, serious, pretty. They'd chatted a bit. He tried flirting with her, but she had not flirted back. There was only that one visit. He'd never been asked back. He drifted away from that crowd. Or maybe they quietly closed ranks against him. It was hard to tell. He had heard stories afterward. The guy whose house he stayed at had been in a car accident. Drunk. Killed a friend. The father—a total bastard, sleazy, double-dealer—had died in some freak accident involving a tree and a thunderstorm. Darius got these pieces of gossip as so many others did: tidbits passed around at a party, something offered up like a canapé.

But these memories were not what kept him there. It was the mountains themselves that appealed to him. It was the density of them. Unlike out west, there were no vistas. You couldn't see the mountains on approach. You were just suddenly in the midst of them, caught in the thick of their deep, forested web. He knew no one here. It seemed a place where he could lie fallow for a while until he figured out who he was, what he wanted to be. Until he reinvented himself as some sort of a more interesting, memorable sort of a man.

Darius rented, month to month, a one-room-with-sleeping-loft, unheated, uninsulated camp. He was supposed to "keep an eye on things," as the owners were splitting up and would be putting the place on the market once the divorce was settled. He wasn't sure what he was supposed to keep an eye on—the owners suggested there might be intrusions by teenage squatters or black bears, but he never saw any signs of either. He stopped at the local feed and hardware store and bought himself some canvas pants and flannel shirts because that was what he saw the locals wearing. He wanted to distance himself from the hiking, antiquing, summering, fly-fishing, seasonal crowd. He had no idea that the contours of his face and speech gave him away no matter what he wore. He tried on the clothes, looked at himself in the mirror, and decided he needed a two-day scruff and ball cap to complete his look. He found an already worn-in hat with a John Deere logo on it on a hook near the door. But the pants and shirts were perplexingly stiff and uncomfortable. He went to the laundromat and washed them over and over. The shirts softened, but the pants still left welts at his waist and on the backs of his knees. He put them on, crawled on his knees in the dirt, rubbed black mud into the canvas, jammed them into a canning pot full of water, boiled them on the stove, and then washed them a few more times. Finally, they were, if not quite comfortable, at least not painful to wear.

He started taking note of the postings on the tackboards at the diner and the hardware store. He took down a few numbers and called about odd jobs: mucking out a barn, stacking wood, cutting brush, shoveling manure. He'd thought that these tasks would give him a sense of the people who lived here, would allow him to step over a line between visitor and resident, a boundary that could be felt but not seen. However, all the jobs turned out to have been posted by recent transplants or vacationers from New Jersey, Connecticut, or downstate, people who said they came for the untamed beauty of the mountain landscape but, once there, spent their money and other people's time trying to beat back and tidy up the nature that surrounded them.

Darius did the work he was paid a few folded twenty-dollar bills to do, and in the evenings, admired the calluses growing on his hands, the muscles starting to create definition in his arms and back. He stopped going to the diner, feeling that he was not yet ready to be seen much around town, that he was still working on developing the man he wanted to eventually reveal. He picked up sandwiches or prepared meals at the local Stewart's convenience store and spent the evenings reading paperbacks he found stacked up on two simple shelves tacked to one wall of the camp. There were dozens of them, all romance and self-help. He had little patience with the romances but read them anyway and found them instructive in methods for charming women, something he'd relied on his looks to do for him in the past. Looks that he hoped were changing, becoming less refined and more rugged. The other books all had titles with words and phrases that were new and strange to him. *Siddhartha*, *Jonathan Livingston Seagull*, *The Book of EST*, *Dianetics*, *What Color Is Your Parachute?*, *I'm OK, You're OK*. Their subtitles and prefaces were puffed up with words like *awaken*, *unleash*, *take charge*, *ultimate*, and *destiny*.

Women's books, Darius decided. *All of them books for unhappy women.*

He told his parents he was staying with a friend and attending community college. They were disappointed by, but also somewhat accustomed to, this erratic approach to his education by now. His mother thought it was partially her fault. She'd had him held back from kindergarten for a year, thinking he was not emotionally ready for school, and feared that had set a pattern. He'd missed a semester in high school when he got sick with mono and pneumonia. He'd taken a gap year between high school and college that had turned into a year and a half of listlessness and hanging out at the country club, where he occasionally taught tennis. He'd always been older than his classmates. Never quite fit in.

In between his dirty jobs, Darius took out a few cash advances, as much as the ATM would allow at any one time. He told his parents, who were watching his accounts more closely than they used to, that the money was for tuition and books, but instead, he stockpiled into a new account in preparation for the inevitable moment when his parents cut him off again. He wasn't sure what he was doing, but he felt sure something would turn up. As it always had before. Then, in the middle of August, he turned twenty-six and received a phone call from a lawyer who had the crackling voice and throat-clearing habit of an old man. This lawyer told him that he now had access to a trust his grandfather had set up for him. The existence of the trust was complete news to Darius. He wondered briefly if his father had known and never spoken of it to him on purpose, or if his grandfather had kept it a secret. The two men were polite to, yet suspicious of, each other and their opposing ideas about whether money was best used for security or show. The lawyer told him there would be an initial outlay of capital, $10,000, and then a regular stipend of $1,500 a month for five years. The lawyer said his grandfather's hope had been that he would invest the money wisely and find himself with a great deal of financial security in his future. Darius rolled his eyes on the other end of the phone.

To Darius, this wasn't much money. Typical of his frugal grandfather. Enough to assist, but not enough for financial independence. However, Darius was beginning to think his material needs were far fewer and less ambitious than he had once thought. In fact, he was beginning to think that the expensive materialism he had seen all around him growing up—$16 cocktails, $50,000 cars, $250 shoes—wasn't for him at all. He liked his $3 premade submarine sandwiches and the coffee he could buy for pocket change.

In two months at the camp, he plowed through every paperback. Some he read twice. He began to seek out books at the little library in town. Then he drove to a bookstore in Plattsburgh. He read about Hinduism, Buddhism, Taoism. He read apocalyptic, speculative, and science fiction titles. He read back-to-nature treatises. For the first time in his life, he considered the degradations of mankind and the abuse humans had heaped on the planet. As the summer slipped away and the days became crisp, when the day approached that he was supposed to be sitting in a college seminar, he cut up the credit cards his parents had supplied him with as a buffer against the bruising uncertainties of the world and mailed them the pieces in an envelope with no return address.

The weathered **FOR SALE** sign was tipped over, sticking from the ground as if it had been struck by a plow the winter before. Or maybe several winters before. A vine had wrapped itself around the post, and a tendril hanging over the board waved at him in a vaguely lascivious way, like a woman at a window. He turned off the dirt road he'd been following onto a pocked and pitted drive. Muddy water splashed out from under his car tires as he rocked and pitched his way down the well-worn, weed-infested gravel. After about one-quarter of a twisting mile, the drive ended abruptly in front of a farmhouse. A dark, dejected, and morose thing sitting slump-shouldered in the midst of overgrown scrub. The porch drooped off to one side, the screen door was canted halfway open, and a couple of once bright-white planters that were now gray with mold hung from the crosspieces. Tattered lace curtains hung in the spider-webbed windows. There was a barn set back from the house. It was more erect—more resilient, apparently, to the abuses of weather and neglect.

Darius got out of the car. When he slammed the door, something skittered under the house. He heard it hiss but saw only two eyes, dark and reflective, before they turned and disappeared. He took a few steps forward and stood in the yard of knee-high grass. He watched another creature covered in fur and stealth slide through a crack in the barn door. A bird called, distant and plaintive. Then silence settled into the overcast air.

Darius made mental notes. The turnoff to the house had to be almost five miles down a poorly maintained and lightly traveled dirt road. The trees, scrub, and twisted driveway made the farmhouse and barn impossible to see from the road. The land around the buildings sloped upward, leaving them in a kind of bowl that kept the site extremely secluded. Darius did not realize this meant that the cold of the coming season would collect here and stay far into the following spring. Those sorts of concerns were beyond his experience. He went to the barn and pushed the door against its rusted rollers, shoving it aside just enough to peer in. Dim light from a few broken windows worked its way past dust motes. He made out a couple of stalls and a separate area with a workbench and wall hooks. He'd never had so much as a pet turtle growing up, but he quickly filled the barn with an imaginary cow, a goat, and a few chickens. He stepped back into the yard and sneezed. He saw, off to the side of the barn, the decayed rib cage of a structure, with tattered strips of weather-beaten plastic flapping in the breeze. It took him several minutes of staring and the sudden memory of a drawing in one of his back-to-subsistence-farming books to realize this had once been a hoop house. Then he quickly imagined the metal structure straightened, re-covered with fresh plastic, and filled with tidy flats of vegetables getting a head start on spring, safe from cold blasts of air, reaching their green fronds toward the wan winter sun.

He walked over to the farmhouse. The steps to the front porch were tilted and springy with rot, but they held as he climbed them. The door was locked, so he stepped back into the yard and looked upward. Two rooflines moved away from each other at hard right angles. He'd never been in an old farmhouse, but he filled in what he could not see with mental pictures of a compact kitchen with a tin-top table; a lumpy, overstuffed chair in a parlor; a few bedrooms at the top of a short, steep staircase. He wasn't sure where these images came from, but there they were, quaint and romantic.

Yes, he thought. *Yes, this will do. This will more than do.*

When he left, he had to get out of his car and step over to the **For Sale** sign, then rub away some moss and mold to make out the phone number. When he called, the agent asked him to describe the house and where it was. Darius tried, but he didn't know what landmarks to conjure; some of the roads near there did not have street signs. He'd only found it because he'd been intentionally turning down smaller and smaller roads and had gotten lost on his way back, finding himself finally spit out onto the main two-lane road three towns above the one where he was living. The agent said he'd have to get back to him. When he called Darius a few days later, he told him the listing had actually expired a couple of years back.

"Do you have any more information?" Darius asked. "Is the house still for sale? Is there someone else I could call?"

The agent said he was new in the office and had no idea who had originally listed it. He suggested Darius look up the deed at City Hall. Darius found three listings with the same last name as the property owner's. He called one number, which rang endlessly. The other was picked up by a person who thought Darius was a salesman of some sort and hung up on him. When he dialed the third, a woman answered. He thought he heard her drag on a cigarette as he told his story of discovering an abandoned farmhouse that he hoped to buy. Darius found it strange to say so many words. He had not had much conversation with anyone for months. Once he started talking, it seemed hard to stop.

"How the hell did you find the place?" the woman on the other end of the phone finally interjected into his steady flow of words.

Darius sputtered to a stop and laughed, relieved to be interrupted. "There was a sign," he said.

"I'll be damned," she said. "I haven't been out there in ages."

"Your house?" he asked.

"No, my grandmother's. She died, oh, five, six years ago. We put it on the market, but no one was interested. Figured the place would just rot back into the ground."

"Well, I'm interested," Darius said firmly.

"Seriously?" Her voice was full of amusement and incredulity. "I mean, why?"

"I'm looking for something I can work on. Get my hands dirty. Make it my own," Darius said with a newfound and totally manufactured confidence.

The voice on the other end of the phone guffawed. "Well, you'll get all that and more with that place," she said.

They made plans to meet out there in a few days. She said her name was Sally. Darius went to the library and checked out some how-to books on carpentry, gardening, and homesteading. He went to the hardware store and stood in the tool aisles, staring at the implements there, daydreaming about their uses, imagining how they might feel in his hands. He was not ready for tools, he knew this, but he bought an ax and a hammer—heavy, useful things that he'd never owned before. He set them by the door in the cabin and picked them up from time to time, ran his hands up and down their shafts, picturing the potential for useful work each tool seemed to hold in quiet abeyance. He went back to the store and bought a tool belt. He put it on in the bathroom of the cabin and looked at himself in the mirror, turning this way and that as if he were a high school girl trying on a prom dress. He admired the way the leather strap sat on his narrow hips.

On the day he was to meet Sally, Darius gave himself extra time to get to the farmhouse, remembering how lost he'd become when he'd left it and trying to retrace his steps home. He had no trouble this time and got there fifteen minutes early. There was already another vehicle there. A truck. Small, dark green, with rust eating away at several places on the panels. Darius was suddenly, sharply, jealous. He wanted a beat-up truck instead of his low-slung Saab. A woman was there, too, standing in the front doorway. A compact, sturdy presence, her hands stuffed into the back pockets of her jeans, work boots laced up on the outside of her pants, her hair tossed into a tumult around her face by the gusty winds of an increasingly brisk September. She raked her hair out of her eyes with her fingertips and stuffed it through the opening at the back of a ball cap. She didn't smile as he got out of the car and moved toward her. He was surprised to find that he couldn't read her expression. Her lips parted in a way that could as easily be mocking as welcoming. Her teeth were a little crooked and overlapping. He wondered why she'd not had braces. It never dawned on him that dental work, for some people, was a luxury rather than a necessity. She was not conventionally pretty, but there was a rough-hewn handsomeness to her face. She stuck out her hand and gave his a couple of firm pumps.

A handshake like a man's, he thought. She appeared to him not unlike the farmhouse itself—good bones, but a fixer-upper.

Sally showed him in and they wandered the half-dozen dusty rooms. Even Darius could see that the house had little to recommend it. There was chipped linoleum where he'd thought he'd find scuffed wood floors, and garish wallpaper where he'd pictured wainscoting with layers upon layers of paint. There was no fireplace, just black spots where sparks had jumped from a long-gone woodstove onto the matted orange carpet. It smelled like cat pee and an old campfire.

Still, he liked it. He'd been alone too much recently. He was ready to like anything.

"What do you do?" he asked Sally as they stood in the dank living room, swiveling their heads around in the thick air of the long-closed-off space.

"Do?" she said. "Do about what?"

"You know, for work." He was irritated by what he felt was her unnecessary stonewalling of his obvious query.

She reached into her coat pocket and pulled out a pack of cigarettes. Cigarettes. No one Darius knew smoked cigarettes. Certainly not indoors. Sally shook one out of the pack and lighted it before answering him.

"I'm a social worker," she said.

Darius wasn't quite sure what that meant. "What sort of social worker?" he asked, trying to cover his ignorance.

"I work for the state," Sally said. "I work with kids. Foster kids. JDs. Fucked-up kids and their fucked-up families."

Darius wondered what a "JD" was but didn't ask. He was a bit startled by her use of profanity. He didn't know any women who swore so freely.

"Sounds like hard work," he said, not knowing what else to say.

"Sometimes. At least the job is secure. Never a shortage of delinquents around here."

Ah, he thought. *Delinquents. Juvenile Delinquents. JDs.*

He wasn't sure what to do next. Sally stared at him and took a long drag on her cigarette. The directness of her gaze made him uncomfortable in a way he'd never been before. He was used to people coming at each other in a certain way. There was a standard set of questions one normally asked, about fathers' last names, firms worked for, schools attended. These queries were always pitched in a tone designed to sound casual and friendly, but the answers were used to place people in a pecking order, to help decide if you were someone to compete with, dismiss, or try to cozy up to. This Sally person was doing none of these things. Darius wondered how old she was. She looked like she'd lived a lot more than he had. That didn't necessarily mean she was much older. He wanted to ask her age, but that was a question he knew was considered impolite. At least among the people he was used to. Maybe it didn't matter to someone like her.

"How old are you?" he asked quickly, before his courage gave out. She gave him an annoyed look. He didn't care. He wanted to know.

"That's a rude fucking question," Sally said. "Not that I care. But still. Twenty-nine."

He nodded instead of apologizing. Looked around the room to avoid looking at her.

"Not from around here, are you?" she asked, squinting against an exhalation of smoke.

He shook his head.

"What do you think of the place?" she asked, then sucked on her cigarette again.

"It's perfect," he said.

"Yup," she said, crushing the cigarette under her boot and into the orange carpet. "Definitely not from around here."

Darius tried and failed to get bank financing. His small trust fund and lack of a job or credit history did not impress the bank officers. He came to Sally with the news, expecting that would be the end of things, but Sally said she'd take his $10,000 down payment and hold the mortgage herself.

"What do I have to lose?" she said with a shrug. "Even if you bail on me, I'm still ahead ten thousand bucks."

They met a few weeks later and signed a simple purchase-and-sale agreement she'd downloaded from the Internet.

"David?" she asked as she looked things over. "Thought you said your name was Darius?"

"My legal name is David. But I've been called Darius for most of my life."

"Two kings," Sally said.

Darius looked at her quizzically.

"A Jewish king and a Persian king?"

Darius was silent.

"Never mind," she said as she handed him a set of keys.

She had brought a twelve-pack of Pabst Blue Ribbon to celebrate the deal. They emptied the cans down their throats while wandering the rooms, then crushed and left them on the floor. As they went, Darius made mental notes about the projects he would take on to fix the place up, an endeavor he unrealistically and optimistically imagined would take only until spring. He listened with half his attention as Sally reminisced about her grandmother.

"She lived here alone for as long as I can remember," Sally said. "Mowed her own yard. Well, more like bushwhacked it, I guess, as there was never anything you'd call a lawn."

The day was damp and the rooms were chilled. The trees were shedding their leaves, and bits of snow spit and swirled in the air.

"She even shoveled snow," Sally said, popping the tab on another beer. "Just enough to get to the barn. Mostly stayed holed up here when the snow got too deep. Ate stuff she'd canned. A deer she killed. Pig she'd raised. Chickens too old to lay eggs. Died in her eighties with an ax in her hand, just about to split a log. Still ran a fucking chainsaw. Don't make them like that old broad anymore."

Darius smiled and nodded as Sally talked. He took no interest in what she said and was unaware that these kinds of stories, told to another sort of person, might make them feel a deeper connection to the house and land. He simply wanted to get started. On something. Get himself set up and ready. For what, he wasn't exactly sure, but having a place of his own seemed a vital first step. He reflexively drank the beers she handed to him, thinking that after the cans were emptied she'd leave and he could walk the rooms that now belonged to him alone, thinking, planning. Instead, when the last can was tossed aside, she folded her legs beneath her, sank to the living room floor, and fingered a joint out of the corner of her cigarette pack.

"Mind?" she asked.

Darius shook his head. Sally inhaled and then pointed the joint toward him. He shrugged, sat next to her on the floor, and took a toke or two. He was not much of a fan of weed but figured helping her finish the joint, as he had the beers, would send her on her way sooner. This, too, did not work out as he planned. Instead, after the slender joint was finished, she gave him another one of her disconcertingly direct looks, then shocked him by shouldering out of her jacket, pulling her shirt over her head, and pushing him backward onto the carpet. Her mouth hit his, her tongue searched for his, and he was stunned into submission. She ground her jeaned hips into his groin, and he was taken aback by how quickly and completely he swelled. He let himself return her rough kiss. Her mouth tasted smoky and sweet, like burned marshmallows. She pushed her pants and underwear down, freed one leg, pulled him from his pants, rode him until she came, then kept going until the moment just before he came, when she expertly pulled back, leaving him with a quickly cooling puddle of semen on his stomach.

It took Darius a moment to bring her face back into focus. She already had her pants pulled back up, her shirt on, and was lighting another cigarette by the time he came out of his orgasmic haze.

"A celebratory fuck," she said. "To seal the deal."

He stared at her.

"Can't say as I've ever been with a rich, preppy boy like you," she said.

"I'm not rich," Darius said.

Sally rolled her eyes. "Right. You bought this place with money you saved in a jelly jar by mowing lawns all through high school."

Darius sort of despised her in that moment. He had thought so little of her, with her coarse manners and cheap beer. When she said that, it occurred to him it was possible she thought even less of him than he did of her. When she left that day, he was glad to see her go. He thought it was all over now. The place was his. She'd leave him alone as long as he sent the mortgage payment in on time.

Yet, the next weekend, her beater truck came up the driveway again. She walked onto the porch with a toolbox.

"Figured you might need some of this stuff," she said. "You're welcome to borrow it. Don't care if you break anything, as it all belonged to my ex, anyway."

She didn't stay this time, just dropped her burdens inside the front door, turned, waved over her shoulder, and left. Darius picked through the items in the toolbox. He was unsure how many of them might be used, what they would be called upon to do, as if they were relics from another culture. Silence descended over the empty farmhouse. In Sally's absence, what had been solitude quickly turned into loneliness.

A couple of weeks later, she stopped by again. This time with another twelve-pack. "Wanted to see how you were making out," she said by way of welcome and explanation.

This time she stayed. Not for long. Just long enough to see that he'd yet to move in. He was still at the cabin, coming out to the farmhouse now and then. He'd done little in the way of improvements. Threw some of the decaying furniture into a pile behind the barn. Ripped the peeling wallpaper back in a few places. Pulled up the carpet in spots. He wasn't sure where to begin or what to finish. Sally clicked her tongue as she assessed his efforts, without making any comments. Darius wondered if she had nostalgia for the house, for some set of childhood memories made there, and if that was why she kept reappearing. As if in answer to his unspoken question, she said how much she had hated the place, how much she had disliked having to spend weekends there when she was a kid, away from her drinking, fighting parents, but alone with her taciturn grandmother, with no television and a plate of boiled dinner.

"What's boiled dinner?" Darius asked.

"Bunch of tasteless meat and vegetables boiled together. Then you chop it up and serve it again in the morning as shit on a shingle."

He grinned at her. He was starting to get her sense of humor.

"I'll make it for you sometime," she said, grinning back.

She wandered the rooms with him again, pointing at things and offering advice on how to remove wallpaper, prep pipes so they didn't freeze, whom to call to get the utilities turned back on, the steps required to refinish the floors. She told him real snow would be there soon enough and gave him the name of someone to plow the driveway, showed him how to secure his garbage so the raccoons and bears wouldn't get in it, and cautioned him about the dangerous listing of the porch stairs.

"My ex was a contractor. Handyman," she said by way of explanation. "'Course, just about anyone who can swing a hammer around here is."

By the time Sally stopped by again, a couple of weeks later, Darius had gotten all the wallpaper off the walls of the dining room and the matted gold-tone carpet out of one of the bedrooms. He'd picked up a few mismatched chairs, a wobbly table, and a random collection of plates, cutlery, and cooking utensils.

"Where'd you get this shit?" Sally asked.

"Mostly junk shops," he answered. "Plenty of those around."

"Guess you're not as much of a rich boy as I thought," she said, setting down the pizza she'd brought in with her.

And you're not as much of a white-trash bitch as I thought, Darius almost said but kept to himself instead.

Darius had also acquired a mattress. This was the only thing he'd purchased new. On sale. No box spring, just a stark white rectangle thrown down on the floor of an empty upstairs bedroom with a twisted sleeping bag curled up on it like something already asleep. After they finished the pizza and the beer—in bottles, this time—Sally spent the night. Their sex, in spite of the mattress, was no more leisurely than before.

Sally started showing up regularly most weekends. And instead of just pointing and giving advice, she would strap on a tool belt and help out. Darius never asked why she'd come over or if she'd come again, and Sally never offered an explanation. Darius would hear the rattle of an old truck and look out the window from whatever task he was at, wondering if it was Sally instead of the toothless manure-smelling guy who plowed his driveway for him. Darius was always vaguely irritated by, but also reluctantly glad for, her company. He loved his solitude, but the weeks were long and unrelieved, the snows were starting in earnest, and there was little to do but work and read. He'd moved on from self-help to spiritual texts about Wicca, astrology, living off the land, and removing your own ego, along with how-to texts on carpentry, plumbing, gardening, raising chickens, basic wiring. He felt he was getting a firm grasp on the lofty tenets of the former set of books but was still struggling with the practical aspects of the latter. He would never admit it, but Sally was an enormous help. Tools came alive in her hands and behaved like willing participants. When she was there, tasks were completed more than twice as fast and in a steady progression. And the results were sturdier, straighter, more complete.

One time Sally arrived with groceries instead of pizza, and together they made boiled dinner. As he washed and chopped vegetables under Sally's direction, it occurred to Darius that he was having fun. Together, they groaned over the bland taste of the parsnips, cabbage, and potatoes and the rough texture of the poor cut of meat. Darius plucked a jar of mustard out of the mostly empty refrigerator and a shaker of salt from the vacant cabinet, and they smirked as they slathered and sprinkled the condiment and spice on their dinner. Sally told him stories of her grandmother pouring vodka into her orange juice in the morning and buying herself a chainsaw on the way home from her husband's funeral because he never let her have one when he was alive. Darius laughed and then realized he could not remember the last time he'd done so.

"Why?" he asked her, the beer and shared domestic activity loosening his tongue. "Why do you keep coming here and helping me out?"

"Would you rather I didn't?"

"No, I'm glad of the help. Glad of the company," he said, and meant it.

"Yeah," she said, "you seem kind of lost out here."

"Is that why you're here? Feel a little sorry for me?" He smiled at her, trying to put on a bit of the charm that used to come so fluidly to him. He was out of practice. He was also afraid she'd say yes. And that she had real reasons to feel that way.

"Don't feel sorry for you one bit," Sally said, surprising him. "You have plenty of options, I'm sure." She shifted in her chair. Lit a cigarette. "I think at first, I was just curious," she went on. "Wanted to see if you'd fail. Honestly, figured you would. Go back to Mommy and Daddy and finish college, and get a job in a nice carpeted office with a briefcase instead of a toolbox. Always suspect I'll drive up and find you've quit the place. I'm actually pretty amazed you've stuck it out."

Darius watched her. He'd never seen himself as Sally did. Someone who didn't give up. Someone who accomplished things.

"Then, well, I guess I just started to like you," she said. "Not many men like you around here. You're not very tough. But very improvable. You're different, that's for sure."

Different. Darius grabbed onto the word. *That's it,* he thought.

He had always felt different from those around him. But in the world he came from, different was a bad thing, something to be suppressed. The goal was to wear the brand of clothes, have the kind of job, go to the sort of school, say the kind of things, behave in the sort of way that signaled to a select group that you were one of them. He'd done that, he'd played by those rules, but there was a small internal treachery that always leaked out and gave him away, made people from the social circle he allegedly belonged to move a few steps away from him as if he emitted a bad smell. This was the first time he'd ever heard someone use the adjective *different* with a positive connotation.

Different. Yes, he thought, *that's what I am. That's what I want to be.*

Through the months of winter while the snow piled up outside, Darius—and often Sally and Darius together—tore out wallpaper, linoleum, and carpet. They sanded and scraped and cleaned and stained and painted. They created burn piles for the debris and flipped through seed catalogs. They often ate only a pizza or a submarine sandwich, sometimes frozen dinners, even as they discussed the best tomato and lettuce varieties they'd grow the next summer. They went to junk shops and collected furniture and tools. Darius's hands blistered and peeled and finally formed calluses. Sally rubbed Bag Balm into his ruined palms and then guided his tingling fingers down between her legs. He'd never done that with a woman before, never performed manual or oral sex. His experience was limited to hurried humping sessions with usually drunk women. He'd never concerned himself with a woman's climax before, just hurried on to his own. He didn't especially enjoy doing what Sally asked him to do, but as he had with the home repairs, he followed her firm lead.

One day, Sally arrived with a duffel bag and a box of her stuff. She said the lease on her apartment, which he'd never been invited to, had come up and she didn't want to renew. She threw her duffel onto the bedroom floor and said it would just be until she found something new. She also reminded him that, as long as he paid the mortgage, the place was his. But the minute he fell behind, it was hers. He felt as if she were lifting her leg on the place, marking her territory. She never bothered to look for anything else, though, and he never asked her to. He didn't really like her very much, but he'd never really liked anyone very much. She was easy to be around, and he needed her help and counsel. Her company settled something in him.

One day, he saw a **FOR SALE** sign on a two-tone truck in a muddy yard next to a double-wide trailer and traded the guy for his Saab. Sally looked under the hood and shook her head at his folly but never told him just how badly he'd been had. She only said he shouldn't have gotten a rear-wheel drive, a mistake he didn't understand until the afternoon he goosed it up the driveway, spun out, overcorrected, got the truck halfway into a ditch, and had to be pulled free by the plow driver. After that they put some bags of sand into the bed, Sally gave him some quick pointers on the difference between his front-wheel-drive, low-slung Saab and this high-clearance, rear-wheel-drive truck, and he drove more thoughtfully. He got stuck one more time in the middle-of-March mud season. But that time, he shoved some spare lumber he had in the back of the truck under the tires and drove himself out of his predicament. As he wiped his muddied palms on his finally well-worn pants, he felt the calm of competence seep into his limbs. He was pleased with himself. This was a new and welcome feeling.

Then, as suddenly as if a switch had been thrown, spring arrived. From the thick, dead silence of winter, Darius and Sally were thrust into the season where frogs sent them to bed at night and birds woke them before dawn. They emerged from their labors in the house to the out-of-doors like children rubbing sleep from their eyes. They shoveled years' worth of compacted manure from the stalls of the barn into raised beds made from lumber they salvaged when they dismantled an old shed. They laid out tidy rows in the dirt and eased the seedlings they'd started in plastic-wrap-covered trays near the kitchen windows into the soft, black humus. They got several chicks and a goat someone was giving away.

There was now enough completed at the house that Darius began to take time away from chores at the property to hike the still-sloppy trails that wound their way up into the steep, flinty hillsides. He also began to visit start-up farm stands and consider what he might do with the bounty he was expecting from his own garden. He took long drives down the twisting roads empty of people and houses and considered that he had somehow made himself a home. He also began to entertain thoughts of what he might make of this home. Gardening and farm stands were not going to be enough for him. Milking the goat and feeding the chickens would not express the restless ambition that was growing in him, looking for a way out of him. He felt he had built something. All the books he'd read and the work he'd done had begun simmering together in his mind, coalescing into a strange philosophical brew of spirit and earth, idealism and practicality, dirty hands and fresh souls. He had kept his vision to himself. He didn't want to risk what he instinctively suspected would be Sally's ridicule. But he was starting to feel the impulse to share. Not through any impulse of generosity—he recognized this about himself—but because he felt he had something to say. He felt there were people who needed to hear what he was convinced he had to offer. He wanted to see them hearing it, to witness what he believed would be their inevitable transformation. That's what the house was for. It was not just a home, it was a platform for a whole new relationship with the world.

One early summer evening, when Sally came home from her day of shepherding paperwork and teenagers, she found Darius weeding in the garden. He'd been distant and moody recently, taking off for aimless drives and extended hikes, returning tired, muddy, preoccupied, turning into bed well before usual, snoring deeply by the time she crawled in. They'd not had sex in weeks. No, more than a month. Maybe longer. He rebuffed her efforts to arouse him, or indulged them to no effect, rolling over and quickly falling asleep once she'd given up. She hadn't decided how to talk to him about it. If she even wanted to. She had enough of talking about things during her workdays.

She brought him a beer from her car, but he waved it away, another new and increasingly frequent behavior. He raised his water bottle at her in explanation, which she recognized was also a passive rebuke of her own drinking. He'd recently asked her if she would smoke only outdoors. If she had to smoke at all. She was beginning to wonder if she'd been had, conned, charmed by this man. Part of her didn't care very much either way. He'd helped her get over her last boyfriend, the one who cheated on her with several women they both knew, practically begging to be caught. Maybe that was all she'd needed Darius for. Maybe it was time to move on. She was starting to notice unsettling things about him. What had at first seemed a rather cute callowness was morphing into an annoying, smug self-righteousness. She found herself thinking she should double-check the paperwork on the house sale to make sure she could get the house back if he defaulted. Or if she just wanted to be rid of him. She found herself noticing the FOR RENT signs she passed on her way to work or saw on the tackboard in the break room. She started thinking she should get some distance from this place, this guy, this situation.

Sally stood in the garden, two open beers in hand. Darius had turned his attention back to the plants in front of him. The mosquitoes and blackflies were thick—it had been a damp spring—but he was serene beneath a netted hat and long-sleeved shirt and pants in spite of the unusually hot, humid air. She made a suggestion about securing the beans to supports. He murmured a bland acknowledgment. She was being bitten by bugs. She shoved one beer in the dirt, the other in the back pocket of her jeans, and swatted at her bare arms. Her palms came back streaked with the black smudges of dead insects and red smears of her own blood. She wiped them off against a clump of grass.

"I gotta get out of here," she said.

Darius looked up and nodded at her.

Something strange in his face, she thought. *He's hiding something,* was her next fleeting, inchoate thought.

She waved the notion away. And the bugs, as well. She was annoyed at the insects, but now also at him. She went into the house with the two beers, dropped her purse on the kitchen table, opened the fridge, and shoved aside a few tofu cakes, a bag of spring greens, and several containers of homemade goat's-milk yogurt to find the wizened lime she was looking to slice and slip into her Corona. She was standing at the counter, cutting into its desiccated rind, when she heard footsteps.

Darius already? No, someone is inside the house.

She turned, knife in hand.

"Hi. You must be Sally."

The person who said these words was a thin reed, someone still straddling the line between girl and woman. She wore a patchwork skirt that fell to her skinny but well-muscled calves. Russet hair sprouted from her underarms, and the outline of wet-teabag breasts showed under her tank top. Her pale gray eyes regarded Sally blankly beneath an overgrown fringe of damp-darkened hair.

This woman has just taken a shower in my house, Sally thought. *She used my towels. This is so not OK with me.*

Sally took a long pull on her beer and said, "And who might you be?"

"Mandy," the other woman said, her eyes unflinching, blank and deflective to Sally's unguarded hostility. "My name is Mandy. I am so very pleased to meet you."

"And what, Miss Mandy, brings you to our humble abode?" Sally asked.

Mandy shrugged her bony shoulders, dipped her head, and grinned. She said one word, the name of the man in the garden, as if that was all the explanation required. She took a few steps into the kitchen toward Sally, moving hips-first, slinky, as if she were on ball bearings. Sally tried to take a step backward, away from the intruder, but was caught against the counter. She held up her knife instead. Mandy stopped. Sally sidestepped her way across the room and out the door. Which she let slam behind her.

"So who's the houseguest?" she asked Darius when she got back to the garden.

"I see you met Mandy," Darius replied, without looking up from his weeding.

"And who the fuck is this Mandy, and what the fuck is she doing in my kitchen? In my bathroom?" Sally tried for a joking tone, but rancor saturated her words.

Darius stared evenly at her. "*Your* kitchen?" he asked. But before Sally could respond, he quickly added, "I met her hiking."

"That's not what I asked," Sally said. "And just in case you haven't done the math, you own not much more than ten grand of this little slice of heaven. I own the mortgage, which means I own the rest."

Darius stood and brushed the dirt from his knees. "I'm not sure I understand the hostility, Sally."

That emphasis on her name aggravated. The overtly calm tone of his voice irritated. She slapped at a mosquito on her forearm, swiped at a blackfly on the back of her neck.

"It's not *the* hostility. Darius. It's all mine, I assure you," Sally said.

"She's a guest," Darius explained.

"And is she staying long?"

"As long as she needs to," Darius said, his voice pitched to soothe, as if he were a funeral director greeting the bereaved.

Sally felt her face prickle with heat. "What is that supposed to mean?"

"Sally. She has nowhere to go. Her parents kicked her out of the house. They're Christian missionaries or something, and they caught her boyfriend in her room with her, and she got stuck here while hitchhiking her way north. She was hoping to get to Canada."

"Canada. Huh. How handy," Sally scoffed.

"What is that supposed to mean?" Darius asked.

"Rich runaways always think they can get easy drugs and out of raps for possession by going to Canada."

"Suspicion is a rather unattractive character trait," Darius said, his voice filled with unguent disappointment. The normal brightness of his eyes was muted by the netting that hung down from his hat.

"It's not suspicion," Sally said. "It's experience." She slapped at a mosquito on her cheek.

"Would you like a sprig of catnip to help deflect the mosquitoes?" Darius asked.

"Catnip?"

"Yes, I planted some. It's coming in nicely. It's proven to be quite effective at warding off mosquitoes."

Sally lit a cigarette. "So is this," she said, blowing smoke in his face.

Mandy did not stay long. She drifted idly about the house, barn, and garden and then disappeared a week later, taking with her all the cash from Sally's wallet, which fortunately amounted to only about forty dollars, a bag of homegrown pot Sally had stashed in the back of her sweater drawer, and a brand-new backpack, bedroll, and pair of hiking boots Darius had just bought.

"Who knew she had man-size feet?" was all Sally said to Darius by way of reprimand about the incident.

She watched with pleasure as he winced at her remark. She had intended to wound him. She knew his reaction was not just because of what Mandy had done, but also because he was sensitive about his stature—he was only five foot eight and had rather small feet. She also knew she got too much pleasure from her thinly veiled insult and from being right about Mandy. She hoped the episode would teach Darius a lesson.

However, it seemed to have no impact on his new, increasingly sanctimonious, air. He told Sally that he and Mandy had had several long, serious conversations while she was there, and in spite of her actions, he was confident she was on the right path. Besides, he said, she had more need for the items she'd taken than he did, and he was glad he could provide her the tools she required for her journey. He reminded Sally that he had repaid her the money Mandy had taken. Sally hadn't told him about the missing pot. But nonetheless, her hackles rose in irritation as she listened to him offer what she viewed as complete non-sense and retroactive justification for bad judgment. This was the same kind of stuff she heard from her cases at work.

Although she disliked talking about her work, wanted to leave it behind at the end of the day, in her increasingly infrequent interactions with Darius, she found herself increasingly telling him stories about the kids she dealt with. She described the varieties of deception and cunning they used to manipulate the adults and the systems in their lives. For sure, they had had tough childhoods, Sally allowed, but plenty of people did, herself included. That was no excuse for acting like you were entitled to a pass from the world no matter what you did or how you fucked up, she'd tell Darius.

She was trying to school him in a subject she knew he thought he already understood. Like a bright but arrogant teenager, he listened to her from a distance, as if she were behind a screen. He went on about his household and garden chores. He wrote in notebooks, pulling a small one from his back pocket while out in the barn and jotting down a few words, or sitting at the kitchen table at night, head bent, an earnest expression on his face, filling page after page of a spiral-bound book with his loose longhand. Sally wanted to read what he wrote, but he kept the notebooks either with him or hidden somewhere. She was curious to see what was happening to him, where these changes were going, where they'd end up. She thought she'd find a clue in his diaries. Slowly, steadily, he was becoming another of her cases. She found herself puzzling over his psychology and wondering if the spell he was under would dissipate and blow away, like the clouds of blackflies would once the summer progressed far enough into July.

Instead, a few weeks later, she found someone named Vanessa shelling peas at the kitchen table. Vanessa explained that she was trying to get clean and had been stranded by her old car as she was fleeing a bad scene with a heroin-addicted boyfriend. Sally watched the woman's bitten-down fingernails work over the green pods and nodded as Vanessa told her that, thankfully, Darius had stopped after so many cars just passed her by on the side of the road. She said he'd saved her life, was full of wisdom, a true old soul. Vanessa took up residence in the guest room, where she was shortly joined by Priscilla, a runaway from abusive parents and a creepy uncle who was inappropriate with her.

"Allegedly abusive," Sally corrected Darius as he told her Priscilla's story.

"Still so suspicious, Sally," Darius said as he shook his head in the guise of indulgent disappointment. "You, who are in a helping, healing profession, can surely understand the impulse to aid someone in need. It's just simple human kindness."

Sally stared at him. "In need? Those two trustafarians in there? Hardly," she said. It was obvious to her that these women were not afflicted with the insults bestowed by low incomes and a poor education, like the people she saw at work. These were refugees from financial comfort, slumming it on purpose to tweak their parents and social class. "And, oh, by the way, who the fuck are you, and what did you do with the guy who used to live here, who used to have a beer and sex with me?" she added.

Darius *tsk*ed his disapproval and walked away. He also stopped sleeping in what had been their bed. A pillow and blanket decorated the sofa, but she rarely saw him actually asleep there. He was always up before she was, always reading or conferring with someone when she went up to her room at night. She wondered if those items were just props and he actually spent his nights curled up with one of the other women. She thought not. The energy between him and the women was all wrong for that. Far too paternalistic and avuncular. Condescending. She also suspected that his impotence was not reserved just for her. He had become asexual, his charms directed toward enticing women to listen to his advice instead of taking him to bed.

Another evening, Sally came home to find a truck with gaping rust wounds in the side panels and a beat-up camper top C-clamped to the bed parked alongside the barn. Two giggly twentysomethings emerged, one with a buzz cut, the other with long dreadlocks, both heavily pierced and tattooed. The bittersweet scent of clove cigarettes wafted over to her on the humid summer air. In the mornings, Sally now regularly dodged a woman—or two—making acrid-smelling teas as she tried to brew coffee and toast an English muffin. She was woken up at night by whispered conversations from the next room. There were frequently damp footprints coming from the other bathroom and only cold water left when she went to take a shower. Sally started locking her purse in her truck at night and stuffing the keys under her mattress. Then a calendar appeared on the kitchen wall. Names had been written into each square for morning, midday, and evening meals. She saw hers had been written in for the following night. She smirked, and on her way home the next day, bought two pizzas. When she dropped them on the table, Darius's face filled with distaste.

"Pepperoni and sausage," he said flatly.

"Yup, our favorites," Sally said, grinning maniacally.

"Astrid is a vegetarian. Vanessa is vegan. You know that."

"Whatever," Sally said. "They can pick off what they don't like. There are plenty of vegetables there, too."

"Sally," Darius said with a tone of great forbearance, as if about to explain something to a small child, "this is a hostile, provocative act—"

Vanessa stopped him with a hand on his arm. "It's OK, Darius," she said, her voice a sing-song. "No bad vibes here. I'll make us a salad. The kale in the garden is beautiful."

Later that night, after the house was quiet, Sally went looking for Darius and found him in the living room, propped up on the sofa, reading a Robert Bly book. She sat in a chair, pulled her feet underneath her, and asked him what was going on.

"What do you mean, 'going on,' Sally?" he said, closing the book over his index finger.

"With you. With these women. What's going on?" she said again.

He stared at her, his face free of emotion.

"Are you fucking them?" Sally asked, wanting to crack Darius's mask.

"Don't be vulgar, Sally," he responded primly.

"Vulgar?"

"Yes, vulgar," he said, reopening his book. "These women are vulnerable. To sleep with them would be exploiting them."

"In other words, it's not just me you can't get it up with."

Darius pinched his eyes shut. "Sally, I am trying to do something here."

"Here, like now, right here? Or here at the house?"

He set his book aside, leaned his elbows on his knees, and spoke to her with the fabricated sincerity that had become his permanent demeanor. He had a vision for the property, he explained. He had been building it in his mind. He felt now that he had been working on this vision for years, even though his clarity of purpose had only recently been made manifest. It was clearly his calling. Just as she had hers, working with youth in the system, he had his, working with people outside the system. He was here to provide a way station, a haven for people in need, in transition.

"You mean for self-indulgent, silly women trying to 'find themselves,'" Sally said.

"These are the people who have crossed my path, Sally. I cannot turn them away."

"How convenient," she said. "For them, certainly."

"There are no accidents, Sally," Darius said, reopening his book.

Oh yes, there most certainly are accidents, Sally thought, toting up the endless unplanned pregnancies she'd seen, the child who died in a house fire when her mother fell asleep with a cigarette in her hand, the guy who peppered his hunting partner in the back with birdshot when he dropped his gun, the teenager who went sailing through the windshield and severed his spine on a rock after swerving to avoid a runaway horse, the rich old guy from Connecticut who had been killed standing under a tree in a thunderstorm when a branch broke free and hit him on the head. She didn't say any of this to Darius. She didn't want to waste other people's tragedies on him.

"So, um, this is news to me," she said instead. "When were you going to let me in on all of this?"

"Sally," Darius said with his new, fabricated, maddening patience, "this has been my plan for some time. You are, of course, welcome to participate."

"Participate?"

Darius stared off in the middle distance and went on again about his dream, his vision, his plans. The property, his property, he told her, would be a sanctuary. He would offer simple work, few distractions, the salutary effects of getting one's hands dirty. He would take these stray individuals into the backcountry and teach them survival skills. He'd get a couple of pigs, a few cows, more chickens, a beehive. They would grow and can and sell wholesome food and crafts at the farmers' market.

He was looking into building a windmill with them. He was thinking of getting a portable pizza oven to use at fairs and festivals, where they'd offer gluten-free, vegetarian pizza. He'd get a pottery wheel. A loom. They would make things, and by making things together, they would create a community together—a community bonded by work and set apart from the materialistic culture of the modern world. They would make and grow and harvest what they needed. They would sell the excess to raise funds to cover their few other needs. There would be no sex and no television. No cell phones or video games. He was especially interested in bringing teenagers there. Runaways and abused kids.

Sally listened, incredulous, but now also fearful. He was ridiculous but also serious. And in that way, dangerous. She modulated her feelings before responding.

"Darius, I honestly don't think you know what you're getting into," she said, her voice filled with genuine concern and perplexity. "I appreciate the impulse. I understand it. I truly do. But I have to assure you, these people, these kids you're talking about, they are not sweet and misunderstood. They are cagey and manipulative. They've had to be to survive. I know. I work with them every day. I've got tens of thousands of dollars in student loans from studying them and their fucked-up psychologies. A little gardening is not what they need. Their problems are bigger, deeper than that. They've been hurt in ways you're just not getting. They've been damaged in ways those women having an extended slumber party upstairs would never understand."

"That's why I was hoping you would help," Darius said, smiling at her now. "Your experience and training. I thought that's how you'd fit in."

Fit in. Sally choked on the phrase. *Fit in? To his master plan?*

She was appalled. "Darius, I work with these kids all day," she said calmly. "The very last thing I want to do is live with them."

"Well, I do want to live with them. And help them. I believe I can offer them something. Something unique and life altering."

"Darius, you have good intentions, a big ego, and a shelf of self-help books," Sally said, even though she didn't believe there was an ounce of generosity in his ambitions. "I'm afraid that's not going to cut it."

He looked at her quizzically. "Sally, if you saw someone drowning in a pool and wanted to jump in to save them, I wouldn't try to stop you just because you're not trained as a lifeguard."

"But because I'm *not* a lifeguard, there's a good chance I'd drown us both!" Sally said, exasperated.

"I will not turn away from them. Everyone else has. They need me."

"You are in over your head," Sally told him. "Growing tomatoes, making clay coffee mugs, and shivering under a tarp in the mud for a few nights will not fix what's wrong with these people."

"It's better than what their parents are giving them," Darius insisted. "Frozen dinners and reality TV. All creating desires for things they can't and won't ever have. This is what causes their sickness. This longing for all these material things. This is what leads them to drugs and other efforts to over- or understimulate their senses."

"Oh my, Darius," Sally said, drawing out the words, trying to tamp down her impatience. "What gobbledygook, New-Age crap have you been reading now? Just because you attended rich-boy camp does not make you a survival expert. Rowing crew at prep school does not qualify you to lead canoe voyages in the backcountry. Volunteering once with Habitat for Humanity because you needed the community-service credit does not mean you can rewire this house. Taking a few psychology courses at college does not prepare you for helping kids deal with low IQs, grinding poverty, and being slapped, kicked, or fucked by their fathers."

"There's no need to be so coarse," Darius sniffed.

"Coarse?" Sally said, exasperated. "You think this is romantic. To you it's just a game. This is no fucking game to them. This is real life for these kids. You have means, money, and rich parents. But what happens to them when they get tired of living out here with you, when they bust a finger or burn something down or start fighting with each other or just want their goddamn Game Boy back? Then they have to go back to their fucked-up families with no skills, no education, no jobs, and no fucking teeth. You get to stay in your little trust-funded utopia and do it all over again."

Darius stood suddenly, dropping his book to the floor. For a moment, Sally thought he might cross the room and slap her. Or better, tear off his clothes so they could fuck their way out of this conversation.

Wrong man, she reminded herself.

That was how things got resolved with her previous boyfriend.

Darius's hands were balled into fists at his sides, and his jaw was clenched. Sally pushed herself farther into her chair. He stepped toward her, kicking Robert Bly in the head as he approached. He stopped. The sound of his teeth grinding against one another and the warm, moist air of late summer rattling through his nostrils was the only thing Sally heard.

"You're a hard bitch, Sally," he finally said.

"You're an arrogant fool, Darius," she returned.

After that night, that conversation, there was not a day that Sally did not think about leaving, moving out, putting it all behind her. But she stayed. She was protecting her investment, she told herself. She was keeping an eye on things. She was doing it for the money, because if she left, Darius might stop paying and she'd have the hassle of evictions to deal with. Plus, staying there meant free rent. She had multiple student loans, had run up her credit cards on basic living expenses, and had two ill, inactive parents living in a modular home and collecting disability—her father for a back strain sustained when he tried to break up a fight at the prison where he had been a guard for twenty-three years, her mother for an infection she picked up as a nurse's aide at the hospital, which, combined with her obesity and diabetes, had meant they had to amputate her foot. Sally had a brother out there somewhere but hadn't seen or heard from him in several years. He had disappeared following yet another drug arrest. He was no help, but at least he was no longer a hassle.

Darius set up a bedroom for himself in the attic. Behind a door he kept locked, Sally noticed one day when she tried to snoop. She kept the room they had once shared and was left to use the small bathroom next to it by herself. The rest of the women filled the other two bedrooms with bunk beds and mattresses on the floor and took turns in the larger bathroom. Given Darius's long hair, facial scruff, and smell of garlic and sweat, it seemed he rarely groomed himself at all.

The changing cast of characters living in the house shifted their weight aside when Sally passed by, a shoal of fish in the presence of a shark. They avoided eye contact and stopped talking among themselves whenever she came into the room. Without decree, she was left half a shelf in the refrigerator and part of a shelf in the pantry—her very few grocery items a stark, shiny, prepackaged contrast to the messy comingling of dirty vegetables, jars of homemade yogurt, bottles of green smoothies, blocks of tempeh and tofu, and bags of nuts and grains that cluttered most of the shelves. Her name was removed from the community meal calendar.

Darius smiled at her politely when they were near each other, left a check in her room every month for the mortgage—always on time— but said almost nothing to her. She tried to think of ways to engage him in a discussion about what he was doing. She wanted to explain things to him, to get through to him, to get him to understand what she knew to be true about the errors of his ways. But he, too, always shifted away from her, making conversation impossible. So she began to avoid the house and its occupants. She worked long hours, ate out, went to the movies, and joined a sportsmen's club where she took up archery and killed time in the clubhouse. But she couldn't stay entirely away. Nor, truthfully, did she want to. She felt compelled to come home and watch what was happening from what she considered a safe, noncommittal distance. Some days, she thought what was unfolding was an elaborate comedy. Other days, she feared it was a tragedy.

Lying in bed one night, staring at the ceiling, wondering why she was still there, Sally finally said to herself, *Who the fuck am I kidding? I'm here because I'm curious. I'm here because I want to see what happens. I'm here because I want to watch it all fall apart.*

DARIUS AND MIRANDA

Miranda met Darius at the farmers' market. She had been toying with the idea of bringing in some of her own vegetables for resale. Maybe making pies. Or jams. Something. Doing something. She was at the farmers' market not to buy vegetables—she had her own enormous garden, well tended and overflowing with produce, much of which she ended up giving away—but to see what others were selling. She was trying to find out if there was a niche there she might fill.

What a metaphor for the rest of my life, she thought.

She paused at a funny little table in a far corner of the grassy field where the market was held because that particular stand was set slightly apart, and so attracted her attention. Or maybe she stopped simply because it was at the end of the line. Maybe because she was tired. Vaguely frustrated. Unsure if she'd found any answers or direction. This miasma of conflicting emotions was becoming familiar, a feeling that seemed to waft in on an errant breeze and then cling, like the tangy smell of manure. It was hard to shake off. She stopped to try and ground her buzzing nerves as much as to examine the odd assortment of wares.

"What's your name?"

Miranda looked into the azure eyes and intense stare of the man sitting at the table.

"Miranda," she replied reflexively, surprised and rattled by the abruptness of his question. "They call me Andy."

She regretted adding that last bit. There was no "they" anymore. Only her parents had ever called her Andy. And her brother. She hadn't even liked the nickname. It had made her feel young, small, vulnerable. She could not articulate, was not fully aware, that the man behind the card table, under the makeshift tent, made her feel the same way.

"Well, Andy," he said, drawing out the first vowel, teasing her or maybe taunting her somehow, "can I interest you in some of our wares?" He swept his arm a few inches above a collection of small jars and twists of metal and scraps of wood on his scarred table. "We have homemade jams, totally organic, from berries foraged locally."

Miranda made her own jam from berries she gathered herself. The scrawled handwriting on the labels and the lids left askew made her smile. He obviously did not know much about canning. She thought his naïveté charming. There was nothing here that she wanted or needed. But she was reluctant to move on. She felt his eyes on her face as she feigned polite interest, picking things up and setting them down again.

"Miranda," he said. "That's familiar to me somehow. You are familiar to me somehow. Surely we've met before."

Miranda tried for a light laugh, tried to compress the expansive feeling that was coming over her. "I don't think so," she said. "This is the first time I've seen your stand."

"Ah," he said. "Yes. Well. Perhaps in a past life, then."

A past life. Silly, but maybe. Why not? Miranda thought as she picked up a twist of wire.

"What is this?" she asked.

"This . . ." he said, letting his breath out as a long pause, as if he was about to reveal something mysterious.

Miranda waited for him to finish his sentence. Instead he stood, reached across the table, lifted her hand from where it hung at her side, and slipped the object onto her finger. She was surprised at how soft his hands were. She was surprised at how warm they were. And at how beautiful the thin strip of matte metal looked on her finger.

"This is for you," he said.

Miranda felt herself flush at the intimacy of the gesture. Then his voice rattled on, the tone changed now, official and practiced. A sales pitch.

"We make all our jewelry from found objects," he said. "Everything is upcycled. We even make our own tools."

We. Miranda pictured a slightly scowling, unwashed hippie wife, a brightly colored bandanna wrapped around long dreadlocks embedded with stone beads and pieces of silver.

"The income from these products supports our other efforts," he continued.

Miranda's hand rested in his, a small weight lightly held. She felt rooted to the spot, the moment. His eyes. So clear, so blue, so empty, framed by the ropes of his dark hair falling around his face. Somehow, he had pinned her down by putting the ring on her finger. She wondered, fleetingly, what he meant by the phrase "other efforts." Then he abruptly dropped her hand, stood back, and scanned her face. It seemed he was looking for something that wasn't there.

"Keep it," he said, wiping his hands together as if they were dirty.

"No, I couldn't . . ." she stumbled. "Let me pay for it."

"No," he said, his voice suddenly deeper, authoritative. "Keep it." His smile was a contortion of his lips. "It will give you something to remember me by."

And then he was gone. He was still there, standing in front of her, but he had turned away, and in that instant dismissed her, his attention on someone behind her, someone she had not noticed. A small woman with a scruff of short, stiff hair, her hands full of wares from the table.

Or was she adding them to the table? This other woman's expression, cold and suspicious, spooked Miranda, and she scuttled away, trying to collect thoughts that had become tangled like dead leaves and twigs swirling in an eddy. She went to the next aisle, reminding herself what she had come here to get: some coffee beans from the new guy who roasted them himself in his home. Some tomatoes, as the blight had gotten to hers—they were always hard to grow in this climate, but the wet summer had been brutal. A chicken, or anything to vary the slabs of venison that still filled the freezer from last fall. She hoped the goat cheese had not sold out yet. Perhaps a bouquet of flowers. Yes, that would brighten the table, the room.

As she walked away she realized, with just a passing thought, that she had not gotten the man's name. She twisted the ring with her thumb and realized she hadn't even said thank you.

Not to worry, she told herself. *He'll be here next weekend. I'll bring him something in exchange. I'll make him something. Something special.*

Not Dix. It was not Dix for whom she'd make something special, for whom she was always making something special. This was an odd, uncomfortable, and yet strangely exhilarating idea. It would be for this other man. This man who as yet didn't even have a name.

The next weekend, Miranda arrived at the farmers' market with a pie in hand. She had made two—both blueberry, Dix's favorite. One for him, and one to give to the stranger who had given her a ring. The pies had used up a large portion of the fruit she had collected, on her knees, from the wild, low bushes full of small, sweet berries. She'd just collect more, she'd told herself as she was arranging the dough in careful strips over the top. Whatever the bears and birds leave behind. And the berry farm. There was always the U-pick berry farm.

She walked down the rows at the market, the still-warm pie carefully balanced in the palm of her hand. She began to feel lost. No, she told herself, stopping at the far corner of the field, she was in the right place. She stared and stared at the spot where she'd had a ring slipped on her finger the week prior, but there was only an empty area of lightly trampled grass at the end of the tidy line of card tables and identical pop-up tents where his ad hoc display and cotton tapestries on bamboo poles had been.

What do I do now? she wondered.

She felt like she'd dressed up and arrived for a party on the wrong date. Silly. Confused. Embarrassed. She couldn't bring the thing home again. Two pies. Such an extravagance. How would she explain what she'd done? She didn't know why not, but she knew she could not. Dix would wonder what she'd been thinking. Why she hadn't just frozen the extra berries. That was, after all, the only thing that made any sense. She'd have no explanation.

She had just passed a table offering raffle tickets. Raising money for the local volunteer fire department. Or maybe it was the library. A local family hit with unexpected medical bills. A child born with special needs or a man with a large family, no insurance, and now a rare cancer. There was always something, someone, in need around here. It wore her down and bummed her out, all these flyers and appeals for people who were so extremely unprepared for the inevitable disasters of life. She took the pie there, to the fund-raising table, told them she'd made two and her visitors were not coming in for the weekend after all, so they could sell it and keep the proceeds. Or add it to the raffle. She didn't know why she made up this story. Another extravagance to justify the first extravagance. She didn't have visitors that weekend, of course. Or any weekend.

Miranda felt more flustered than seemed warranted by the small mix-up in her intentions, the thwarting of her picture of how this little interaction was supposed to go. She had anticipated pleasure at the strange man's imagined delight with her gift. She had thought he'd dig into the pie right there in front of her, magically produce a fork, make appreciative noises over her culinary skills and generosity. And now . . . now she didn't know what to do. So after she freed herself of the pie, she left the market without buying anything at all.

The next weekend she came with a list she had scribbled with the intention of keeping herself on track. She avoided the aisle that had held the funny table, but then, while fingering some skeins of bulky yarn—she was trying to learn to knit—she saw in her peripheral vision the colorful cotton bedspreads draped over bamboo poles, and the head of thick, dark, wavy hair. Miranda turned to look, and as she did, she knocked a soft ball of wool off its perch and into the grass. She squatted to pick it up and realized that it was not him at the table after all. The wares were the same, but the hair belonged to a woman with brown eyes, dark in a way that had little to do with their color. Suddenly, Miranda felt that she'd imagined him. Not just then, but the other day as well. He was a dream, a fantasy. There were two other women at the table. One with graying hair falling in corrugations down her back and another with blonde hair roughly cut to just below her chin. It looked, Miranda thought, as if someone had gathered the woman's hair into a ponytail and chopped it off with pruning shears.

She twisted the ring on her finger. He had to have been real, she thought. She had the ring to prove it.

She bought two large boxes of imperfect tomatoes and a bag of onions. They'd been grown in hoop houses, she figured, so they'd be less flavorful than what she'd get later in the season, once the summer was in its full hot-and-humid swing, but these would be fine for making salsa and sauce. She'd can a bunch for the winter. The task would keep her busy for a few days with chopping, cooking, boiling. She loved listening to the satisfying pops of the metal lids sealing themselves as the jars cooled. The sauce would be delicious with those thick, almost-obscene ropes of venison sausage.

The market was winding down for the day. The tourist season had been slow this year, the weather uncooperative, the blackflies brutal. The locals didn't come much. They couldn't afford to buy organic produce. Most people around here gardened organically by default—not because they cared about pesticides but because they couldn't afford them. Miranda came back to the market only a few more times that summer. She didn't really need anything. Picked up some yarn and a variety of squash she didn't grow herself. More of that coffee that she liked. The stuff Dix called "fancy." She never set up a stall herself. And the table with the twisted lids on jam jars and jewelry made from scrap did not appear again.

What Dix noticed was not the ring, not at first, but the new and nervous motion of Miranda's fingers. Thumb tucked into the palm, pushing, twisting, fluttering as she spun the little metal spiral. He felt that Miranda was both unconsciously challenging him to notice and also counting on his not noticing. She thought he didn't notice much. Especially when it came to her. This was a new complaint, fresh and sharp as the first cold snap of impending winter.

"There could be a bear in the living room and you'd walk right by without breaking stride," Miranda had said recently, apropos of nothing.

"Not noticing and not minding are two different things," he'd replied. "Besides, the bears around here find berries a lot more appetizing than me."

He had said that hoping to make her smile. Something that seemed harder and harder to do.

"Anyway, if there was a bear in the living room, it would probably be just looking for one of your delicious pies."

She stared at him, hearing his words but not taking them in. There was that sheen of sadness again, a spill that she sometimes blinked back and that other times seeped over the entire surface of her eyes. This was a new sadness. It hadn't been there that first month, when she lived in the cottage, when he'd have expected it, after all the tragedy had come and gone and left its path of quiet destruction behind. It wasn't there when she started spending more time with him in the house, sharing the meals she cooked as a thank-you for the cottage. It wasn't there that first time he'd kissed her, which was the last night she'd slept in the cottage. It wasn't there when her mother died, in the deepest part of the winter. She'd seemed sad then, of course, but also relieved that the woman was out of her misery. And that Miranda was also out of hers. No, it had come into her eyes a few months ago. A darkening of the light that had once and always seemed to radiate outward from her pale blue orbs. It came on with the spring, an inverse of the season.

"You mean not caring," Miranda said, her thoughts lingering back before his joke.

"What?" he asked, not following her train of thought.

"It's not that you don't notice because you don't mind," she said. "It's that you don't notice because you don't care."

He wanted to tell her that not caring was not necessarily a bad thing in a lot of situations. Caring about inconsequential things took up time and space and energy that could be used for other, more productive things. Like adjusting the sagging barn door so it would close properly this winter.

"I care about you," he said. "I care about you very much."

He hoped this statement, true and sincere, would bring her to him, send her into his arms. But instead, she turned her head away, frustrated that he would not argue with her, and left him there at the kitchen counter, alone, where they had been standing side by side, sipping tea.

Dix wondered if she was mad at him for something. He mentally skimmed over his behavior and their interactions recently, and he could find nothing obvious to point to, nothing tweaked in the companionable rhythm they had eased their way into. He figured, at some level, this moodiness was her understandable, if delayed, melancholy working its way out, a splinter that had dug itself in under the skin and was starting to erupt, carried forward on a small wave of pus. He also thought she was trying to provoke him, punish him somehow for something that was not of his doing. Because who else was there to punish for all she'd been forced to bear? Everyone else was dead. He forgave her. Over and over, he forgave her.

There was also the pregnancy. Or the lack of a pregnancy. He didn't understand why she was in such a hurry. At first they'd just been careless with birth control. They had been so hungry for each other. It was as if, after all those years of knowing each other from a distance, hired hand and employer's daughter, they had some kind of catching up to do. They spent hours in bed, exploring each other's bodies, discovering the parts of each other that had been kept hidden. Miranda started joking that if they weren't more careful, there'd be little Dixes running around. She had moved very quickly from teasing to disappointment, though. She started wondering if something was wrong with her. She became fearful that she'd never be able to be a mother. He soothed her and made love to her and told her to stop worrying. It didn't help. She insisted he get tested. She insisted she get tested. There was nothing wrong with either of them. He was excited by the idea of becoming a father but was in no hurry. He kept reminding her that they had plenty of time, that she was so young, just twenty-four years old. The doctor said the same thing. But she was impatient. An impatience Dix felt had to do with more than just waiting for a child to come. He was afraid she wanted a child so badly to replace the family she'd lost. Or, perhaps worse, to give herself something to do. To find a way to fill the emptiness of her days and postpone the more difficult quandaries of deciding what she wanted to make of her life, of figuring out who she wanted to be. She was young, he reminded himself. Again. The same excuse he used for her over and over.

He didn't understand her increasing irritation with him. He knew he was somewhat maddeningly un-provoke-able. He tended to walk away from arguments. He didn't much mind about the twisting tunnels of feelings that so many people got tangled up in. If a person wanted to get lost in the dark passages of her own emotions, well, fine, but he had no time for such things. He also did not know what to say or do to fix other people's feelings or those sorts of things. His practical experience told him that when you tried to repair something without fully understanding how and why it got broken in the first place, you tended to make things worse. He thought he knew how Miranda had gotten out of true; he'd seen the events that warped her emotions, but he did not know how to help her get realigned.

So he watched and waited, and Miranda's face did what it often did these days. It got still and flat, and in that stillness, he knew there was some particularly female sort of pain he might never be able to comprehend. He watched as she began to fret over all those things that not only didn't matter to him but hadn't ever mattered to her, either. Things like a few flecks of mud falling from the bottom of his pants to the floor. Another chicken killed by a fox. The tangy smell of manure that wafted through the valley when the farmers spread it on their fields. These were all just normal country things. Things she used to laugh about.

And there were those other things she worried herself over now. Why the Simpsons hadn't asked them back after that one party. Whether she should serve fish or just put burgers on the grill for the two of them on a Sunday night. Should she volunteer somewhere or take a class? If the people at the local garden center would be mad that she hadn't come to buy hanging baskets this year, like she had the previous spring.

"They won't care," he said, confused. "They won't even realize."

"You don't understand," she said, pushing her lips together.

"You're right," he replied. "I don't understand." He also didn't understand why she had starting fussing with her hair, asking him whether it looked better pulled back or left loose. "Wear it whatever way is most comfortable," he'd said. "You're just going to the store." And then, knowing he'd said the wrong thing, added, "It's beautiful. You're beautiful either way."

He meant what he said, and he also hoped his words would soothe her. Would keep her from the bathroom, where he found her more often than ever, bent over in front of a small magnifying mirror picking at imaginary flaws on her face, rubbing thick white creams from small pots onto her skin, and even applying makeup, which simply ended up smudged beneath her eyes and on the sheets in angry streaks of black.

Nothing he said seemed to help her. Words were clumsy tools in his hands.

"No one cares what your hair looks like."

He meant it as a comment about them, a way to diminish those others whose opinions seemed to matter to her in a way they never had before. It didn't come out right. She glared at him.

"I'm sorry," he said. "I can't seem to say what I mean. You're worth ten to anyone else in this whole valley. You don't need to give a damn what anyone else thinks."

That dark, reflective shimmer invariably came back into her eyes. She was singed, somehow. And he was frustrated. So he would go outdoors to find something he could fix. And she would go to the kitchen, where there was something she could clean.

That was why he didn't ask her about the ring. Not because he didn't notice. Not because he didn't care. Because he was afraid he'd ask the wrong question, say the wrong thing, hurt her in ways he could not comprehend or control.

Taking care of other people's property reliably supplied Dix with chores that settled his mind. His own property also supplied him with an endless stream of must-, should-, and could-dos. The chore that faced him the morning when Miranda left him standing at the kitchen counter with a cold cup of once-warm tea was a dead tree he had cut down and bucked up. The kegs of wood were piled next to the barn, where he'd dumped them. They needed to be split and stacked. So he went outdoors to the familiarity of his compliant tools, hanging against the wall of the barn.

The barn had two stalls. His mother had kept a placid quarter horse that she used for trail riding. His father never took to animals the way she had. Which seemed fine with her. The barn and woods were for her, as they were for Dix, an escape from the confines of the house. She loved her house but also loved to leave it for a while, partially so she could have the pleasure of returning. She'd kept a goat as company for the horse—but also as entertainment for herself—and chickens. Always a rescued dog, sometimes two, and a few cats, which tended to live in the barn instead of the house. The animals had died, one after another, during the years of her illness, as if in solidarity and foreboding, and Dix had not replaced them.

Miranda had talked of getting a dog but was insecure about her ability to manage one, to train and care for it properly, not having grown up with pets. She wanted to do things well but was also afraid of having to get herself through the failures it took to learn how to do a thing well, a tendency that led her increasingly into spirals of self-doubt. She wanted chickens, so Dix repaired the old henhouse, an effort that had given her the necessary courage to pick up a pamphlet and a box of fuzzy chicks from the Agway this past spring. Their number had decreased and needed to be supplemented a few times—a natural inevitability of living alongside raccoons and foxes and coyotes, he assured her. Still, she took the losses hard, cried over the disparate trails of feathers when she found them. Cried too hard, he thought. Cried over the chickens, but something else as well. Something neither of them could name.

When Dix entered the barn, he was comforted by the intertwined sweet and sour smells of sawdust and grain, manure and gasoline that lingered where animals and machinery had been housed together. He took off his canvas shirt and hung it on a peg—he loved the strange magic trick barns performed of being warm in the winter, cool in the summer, and a mirror of the temperature outside during the in-between seasons—then flicked on the fluorescent lights over his workbench. Working in a gray T-shirt, he found his ax and a file and began sharpening his tool, the dull metal brightening to a silver gleam as he filed away the rust and dents. He tested the edge with his thumb and then stepped out the back side of the barn and into the bright day. The logs were in a pile the size of a small car, right where they had tumbled off the back of his dump truck.

He swung the ax into the smaller pieces of wood right where they lay in comforting disarray. With every strike of the ax, he felt a piece of tension, a mote of worry, leave him. Strike, breathe, release. He soon felt emptied out, a pail scrubbed clean. That peaceful void stayed with him for the next hour. He got into the bigger pieces, picking them up, setting them on the splitting stump, working harder now, bringing the ax overhead for extra leverage. Swing, split, stack. But then, drop by drop, he felt himself start to fill again with something cold and wet. He paused, wiped his forehead on the short sleeve of his T-shirt, and looked into the dark wall of native forest that ringed his cleared acre and a half of home, cottage, barn, garage, storage shed, raised garden beds, perennial and shrub borders, and small patch of lawn. He didn't really believe in lawns—this one was simply a means of keeping the forest from taking over.

He looked over his shoulder toward the house. It seemed empty in there—it was so quiet and still. He wondered if Miranda had left. No, he'd have heard the car. Maybe she was taking a nap. Reading a book. Trying to knit again. Cleaning. Fretting over her face. He didn't normally wonder about her in this way. It felt strange and suspicious.

He went back to splitting.

He went back to remembering.

The first activity was familiar, the second less so.

Dix was someone who rarely looked backward. But recently, he found himself retracing his steps through his time with Miranda, trying to find the moment, the event or failing that had turned her from him. She had moved very little with her into the cottage. Just a suitcase of clothes, a few books, and one faded stuffed bear her father had given her as a child. She was hardly noticeable out there, but after years of living alone, Dix felt her presence the way one notices how a borrowed jacket doesn't fit quite right because it has worn itself to the contours of another's body. In the mornings, after he made coffee and ate breakfast, he would look out the window of his kitchen and stare at the small gleam from the cottage filtering through the trees. He was always up well before her light came on in those chilled, damp fall mornings, and as he drove away, it gave him comfort to think of her tucked in the cottage where he felt she was safe and secure. In a place where no more harm could come to her. That was his hope, anyway.

When he returned, the shorter days sending him home in the late afternoons, he'd find some small evidence that she'd been in the house and he'd smile to himself, satisfied. He'd told her to make his kitchen her own and was happy that she was. At first, he'd find just a coffee cup or bowl in the drain tray. Then a new box of cereal in the pantry or container of yogurt in the refrigerator. It gave him pleasure to see her things, not really mingled, but shyly set alongside his own.

Then she began to leave things for him. A plate of cookies she had baked. A loaf of homemade bread. A pot of soup. He reciprocated. He left a small trout in the refrigerator one day when he had to be out of town and wrote her a note telling her to cook it for herself. He brought some mismatched eggs from a neighbor and told her to help herself because there were too many for him alone. For a couple of weeks, they tiptoed around each other in this way, leaving their notes and offerings, waving from a distance, unsure how to step across the comfort of their friendly and formal distance—or if they wanted to.

Then one day there was the pie. It was a thing of beauty, with a delicate latticework of golden crust. The buttery pastry dissolved against his tongue and melded with the warm and syrupy apples that made up its filling. For this he had to thank her. In person. He cut two fresh pieces, scooped some vanilla ice cream he had in the basement freezer, and with a flashlight in his teeth to illuminate the way, walked toward the small patch of light that was her cottage. When he got to the door he stood there, unsure how to knock when his hands were occupied with the two plates. He kicked gently with the toe of his boot. She opened the door, and her face had registered caution, then surprise, then pleasure, in quick succession. She removed the flashlight from his mouth and ushered him inside. He took the rocker and she the upholstered chair, and they dug into the pie, the murmuring sounds of gustatory pleasure the only explanation required between them.

"Where did you learn to cook?" Dix asked once his plate was clean.

"My grandmother," Miranda replied. "My father's mother. She was an immigrant from Italy. She married an Irish man. They were very working class."

Dix raised his eyebrows.

"I know. Everyone thinks my dad was the perfect WASP. But he wasn't. Maybe that's why he worked at it so hard, out-WASPed the real WASPs like my mother."

"The converted are always the most devout," Dix said.

Miranda laughed, which pleased him.

"His parents were not like that at all," she continued. "Very simple. Very decent. Showed their love with food, not money." She paused to finish her last bite. "I think they kind of embarrassed him. But I loved spending time with them. Especially my grandmother. In the kitchen. Cooking. I think it's the only thing I'm any good at. Thanks to her."

This was a lot of conversation for them. A lot of revelation.

"My mother taught me to cook," Dix said.

Now Miranda raised her eyebrows. "Seriously? My mother's idea of making a meal was to make reservations."

Dix gave her a knowing look. "Yes, I remember that about her. My mother was a bit different. She wanted me to be self-sufficient. I even know how to mend and iron."

Miranda laughed again, a light, easy sound that filled the small room.

"Come up to the house tomorrow night," he said, surprising himself as much as Miranda with the invitation. He began collecting the plates, distracting himself from what he'd begun, from the fear that she'd protest. "I'll show you. You'll get to meet my mother through my cooking."

And then before she could say no, he left the cottage.

When Miranda arrived the next evening, Dix could not help but notice that she had dressed up. Just a bit. Her hair twisted against her head in a knot rather than pulled back in a ponytail. A long skirt rather than jeans. A touch of color in her face. He watched her as she came into the kitchen, saw her noticing the dining room table set with cloth napkins and candles, and asked if she wanted a glass of wine.

"Are you having some?"

"A beer," he said.

"I'd like a beer, too," she said, looking around the bare kitchen counters, vaguely confused. "Am I too early? Can I help you get started?"

In answer, he opened the oven and a wave of smells, rich with spices and earth, permeated the room. "It's almost done."

"Ah, you're one of those who cleans as he goes," Miranda said. "I make a huge mess and clean it all up at the end."

"Well, I wanted to make something that didn't require a lot of fussing. Venison stew," he said. "Cornbread. Salad. Leftover pie for dessert."

"That does not smell like any stew I've ever eaten!" Miranda said. She laughed and a strand of hair fell free of its clip, framing her jaw. Dix was flooded with the urge to reach forward and push it back behind her ear. The sensation was so raw and unsettling, he turned away from her and busied himself with the salad bowl.

He asked how the cottage was working out, how her mother was, if all the real estate transactions had been completed. Small talk. The kind of thing he was unused to. It was not just that he had lived alone for so long. His parents had not been much for chitchat, either. They spoke to each other about their work. They spoke to each other through their work. Having someone in his home for dinner was strange and thrilling for him. He was also nervous, another thing he was unused to.

He served, they sat, and Miranda ate slowly, taking her time with each bite, asking after his techniques and flavorings. They shared stories of their family meals, hers always centered by pasta and red sauce, his by game from the mountains and vegetables from the garden. They stayed at the table for a long time after the plates were emptied. The candles sputtered a bit. He thought of asking her if she wanted to sit in the living room, but something kept them right where they were. They talked of their mothers' illnesses. He told her how his father had died soon after cancer took his mother. A heart attack.

"Well named," Dix said as he folded and unfolded a napkin. "Losing her broke his heart."

Then he looked up, and in the clear blue lakes of Miranda's eyes saw a sorrow of his own reflected. It was a sadness he hadn't fully realized he felt, and its revelation made him realize how lonely he had been—and how accustomed to loneliness he had become. In that moment, her eyes were a gentle press of light and warmth that seemed to dissipate the shadows of those feelings. And offered a promise to hold those feelings at bay, indefinitely.

They both got quiet, emptied of words. She yawned. He stood in response. She seemed reluctant to rise, but he attributed this to tiredness, the late hour, not to a desire to stay at the table any longer. She reached her arms over her head and stretched before getting to her feet and going toward the door. He held it open for her. The air, touched that night with the cold of the imminent winter, drifted in the gap. She thanked him. For dinner. For everything, she whispered. At the door, at the end of that evening, he went ahead and pushed the loose strand of hair behind her ear. She tilted her head toward his hand. His fingers grazed her cheek. Then she was gone.

A few evenings later, the lights were on when he drove up to the house. The smell of sautéing onions wafted toward him. Music was playing, some low, female vocalist. Miranda was at the stove when he came in the door, but crossed the kitchen with a cold beer in hand for him. She was smiling. Her hair was loose. There was flour on her cheek.

It was her turn to make him dinner, she announced.

After that meal—a veal dish, something he'd never had before—she didn't go back to the cabin. He could still recall the taste of wine and berry sauce on her lips when, washing dishes side by side, he had bent his face to hers. Without words, she'd let herself go soft in his arms, and then they'd wandered, side by side, to his bed. He remembered how strange his coarse hands felt on her smooth skin, the contrast of his lean, hard musculature against her pillowy, delicate body. How odd it seemed to dress in the morning, tiptoeing around his own room while she slept in his bed, her hair a spray of dried grasses spread over his pillows. How quickly he got used to hearing music in the air and something sizzling in a pan when he came home at the end of the day. How much he enjoyed the lunches she packed for him, thermoses of soup and sandwiches on thick slabs of homemade bread. How accustomed he became to her appearing in the barn with a cup of hot coffee for him when he was working.

She told him she seemed to be like her grandmother—she showed her love through food.

And on that day, that afternoon when three full seasons had passed since he had first pressed his chapped lips to her moist ones, as he stood in the sun splitting wood and tasting his own sweat as it drizzled into his mouth, wondering when and why things had changed so much between them, he slowly realized that he was waiting for that cup of coffee. He was waiting for her. And it didn't look like she was coming.

While Dix waited for Miranda, she watched him. She had gone to the garden, seeking a simple task to settle her mind. She was being irritable and she didn't know why. She was being short-tempered with the one person who deserved it not at all. She was being what her mother would have called "a brat." She disliked herself for it. She picked a few tomatoes and ears of corn and returned to the kitchen. From the sink, with the water rushing over her gleanings, she watched Dix's deceptively effortless competence on full display. He swung the ax with an economy and precision of movement that made it seem as if the logs were splitting of their own accord. She'd watched him do this before and loved the rustic choreography of his efforts. She admired him and was jealous of him. She adored him and was besieged by doubts as to why he loved her. She toted up all the comforts and kindnesses he had given her and feared she had offered little in return. Everything he gave her seemed like a revelation, a shiny, new object unpacked just for her, and she felt she came to him empty-handed. She couldn't even get pregnant. Tears began to drip down her face. Dix appeared to her as if he were underwater.

"God," she said out loud. "What is this ridiculous self-pity?"

She felt weak in the face of his exquisite self-reliance. The comparison stung. She turned off the water and rubbed her hands in a towel, reminding herself of all the reasons he said he loved her. She was calm, peaceful, quick to smile, unselfconscious, generous, kind, not made up or given to airs. He had told her over and over again. But these were all things she felt she had not earned, things that just seemed like dumb luck. These were also things she felt less able to find within herself these days. She was more peevish than peaceful, more irritable than generous, quicker to find fault than to smile.

Why? she wondered. *Because I have not figured out who or what I want to be.*

She had not found a place for herself in this world, a job or task she could set before herself to make her mark, to make a life. She had been looking forward to the happy occupations of motherhood, the absorbing busyness of giving oneself over to another's life. A baby was going to be her answer to the question of what to do. But that answer was proving as elusive as all the others.

Dix kept reminding her it hadn't yet been a year. They weren't really "trying," just forgoing birth control. She was only twenty-four years old. He was only thirty-one. There was so much to look forward to. There was no hurry. Yet she felt anxious all the time now. As if she was missing something. She wondered if they should get married. He'd always said there was no need. Nothing a courthouse could give them that they didn't have already. She'd always agreed. Besides, there was no one to come to a wedding. But now she wondered if being married might settle something inside herself. If it might be a tonic to some restlessness in her soul. She was starting to realize she was lonely in a way that had nothing to do with the presence of other people but had to do with something missing inside herself. She was mad that she wasn't whole, and frustrated that she wasn't finding whatever seemed to be lacking. And she felt silly and stupid for feeling so bad when there was so much good in her life.

Miranda watched the man she loved split logs in the long drafts of yellow, late-summer light, the ax moving in an elegant arc overhead and then down against the hard wood without hesitation or doubt that the desired goal was a given. She felt her tears dry, leaving sticky salt residue on her cheeks. She wanted so much to go to him, but she didn't know what to bring to him, and she felt that just herself could not possibly be enough.

That first summer together, Dix and Miranda stumbled in and out of the shadows of their relationship. Some days there was more light than others. Miranda might suggest a hike and a picnic for them, and Dix would push off a client so he could say yes to her. Dix might reach across the darkness of their bed and pull her in between his arms. They'd laugh together at the antics of one of the chickens. They went to the grocery store together, had lunch while they were in town. The stuff of life kept reestablishing their threads of connection even after their occasional emotional fumbling strained or broke them.

Sometimes, when Dix went to check up on a house, if there wasn't too much work for him to do and if the owners were away, Miranda would pack a lunch and tag along, turning the chore into a kind of date instead. One day, as they drove down an unfamiliar road toward a new log home Dix wanted her to see, she watched the trees click by outside the passenger-side window. Fall had settled in and brilliant red and yellow leaves had begun to drift down, leaving the deciduous trees partially naked among their evergreen brethren and creating seductive gaps in the landscape that allowed glimpses of homes and hillsides that were usually hidden. She was watching for these new sights, these peeks from a distance into otherwise private worlds, when suddenly, something close in the road jumped into her line of sight, startling her so that she flinched backward. It took her a moment to realize it was just a man standing at a listing mailbox by the side of an otherwise-deserted street. It took her a moment more to recognize something familiar in his passing profile.

"What's going on?" Dix said.

"Nothing," Miranda replied, trying for a nonchalance at odds with the unexpected thumping in her chest.

Dix glanced from her to his rearview mirror a few times before saying, "That's the hippie guru guy."

"What?" Miranda asked, honestly confused. "What are you talking about?"

"That guy you were looking at. The guy by the mailbox."

Of course Dix had seen the man by the side of the road. She said he didn't notice things, but, in fact, almost nothing escaped him. He saw critters rushing through the underbrush. Birds hidden in dense trees. Things that were on the verge of disintegrating and would benefit from repair. Her feelings. Even though neither he nor she could readily identify what her feelings were, what they portended, what to do about them, it did not mean he didn't notice them. Miranda involuntarily twisted the ring on her finger. Dix's eyes dropped to her hand, then went quickly back to the road. She was too distracted to notice the trajectory of his gaze.

"What do you mean the 'hippie guru guy'?" she asked.

"Some guy bought an old farm that had been abandoned for a long time. No one wanted it because it's in such a damp spot. So little sun. Old woman died out there, alone, one winter many years ago. Anyway, he's been there, I don't know, a year maybe. People thought it strange that he bought the place, then there's been talk that it was just him and a bunch of lost, random women—that's how the guru stuff started, especially because the women were so somber and always came into town together. Like a pack. Some thought he was a Mormon or some such. You know how folk talk. But then more recently, he started taking in kids. Runaway types. Some went back home after being there and told stories about him and the place."

Dix paused. Miranda wondered if he was afraid the talk of town gossip upset her. Sometimes it did. There had been so much chatter about her family. About her. Her and Dix. She hated it. But she tried to steady her mood. They were having a nice day. She wanted to keep it that way.

"Who knows if any of it is true or not," he went on. "People make stuff up. Especially kids."

That last bit was for her benefit. He was always telling her to ignore gossip. That people just fabricated stories and didn't care if they hurt people in the process. Miranda realized she was spinning the ring. She stopped, but she had a strong feeling that Dix knew where it came from. It seemed impossible, but then again, he knew so much. Kept most of it to himself and brought out his knowledge and understanding only when required. Like his tools. Kept in immaculate repair, in a tidy box, until they were needed for a specific task. She didn't want him to know where she'd gotten the ring, and she didn't want to know why she didn't want him to know.

"What kinds of stories?" she asked, trying not to seem overly interested. "What do the kids say?"

"That he's got all these ideas about the evils of modern life. No television, computers, cell phones. Trying to stay apart from the modern world. Its corrupting influence. Like some New Age Amish person. Guess that's why so few kids stay out there. Try it for a bit. Then back to the video games. Even if it means putting up with Daddy smacking them around."

He was quiet for a bit, looking for the driveway to the house he was taking her to.

"Who knows, though?" he said. "You know how kids talk. How town people gossip. He could be a monk who gave a kid a ride once and they'd turn the story and make him a serial child molester."

He was through talking now, Miranda could tell. That had been unusual for him, saying that much, in that way, about a person he did not know. He would not condemn. Not unless he had the facts. And even if the facts were bad, he would simply avoid that person. Until he or she was in actual need or trouble. Then he would step up, as he always did. His straightforward civility had always been a marvel to Miranda. She wondered why it was starting to be an irritation.

"Yes," Miranda said into the quiet that had settled between them. "I know how town people are. How much they gossip. How little they care for the damage their meanness can do to people."

As much as she was trying to stay cheerful, she allowed her voice to become rancid with memories. She had almost stopped going into town because she was tired of how what started as idle chitchat so often wheedled itself into questions that were designed to extract incriminating information. Someone asked how her mother was, even though Miranda suspected they already knew she'd died, robbed of her senses by strokes. People continued to ask what had ever happened to her father's house, did she know who bought it, what was going to happen with it, even though it was long abandoned. They asked where she was living, knowing that she was with Dix, and then expressed surprise that she was "still" there.

She had learned that her answers, which she had once given so freely and without thought, would often become some other person's currency, something they traded, after considerable embellishment, to show that they knew what others did not. She had experienced too many times the discomfort and pain, the feelings of hurt and treachery, when someone remarked on some aspect of her life but gave it a sinister and spiteful twist.

"Heard you made a pretty penny when you sold that land," someone she barely knew said to her in the hardware store.

"Never did understand how your dad got the rights to build what he did up there," another person remarked as she picked up a package at the post office.

"Guess that nursing home didn't take such good care of your mom."

"You musta learned by now that Dix just ain't the marrying kind."

"You still here? Thought you'd move back to Connecticut by now."

"Must be nice not having to work or nothing."

Wink, wink, nudge, nudge.

Dix had tried to explain that certain sorts of scarcity and ignorance could make people want others to do poorly instead of well, could make them suspicious and resentful. But it didn't help. Miranda was stung and bruised by their comments. She found herself staying increasingly at home. She gardened, canned, cooked, and baked. Tried to learn to sew and knit. Watched the chickens scratching in the yard. Had considered having a pig but knew she'd get too attached to butcher it. When she did go into town, she tried to go at off hours, when there were fewer people at the post office or store. Sometimes she sat in the library, leafing through picture books as if she were a child, but when the real children arrived after school let out, she would get up from the table, return her books to the shelf, and head home.

She felt isolated, almost caged by the boundaries of her life on Dix's twenty acres. But at the same time she felt safe because the thick trees and old fencing that marked the perimeter were a frame that kept others out as much as they kept her in. Her forays to the farmers' market had been the start of an effort to find a new way out of her self-imposed walls.

"I've never met the guy," Dix said, unexpectedly taking up the thread of their stalled conversation as he turned into a steep driveway. "So I can't say much about him. But if he's taking in kids in trouble or from crappy homes, I have no beef. There certainly are plenty of those around here. Anything to get them away from getting popped upside the head all the time. Or worse."

He threw the truck into park in front of a mammoth log home not dissimilar from the one her father had built.

"I've met him."

Miranda's words surprised her. She waited for Dix to react, to ask her something. She watched the side of his face. The creases around his eyes seemed deeper than she remembered. There were discolorations that were not quite freckles here and there. He kept looking out the windshield, staring hard ahead of him at nothing in particular.

"Really?" he finally said.

Miranda listened for false nonchalance but couldn't find any. She wondered if that was because there was none or because he was better at hiding it than she was.

"Where?"

"At the farmers' market," she replied, finding herself unable to say more.

It was Dix who had suggested she go to the market. It was he who suggested she sell her pies. Extras from their garden. Maybe make some sweaters, even though she was still struggling to learn to knit. She knew he was really just encouraging her to get out more. To meet people. To have a life beyond him and their property and worrying about when, or whether, she'd get pregnant. She knew he felt that she needed to find something productive to do. She also knew he was undoubtedly right. But she felt herself in some kind of enervating psychic quicksand. She was embarrassed to think of how many days she lay in bed long after Dix had headed out in the morning, of how many afternoons she spent staring out windows for hours at a time.

Dix had pointed out that most of the people who went to the farmers' market were summer people, not locals. Miranda knew that "summer people" was his code for those who talked only about people back home in Connecticut or Long Island or New Jersey. To them, the locals were just servers at the club, fishing guides, house cleaners, caretakers, and driveway plowers. People good with tools and machinery and not much else. People with bad teeth, poor grammar, and even worse parenting skills. They both knew this was how her father and mother had viewed the locals. This was how they had even seen Dix, she hated to admit, in spite of his excellent diction, reliability, and mouth full of straight, white teeth. In spite of how much they depended upon him. Dix was staring at her now, his dark green eyes silently asking her to continue her story about how she met the man by the side of the road. She had to swallow hard against an unexpected wad of dread and emotion that had lodged in her throat.

"He seemed nice enough," Miranda said carefully. "Not crazy or anything. Just selling jams and crafts. I guess he was a little, I don't know, intense. I didn't know he was taking in kids. That's really nice."

She found herself registering the location of the mailbox where she'd seen him. Found herself thinking of the route they'd taken to get here. Wondered if she had any business up this way. If she could find a reason to come back. Ridiculous, of course. They were out in the middle of nowhere. There was no reason for her to be on this road on her own, only because she was riding along with Dix. She also found herself searching for something else. She wasn't sure what it was until she heard what next came out of her mouth.

"I've always wanted to do that," she said.

"You've always wanted to do what?" Dix asked. "Take in juvenile delinquents?"

There was a faint smirk in his remark. Maybe Miranda's insecurity caused her to imagine the whiff of a sneer. She had a brief flash of panic that he was mad at her for something. But he was never mad. Mad was not something he did.

"No, not that," she said. "Not foster care or anything." She was making this up as she went along. Yet, as she said the words, she realized she was expressing an until-then-unrealized desire. "More like a Big Sister kind of thing. A mentor thing. You know." These revelations were surprising, and relieving her of something at the same time. "I never had a little sister. Always wanted one."

This was not really a true statement, she knew. She'd loved being the baby sister to her big brother. It was a role she would not have willingly given up. But now that he was gone, her parents were gone, a kind of long-delayed but achingly deep desolation had descended upon her. Being with Dix had kept it at bay for a time. She hoped having a baby would drive the feeling away forever. That wasn't happening, and she was struggling to find some way to keep this latent sadness from consuming her.

"I've thought about joining one of those programs," she said, a statement also not wholly true. "I don't think they'd be right for me. Those formal programs."

Dix turned his body toward her and his expression, full of the deep and thoughtful consideration she so admired in him, was now both encouraging and intimidating to her.

"I just like kids," she said.

She felt tears gather in her eyes. She blinked them back. She knew she was picking at the edges of the wound between them, but it was a wound she thought affected only herself. She was also working her way toward something. She was testing him and testing something between them.

"I wonder," she said cautiously. "I wonder if that guy needs any help out there. With the kids." There. She had said it and she couldn't take it back. "Maybe I should stop by sometime." She heard her words as if they'd been said by a different person. "See what they're up to. Maybe I could help out. Tutor. Maybe. Maybe I could find out if I'm any good. Good, you know, with young people."

Dix's eyes, which looked as if they'd absorbed their color from the mountains around them, drifted from her face to the house to the woods and back to her face. Miranda stopped talking and waited on him, afraid of what he might say. Afraid of what she'd just said. Finally he reached out and wrapped his long, heavily knuckled fingers around hers where they were fluttering nervously on her thigh.

"Honey," he said, leaning toward her, "I'm sure you'll be good with them. They'll love you." He reached up and rubbed her cheek with the back of his hand. "They'll love you just like everyone does. Just like I do."

He patted her hand. Then he smiled, rolled his neck, opened the truck door, and got out. Enough talk. Time for work. She stayed where she was.

His answer was so like him, she thought. So sweet and right and full of hope and promise and confidence in her. Why then, she wondered, full of frustration and bile, did it make her feel so weak, so inadequate, so much like bursting into tears?

A rash developed under Miranda's ring. Thinking it was some sort of reaction to the metal, she changed her dish soap. That didn't help. She tried painting the inside of the band with clear nail polish, but it wore off quickly and the bloom of small, itchy bumps and dry, flaky skin came back. She told herself to just take the ring off, put it away. It was nothing special. But she resisted removing it. She'd hold her hand out in front of her face and admire the way the ring accentuated her finger, gave her delicate hand some heft. The ring was symbolic of something, meant something to her beyond mere adornment. She knew it was trying to tell her something; she just wasn't sure what it was. The rash added another layer to the mystery message. However, instead of listening to it, she fought against it. She'd remove the ring, leave it in a drawer for a few days while the rash cleared up. She'd apply some Bag Balm and then try it on again. Nothing worked.

One day she was clawing through the soft, cool, crumbly potato mounds, feeling around for the firm bumps of the hiding tubers, hoping to find a few end-of-season stragglers. Her fingers landed on a cluster of small potatoes. She laced her forefinger and thumb around the clump and pulled them through the earth. She knew, the minute they were free, before she'd settled them in her basket and wiped the dirt from her hands, before she even looked, that the ring was gone. Left behind in the potato mound. She had no desire to search for it.

Now I know where it is, she thought. *Now I know it's safe.*

The irritation cleared up, but her thumb still searched for the ring. She still itched at the fresh, smooth skin. Her hands were restless and so was she. Dix was busier than usual with end-of-season chores. She could find little to engage herself, and the hours between when he left and returned dragged. The light was low, with the morning darkness lingering and the evening gloom rushing in before its time. It was often difficult for her to judge what part of the day she was in. Was it time for breakfast or for afternoon tea? The tasks she had once enjoyed—weeding, cleaning, canning, trying a new recipe, making some fresh curtains, learning to knit—went undone or remained half finished, their former charms falling flat for her. Time seemed to be not an opportunity but a void.

Then Dix went away for a week to do some work on a property up near the Canadian border. Miranda's days were now not even punctuated by the simple fact of him, by waiting for his lanky frame and slightly bowlegged gait to appear in the early evening, his knobby fingers running through his unkempt hair. It was into the long emptiness of the fourth morning after he left that she found herself in front of the bathroom mirror, staring at her just-washed face.

"Enough stalling and wasting away," she said out loud.

She gave her hair a brisk brushing, pulled a few strands into a barrette, wiped some gloss on her lips, and walked to her car. She retraced the drive she'd taken with Dix weeks earlier, made a few wrong turns and had to double back, but eventually she found the unmarked black and rusty mailbox on its canted post. She stopped and stared at it. No cars appeared in her rearview mirror, and none passed on the other side of the dirt road. She could sit here in her idling car as long as she wanted. She could keep driving and wend her way down these unfamiliar, narrow roads back to the comfort of her home. A comfort she had once snuggled into but that now felt stifling.

She made her choice. She turned the car and drove it very slowly down the rutted, narrow, barely graveled drive. She stopped again before any sort of building came into view. She wondered what she was doing, what she'd say once she got to whatever was at the end of the driveway. She looked for a place to turn around. Reversing was impossible. She was afraid she'd put the car in a ditch. She had no choice but to go forward. She soon found herself in a muddy clearing fringed by scrappy bushes. There was a long-unpainted, compact farmhouse at the far edge of the opening in the scrub. It seemed to be reverting back to the wild, its cupped siding fading to the same color as the bracken and dirt around it.

A feral house, she thought. Like the cat that had started hanging around the barn at home.

Home. The word lodged in her throat. Home? Her home? Or was it Dix's home? It was supposed to be theirs. But she still felt like a guest, she realized. Just like she had in her parents' house.

Not mine, she thought. *None of it is mine. I'm just a visitor in other people's lives.*

She shook the thought away and looked around. There was a pop-up camper parked next to a medium-size barn. And farther away, beyond the garden, at the end of a small, muddy path through the yard, there was a trailer. She could see its concrete-block foundation through the broken skirting. The camper tilted drunkenly at the corner where a tire was flat. The dilapidated buildings seemed like a collection of fantastic hags, full of secrets and recipes for wicked brews. Miranda had expected activity. Some sort of comings and goings. Teenagers in the yard. A woman carrying a wooden garden trug overflowing with flowers and vegetables. A cat arching its back in the barn doorway. A dog trotting out to greet her, barking tentatively. A cow lowing. But it was silent. Even the chilly breezes that might have freshened the area did not reach this hollow. She didn't know what to do. She considered tapping her horn. No, that would be too confrontational. It was something her father would have done. She sat in her old Subaru and waited. She scanned the view outside the familiar confines of her car. She watched for movement of any sort.

It came from a window in the trailer home. A faded sheet tacked there moved a few inches and then dropped back into place. Then a door opened at its far end and a woman with a kerchief over her head, wearing what appeared to be men's clothes, walked down the steps, along the path, across the yard, up onto the porch of the farmhouse, and entered the front door—without ever looking in Miranda's direction. A dog crawled on its belly out from under the porch of the farmhouse, stretched backward from its front paws, and threw itself into a small patch of trampled, dead grass in a sudden spot of sunshine. All these small movements seemed to her to be connected, as if some sort of silent communication was taking place.

Minutes passed. The farmhouse door opened again, and then there he was, standing on the porch. He was shorter than she remembered. Smaller overall. He looked directly at her, his eyes glowing across the space between them.

Cold, she thought, surprised as her breath caught in her chest. *I didn't know blue eyes could look so cold.*

Then he smiled and his entire demeanor altered, an actor slipping into character. Somewhere deep inside herself Miranda recognized that he was giving a performance, and yet she did not care. It didn't seem to matter. She was willingly transfixed by the play. He came down the steps, skipping over the last one, and strode to her car. She remained frozen in her seat. He bent at the waist and looked in her window.

His eyes. Lit from within on this day of moving and mottled light. His smile. So much conviction of some sort behind it. None of the sweet, stable, unobtrusive deference she was used to from Dix. Dix who seemed to not even displace the air he moved through. This man's face, his expression, was that of an animal scouting for prey. The click of her door handle startled her out of her reverie. A blast of cool air, as if he had brought it with him, surrounded her when he opened the door.

"Welcome," he said, reaching forward with his hand to help her from the car, his voice an oily caress. "I am so glad to see you. So very glad you found us."

She was shocked that he recognized her. She'd been so nervous that she'd be intruding, that he'd question her and her intentions with a burst of brusque skepticism. She was so relieved by his welcome that she obediently swung her legs out from under the steering wheel and placed her hand in his. She had no idea what to say; the simple act of getting out of the car took all her concentration. She stood. He remained standing a few steps from her. She felt pinned between him and the car. It was not an unpleasant sensation. He dropped her hand, crossed his arms over his chest, and ran his eyes up, down, and over her. His look was an unembarrassed, proprietary assessment without a whiff of sex or flirtation.

"What brings you here?" he finally asked.

"I . . . I . . ." She found it impossible to hold his gaze. She dropped her eyes to the dirt, as if she might find an answer there. "I thought maybe I could help out."

"Help out?" he said, not a question to her, more a question to himself.

"Yes. I . . . I . . . I heard you take in children, um, teenagers, who . . . who are having a tough time. I don't know what kind of an operation you have—"

"Operation?" There was something teasing, maybe even mocking, in his tone.

"Well, you know, like what services you offer. What you might need. If there are formal programs or if it's more, I don't know, ad hoc."

He shifted his weight, cocked a hip. A smile played on his lips.

"Formal," he whispered, trying out the word. "Ad hoc. Hmmm."

Miranda was entirely captivated and squirmingly uncomfortable at the same time. "I don't know," she finally stammered, giving in to the awkward feeling that consumed her. "I just thought that maybe I could be useful."

"Miranda. Andy," he said.

She nodded. She wished she knew his name.

"I know you," he said.

"You do?" she replied, alarmed.

He nodded.

"What do you mean, you *know* me?"

"Ah," he said. "Not to worry. I merely mean I know where we've met before."

"Yes, at the farmers' market."

"Yes. And no. From before that. Long before that."

Miranda was getting confused. "What do you mean?" she asked.

He smiled at her, his grin a refusal to explain.

Miranda was rattled. All the social niceties she was so familiar with did not apply here, in this yard, with this man, who was familiar and strange at the same time. "May I ask your name?" she said.

"My name? I am Darius."

"Darius. I don't know anyone named Darius."

"No, I don't suppose you do."

Miranda narrowed her eyes at him. His features were impossibly regular, balanced, symmetrical, a dictionary definition of what handsome was supposed to be. She was surprised she hadn't noticed that about him before. But she hadn't been looking at him so directly or with the intention of trying to grasp something, anything about him. There was nothing crooked about the smile, no faint scar that might have a story behind it, no hint of ethnicity in the features. She looked for something recognizable but didn't find it. She wondered if he was teasing her. Something her brother used to do. His friends, too. Other girls would have called it flirting. To her it felt more sinister. Like baiting. Miranda knew she didn't have enough experience with men to distinguish between flirting and charming, to understand that the former was to compliment another, and the latter was to compliment the self. Darius shifted his weight, straightened his spine, and changed the subject. Miranda was thrown off balance again, this time in a different direction.

"What do you want, Miranda? What is it that you want?" he asked her.

His expression was so neutral, his voice so bland, the question so large, that it sparked a wave of existential dread in her.

"What do I want?" she repeated, stalling for time, trying to bluff her way through feeling so completely confounded and rattled.

"Yes," he said. "Why have you come? Why have you come *here*?"

"I met you at the farmers' market," she said, trying to find an adequate explanation, some solid ground.

"Yes," he said, "I know. We've established that. I remember. I gave you a ring."

Now, added to the mix of her bubbling emotions was the mortification that she wasn't wearing the ring and panic that she'd lost it. She was totally unprepared for his interrogation. She felt exposed, scrutinized by him, and also by other eyes she could not see yet suspected were peering out at her from behind the curtained windows. She returned to the script she had tried out loud first with Dix, in the truck, that day they first passed here, a day that seemed strangely long ago, and then silently with herself, adding to it, embellishing it, over the following days. She cleared her throat.

"I heard that you do work with teenagers here," she said. "That you help out kids who maybe have a rough home life. I admire that. I've always wanted to do volunteer work with kids. There are not many opportunities around here, and what programs there are don't appeal to me. I did some mentoring and tutoring in college. It's been a while.

I thought I might get into it again. I thought . . . I thought maybe I could be useful."

"Ah," Darius replied, jutting his square chin slightly forward. "Useful." He nodded. "You keep using that word, Miranda, Andy. Yes, useful. Isn't that something we'd all like to be? Useful."

He made the word she'd meant to be generous sound like a selfish conceit.

"Well, yes," she plundered on. "Useful to the children in some way." "Useful."

Why is he repeating that word? she wondered. *Like it's a bad thing. Isn't that a good thing to want to be? Why am I feeling so mixed up?*

"Yes," she said, working her jaw against her mounting confusion. "Helpful. I thought I could maybe help with homework assignments. Maybe, you know, just be another adult they could talk to."

He looked away. She watched his eyes flick over distant things in the landscape, a moving bird, a swaying branch. He nodded a few times at some internal thought before turning his attention back to her. His voice was urgent now, almost a growl.

"And why, Miss Miranda, do you think anyone here, anyone to whom we are offering shelter, would want to talk to *you?*"

He stared at her intently. She began to tremble. Her mouth opened but nothing came out. They locked eyes in silence.

"Well, well," he said, satisfied by her stupor. "Why don't you come back sometime when you have an answer to *that?*"

He spit out the last word, spraying her face with a few drops of saliva. Then he turned and left her. She stared off into the middle distance, into the space he'd just occupied, her eyes unfocused, her skin tingling with goose bumps.

Miranda went home and tried to rid herself of the tumult of feelings the strange experience out at the farmhouse had created. She got online and looked into other mentoring programs. There wasn't much going on locally, and besides, she was concerned about working with kids from families she might run into at the hardware store. She looked into programs up in Plattsburgh. It was a drive, but she had time, she reminded herself. She'd make it into an overnight. See a movie. Take herself to dinner. Do some shopping. It'd be good for her to get out. But the truth was, she didn't want to get out. She didn't want highways and restaurants, sidewalks and traffic lights. People. Lots of people. Having to decide what to wear, if she should fix her hair. She didn't want to leave the confines of the mountains that surrounded her. The more time she spent under their stoic embrace, the harder it was to extricate herself.

When Dix came back from his trip, she didn't tell him that she'd gone out to the "guru's" place. It felt like a betrayal to keep this detail from him, but also like a gift to herself. He knew everything about her life, her past, her family, every embarrassing moment of weakness and shameful episode. Holding back information about her visit and her internal struggle felt like a necessary act of defiance over the imbalance she was experiencing in the structure of their relationship.

She tried to brush it away, but the question Darius had asked kept making itself manifest. As she was sweeping the floor, turning the compost, feeding the chickens, she found herself wondering, indeed, what she had to offer. Why would kids from rough backgrounds open themselves up to her? Why would anyone open themselves up to her?

"Well, I never had, but always wanted, a little sister," she responded under her breath to an absent interlocutor. Or, she'd try this for an answer: "I took a lot of education and psychology courses in college." Sometimes she murmured, "I would like to give back—I've been so fortunate."

Even as she said them, she recognized that all these phrases sounded canned and trite. They were also answers to some other question Darius had not asked, only implied. She realized she was describing holes in herself that working with these kids could fill for her, not describing what she might be able to give someone else. She knew nothing about the kids Darius was allegedly helping. She had seen no sullen teenagers at the farmhouse. She had seen a few around town from time to time, their hair hanging in greasy hanks around their excessively pale faces, with their big cheeks, soft chins, and too-small, too-close-together eyes, but she had never so much as said hello to one of them. In fact, she avoided them. They sneered at adults, and when they spoke among themselves their sentences were filled with casual and repetitive swears and slurs that took her breath away. She imagined their dirty trailers, mangy dogs, and overweight and underemployed parents.

She began to realize that she thought of the people who came from these mountains in a generalized way as "disadvantaged." She knew herself to be "advantaged." She thought the distance between these two conditions was something she could help a teenager or two, maybe as many as three or four, bridge—not with money but with exposure to ideas about education, engagement, ambition, curiosity. It never occurred to her that these kids might be completely disinterested in whatever she offered. That their parents might not want them to cross that bridge and leave their family behind. She'd already, or perhaps willfully, forgotten the frustrations of her earlier experiences tutoring local kids.

On an uncharacteristically warm day in mid-October, when she was sick of her own swirling thoughts, Miranda grabbed a sweater and her knitting and found a spot on the porch, protected from the breeze, in a patch of increasingly infrequent sunshine. She tried to focus on deciphering the pattern in front of her, of working out the code to a new stitch, and making her knitting needles behave. She heard Dix's boots on the floorboards. The yarn was puddling in her lap and at her feet, and she felt surrounded by a fog of frustration and discontent. She knew she might cry, so she didn't look up as he approached. She was sick of seeing her own sadness reflected in his eyes, in trying to explain feelings to him that she didn't understand herself. She didn't look up even when she felt him place a light blanket over her shoulders. Not even when she realized that, yes, in fact, she was cold, that the blanket was welcome. Dix was like that. He didn't wait to be asked. He saw what was necessary, what was needed, and took care of it without drawing attention to the act.

"How's the sweater project?" he asked, squatting, closing the gap between his standing height and her seated self.

Miranda felt an unexpected wave of relief at his presence, but she was not quite ready to give up the perverse comfort of her irritated mood.

"Damned needles!" she said in mock exasperation. "I swear they are out to get me!"

"Come sit here," he said, patting a footstool.

Miranda complied, and as she did so, he took the needles from her hands and smoothed the tangled strands of yarn as if they were hairs on a truculent child's head. Then he wrapped his arms around her from behind and gently guided her fingers through the motions of creating one smooth stitch after another. She allowed herself to be led and watched the knitted stitches obediently line up, one after another, on the needle. Then he turned the work and guided her fingers over the purl row.

"How do you know how to knit, Dix?" she said. Then, before he could answer, she added, "Is there anything you can't do?"

She was glad he was behind her and could not see the hot tears that sprang to her eyes as she was once again stung with a feeling of deep inadequacy. She wanted desperately to be good at something. Really good at something. She just couldn't seem to find what that thing was.

"My mom was always knitting," Dix replied quietly, ignoring, as he always did, the jab of her last remark.

Miranda couldn't even be successful at getting a rise out of him.

His fingers touched and nudged hers, helping them find and make the stitches.

"She knit my father and me sweaters," he continued. "She also knit lots of stuff to give away or sell at the church bazaar. Her hands were always busy making something."

"My mother's hands were always busy drinking something!" Miranda said, surprised at the anger in her own voice.

Her fingers stopped cooperating with his, and the work fell into her lap. He let it go and scraped a chair up beside hers. He kissed the top of her head before sitting down. He took her hands out of her lap, where they were tangled with yarn, and held them in his own. He said nothing. He looked into her face and waited.

"I wish I was good at something, Dix," she sighed, her voice now quiet, defeated.

"Would you like me to tell you all the things I think you're good at?" he asked.

"Oh, sure," she answered for him. "I'm good at gardening and canning and making pies. But those are easy things. I want to be good at something hard."

"Do you have any idea what that hard thing might be? What hard thing you want to take up? I have no doubt you could become good at anything you put your mind to."

"No," she said, embarrassed that her voice sounded like a petulant child's.

His thumbs rubbed the top of her hands.

"It's just that . . ." she started, then stopped. "I'm sorry. I don't know what's gotten into me. You know how to do so many things," Miranda said. "Everything you do, you do better than anyone else does without even seeming to try. Shit, your jam is even better than mine, and you know it."

Dix let her hands go and sat back in his chair.

"Miranda, everything I do well I learned how to do from my father or my mother or my professors or some other person who had tons of experience. I made lots of mistakes, but I learned from those mistakes. That's just part of the process. There's no secret about how to get good at something."

"All my father knew how to do was make money," Miranda said. "And all my mother knew how to do was throw cocktail parties."

"When you're good at making money, you don't need to be good at other things," Dix said quietly.

"I don't even know how he made all his money," Miranda said. "Wall Street. As if that's the only explanation anyone needs."

"Well, we know how he lost it," Dix said. "Maybe that's the more important thing to know."

"On lawsuits and nursing homes," she answered, her voice a cold snap bursting into the warm day.

"By being in opposition to the world," Dix said quietly.

"Thinking the rules that apply to others don't apply to you," Miranda added. "Thinking you have all the answers."

And in that moment, she knew what she would tell Darius. She knew exactly what she had to say.

The cluster of seen-better-days buildings was again eerily quiet when Miranda drove up the muddy drive for the second time. The silence was not a no-one-is-home sort of stillness but a we're-home-but-don't-want-you-to-know kind of hush. Unlike her first foray, when she pulled into the yard and sat in her car, this time she immediately stepped out and slammed the door, full of conviction and intention. She stood there and waited. She'd imagined Darius would show himself. Immediately. Almost as if he'd been waiting for her. She stood at the side of her car, suddenly unsure what direction to take. Her courage began to seep away, a small cup of water in dry sand. She hoped someone—preferably Darius—would show up before it dissipated entirely. She craned her neck, looking to see if there was activity in the dark cavern of the barn, but the interior was too dim to make out animals or people. It was the middle of the day. Where was everyone? Where were the women and teenagers? A slight squeak of metal on metal interrupted her thoughts. She looked toward the sound. In the far corner of the farmhouse's front porch, shadowed by a scrappy, overgrown alder, was a swing. Darius was there, gently pushing himself forward and back, forward and back. He'd been there the whole time, she realized. She suspected he had enjoyed watching her squirm in the driveway.

"So," he said, his voice pitched to carry just to her but not farther. "You've returned."

Miranda nodded and took a few steps toward him, attempting to be undeterred by this strange reception. She saw his stare harden. She stopped.

"And what," he said, "do you have to tell me this time?"

"I have an answer to your question," she said.

Darius narrowed his eyes and nodded. A cackle of laughter, quickly shushed, came from an upstairs window. Miranda shifted her weight back and forth between her feet.

"Do go on," he said. "I'm dying to hear."

The swing squeaked rhythmically.

"My answer to your question . . ." Miranda began, lifting her chin, trying to project her insubstantial voice. "Is that I don't have any answers."

She pushed her heavy honey-colored hair over her shoulders. She wasn't sure if she should go on. She was waiting for some sort of sign from the man on the porch. He gave her none. She knew that this was some sort of a test and that she had to persevere.

"The truth is, I don't know if they'll talk to me," she went on. "I don't know what I might be able to contribute. But that's what I'd like to find out. I admit it—this is more about me than them, right now. I think, I believe, if given a chance, that will change. I intend to make sure that changes."

Darius stared at her, his face expressionless. She tried to hold his unflinching gaze but eventually gave up, looked away, up into the more forgiving but equally chilly blue of the sky overhead. She felt the vexation that seemed to be always simmering in the pit of her stomach these last few months threaten to bubble over.

"I know why you're here," Darius finally said.

Miranda furrowed her brow. "What?" she asked, puzzled. She tried for a light laugh, but it came out as a choking sound. "You do? OK, you tell me, then," she said.

"You want to make amends," Darius replied, his voice heavy with seriousness.

His tone scattered whatever Miranda had been feeling and replaced it with something more ambitious, more enticing. Something also dangerous.

"Amends? To who?" she asked. An icy heat was spreading outward from beneath her navel.

"Oh, it's not to who," Darius said knowingly. "It's for what."

They stared at each other for a few moments.

"Listen, Miranda," Darius said as he stood up. He leaned against the porch post with his arms crossed. "Andy. I know you have some unfinished business. I know you're hurting."

Miranda shivered at his words and longed for the sweater she'd left on the passenger seat in the car. "Hurting?" she said.

"You're carrying the hurts of others," Darius continued. "Your father. Your brother. What they did. The pain they caused."

The hair on the back of Miranda's neck lifted, and goose bumps rose on her arms. "What are you talking about?"

"I knew your brother," Darius said.

Flashes of the past came to her as if she were flipping at high speed through a photo album. The back deck of the log house. Her brother and his friends out on the lawn playing badminton or croquet or bocce. This other man—boy, really, back then—not with them. Instead, with the younger version of herself. This teasing, knowing way about him, it had been more cajoling back then, less confident. But still. She remembered how unsettled she had felt with him then. And now, here, again. Back then, the feeling had repelled her; now, she was drawn to it. Being near him gave her a dizzy, lightheaded sensation, as if she'd just stepped off a roller coaster.

I miss that house, Miranda thought. *So much. I miss my brother. I miss his friends. I miss my parents. I miss that life.* She stared at Darius. *So strange that this man knew my brother. He was in our house.*

And then, *He is so handsome.*

"You knew my brother," she whispered.

"Yes," Darius said.

Miranda watched his eyes flicker for a moment, as if he was unsure of what he was about to say.

"I knew him well," he continued, with sudden conviction. "Admired him. Great guy."

"He was," Miranda said, her eyes filling with tears. "I loved him so much."

Darius smiled. He seemed spurred on by her emotion. "The problem is, Miranda, because your father and your brother are no longer here, they can't face the consequences of what they've done," he told her from his perch on the porch. "They can't make amends. The universe can't conduct its karmic balancing act on them. Of course, they paid a price, Miss Miranda. You've paid a price, too, Miss Andy. Perhaps a bigger one since you're still here and living with their tattered, sad legacy."

Miranda wanted him to stop saying her name. She wanted to understand what he was getting at. She wanted him to stop insinuating things about her family, stop clicking his tongue in judgment and condemnation over their failings. Everything Darius said seemed true and false at the same time.

"There is the law of man, Miranda," Darius continued, spreading out his hands. "And then there is the law of nature. Mother Nature keeps her own score. The natural world is always finding ways to rebalance, to heal wounds, to restore itself after insults. To restore her children, which we surely are, as much as the deer in the woods and the plants in the garden and the fish in the stream are. This balance will be—must be—restored, Miss Miranda, even if it takes generations."

Miranda began to feel, deep inside herself, that what this man said was right. She felt bitter relief at admitting to herself just how right he was.

"That's what we do here, Miranda," he said, sitting again, squeaking the swing, elbows on knees, his voice now soft and professorial. "We restore balance. We restore balance by showing respect for nature and natural rhythms. We restore balance to the world by removing ourselves from the world."

Balance. Yes, that's what Miranda wanted. That's what she had been missing. And amends. That, too. She did have amends to make. She felt terrible about what her father had done—cheating, bending laws meant to protect the natural world. She was also ashamed that her brother had taken another life by driving drunk. People had said it was just an accident, he was barely over the legal limit—no, it was a stupid, arrogant action. Both of these men had destroyed life and welfare. They had manipulated the system and taken advantage of the world. They had been takers, not givers, greedy guzzlers of resources. They had destroyed themselves in the process, but they had ruined so much else before their deaths had halted them. Her mother had done nothing to stop them or to try and fix things. She'd been a sponge, soaking up whatever came her way. Her passivity made her complicit. Miranda had never realized, up until that moment, just how bad she felt about it all. She didn't want to carry her family's legacy forward. She wanted to create a new future, to erase all that had come before. She wanted to leave things better than she found them, to be someone who evoked smiles instead of sneers. She began to slowly, unconsciously, nod her head.

Darius smiled, his teeth large, white, lined up perfectly like soldiers. He stood, moved to the porch steps, and held out a hand. Miranda came forward and took it.

Soft, she thought. *So much smaller and softer than I thought it would be.*

"So what exactly is it that you're doing out there?" Dix asked.

Miranda had been humming as she chopped onions. She stopped when he asked this question. He was surprised at how relieved he was. He hadn't realized how much her incessant background noise had been annoying him, a fly banging against a window, trying to get out.

"You sound skeptical," Miranda said in a breezy voice that was new to her. Laughter seemed on the tip of her tongue.

Dix was grateful to hear the lightness in her tone. This was something that had changed, for the better, since she'd been spending her afternoons at the farmhouse.

Or was it more than her afternoons? Was it all day? He didn't really know. She didn't really say.

She was home when he left in the morning and when he returned. Most of the time. He knew that when he drove back into the driveway in the early evenings and her car was absent, he was disappointed. Irked. He hated to admit that last part. She had started to smile more, even as she had become more vague and evasive about how she spent her days. He was relieved that she had found something that made her happy, but it was true, he was skeptical. Which she didn't seem to mind. Which made him more skeptical.

"I'm not questioning you. I'm just interested," he said, touching her back, trying to mean what he said. "Just curious."

She was already firmer and more muscled than she used to be. That told him something. Her appetite had increased, too. At dinner, she ate almost as much as he did. And her appetite for him had increased as well. That was a change that he didn't mind but still found unsettling.

"Curiosity," Miranda said, whacking him gently with the back of a wooden spoon, dodging his query. "We all know what that did to the cat!"

Dix leaned back against the counter and crossed his arms. "Seriously, Miranda," he said, his voice now reflecting his words, "what goes on out there?"

She looked at him over her shoulder. "Seriously, Dix," she said, lightly mocking his change in tone, "nothing you need to worry about."

"I'm not worried," he said, although her cagey avoidance of his question was making him that way. "Just wondering why it's all such a big secret."

"Because it's sacred, that's why," she said.

Dix scoffed. He thought she was making a joke. She wasn't.

"It *is* sacred, Dix," she insisted. "And it's personal and private. Besides, you know how people can be. How people are. How they talk and make everything mean and ugly, even when it isn't. Especially when it isn't."

"I'm not 'people,' Miranda," Dix said. For the first time since they'd been together, he wished he could say, "I'm your husband," and exert some kind of relational influence over her. Instead he said, "I care about you, Miranda. If something is this important to you, I'd like to know more about it."

"And you want to know if the crap you're hearing in town is true, right? Don't deny it, Dix," she sniped back at him.

"Sure, of course, I want to hear things from you, not just idle gossip. Jeez, Miranda, you make it seem like I'm not on your side."

"There are no sides, Dix."

Dix fought the urge to shake his head.

Where did she learn this maddening and oblique way of talking? he wondered. *She used to be so straightforward.*

"I don't think there are sides, either," he said. "That's why I can't understand why you're so evasive about that place. Remember, I was the one who said I supported his efforts. Before you even went out there, I defended him. But if you act like you have something to hide, people get suspicious. It's only natural."

"We don't have something to hide, Dix," Miranda said. "We have something to protect."

She stirred her onions. She sliced some tofu. She was giving up meat. They were increasingly eating different dinners, together. She was still cooking for him but using only specially designated pans for what she had begun referring to as "flesh." Dix sighed and rubbed his cheeks. He watched her flick her eyes at him. She seemed to be assessing or testing him. As if she wanted to see how far she could push him. He'd always indulged her. He realized that. Maybe it was time to set some boundaries. To stick up for himself more. He'd never had to do that. He wasn't sure how. He felt frustration building, a pressure in his head and chest. He sighed again. Shuffled his feet. Refused to look at her. These small expressions of exasperation seemed to have an effect.

"OK," she finally said. "I'll share. A lot of what we do is just simple work. Taking care of the animals. Repairing the house and barn. Of course, in the spring, there will be gardening. Right now, we're planning. Building a cold frame. Thinking about a small greenhouse. The inherent value of hard work is part of what we're trying to teach these kids." She sprinkled tamari over her tofu cubes. "Sometimes we just talk. Try to get them to open up about what their lives were like, what they could be like."

"Who's we?"

"What do you mean?"

"Other than you and Darius, who else is out there? How many kids, how many adults?"

"Quite the inquisition."

"Just a conversation."

"Right. Well. The number changes. The mix changes. We have just a couple of kids right now. There are four other women besides me. One has a teenage daughter. They all live there full-time. And Darius. And Sally. But she's not really part of our program. She just rents a room there, I guess. She's like Darius's cousin or something. I don't know. That's what he said. We're supposed to just leave her alone. Anyway, the rest of us do everything together."

"Women, children, and Darius. You can see how folks might get the wrong idea," Dix said.

"Women and children are vulnerable in our society. They are the ones most in need of sanctuary," Miranda said. "And sanctuary is what we provide. Sanctuary and healing."

Dix winced. That was not her voice. Those were not her words. She was channeling someone else, repeating phrases and ideas given to her. She had never been given to this kind of psychobabble. "And how does Darius provide 'sanctuary'?" Dix asked, trying not to allow his tone to become exasperated.

"He does many things. He leads us in spiritual exercises. Things like meditation. Focused breathing. Becoming more conscious of our energy flows. Looking for energy blockages. He guides us, teaches us the truths he's learned through his extensive studies."

"That all sounds perfectly groovy," Dix said. "What about, you know, school for the kids?"

"We are homeschooling. Traditional education is tied into the dominant hierarchy, and we're trying to create a different path for people, a different way to be in the world. Darius provides us with a place to step away from the material concerns of our consumer culture so we can recapture and reconnect to natural abundance. This is the core of what The Source is all about."

"The Source?"

Dix was accustomed to seeing the occasional back-to-nature, tie-dye-clad hippie around town. Had seen flyers for various spiritual retreats that promised everything from "rebirthing" and cures for illness to simple peace of mind and happiness. But this was different. What Miranda was describing was more of a commune. Dix was starting to think that the gossip and suspicion he had heard grumbling around town was more accurate than he'd originally allowed. He was starting to think he'd given this guy far too much benefit of the doubt. He began to worry he was taking advantage of people. And especially of Miranda's naïveté.

"Yes, that's what our sanctuary is called," Miranda said.

"Does he ask for money? How is this place supported?"

"We sell crafts and goods at the farmers' market and at shops."

We. She'd never sold anything at the market, but she was already claiming kinship with things they did before she had even joined them. Now she was part of a "we" that was not their "we," the "we" of Dix and Miranda.

"That can't bring in enough to support that many people," he said.

"We live simply. We grow much of what we eat."

"Still."

Miranda cleared her throat. She tossed the tofu into the pan, where it sizzled almost like real meat. "People are encouraged to give as they can. What they can."

Dix held his breath.

"Sometimes this might be a particular skill. Other times it might be money, yes. To go toward programs and upkeep," she explained with a practiced casualness.

"But he owns the property. He gets the advantage of the upkeep, the improvements," Dix said.

"Gifts, Dix. We each give what we can, what we choose to, what comes naturally to us, without expectation of return. That's what a gift is. The reward is in the giving itself, not in the expectation that you will get something by giving something."

Dix wondered how much she'd given Darius. She had far less than people thought she did. She was not savvy about financial matters. She'd never had a reason to be. Until the house of cards her father built had crashed down. But even that hit she had felt emotionally, without it really registering financially. He recognized that this was partially his fault. He'd taken care of her. She had no real expenses. She had perhaps stepped too quickly from her father's home to his. He would not ask her if she'd given Darius money or how much. Her money was hers to do with what she liked. He also sensed that any discussion on that topic would lead to an argument. Neither of them had the temperament for arguments. More than anything, he was worried about her drifting away from him, from them as a couple, and felt a misstep on his part would send her even farther out into Darius's sea.

"Dix?"

Miranda's voice was tentative and serious, now more her own, the voice that was familiar to him. It drew him out of his private worries.

"Do you want to come out sometime with me? See what it's all about?" she asked.

Dix felt a stubborn resistance rise inside him.

"You could see how lovely it all truly is. You could meet Darius, the kids."

"Would I be welcome?" he asked.

"Of course!" she said, turning to look at him, her broad mouth breaking into an inviting smile.

Dix felt himself soften toward her.

"Besides," she said, going back to the stove, her voice now dropped into a more pragmatic pitch. "Frankly, we could use your expertise. You could give us some advice. We're trying to convert a school bus into a bunkhouse. So we can house more kids. Maybe you'd have some ideas. You're so good at that stuff."

Dix stiffened again. He had no interest in gifting his skills or counsel to Darius's operation. He suspected they'd want him to gift materials and labor, too. He resisted the unwelcome thought that now Miranda, through Darius, was using him. Or trying to. Maybe it was just Darius using her to get to him, manipulating her and taking advantage of her good nature, gullibility, generosity.

"More kids, Miranda?" he asked, avoiding responding to her invitation. "Are there any real social workers out there? Does this guy have any supervision, accreditation? He seems to be a doctor practicing without a license."

Miranda stared at him with an expression he had not seen before. She was suddenly cold, hard, and walled off. "I refuse to be brought down by your negativity," she said sharply. "I knew I shouldn't have told you all this. I knew you wouldn't get it."

"I'm sorry, Miranda," Dix said. He was sorry, it seemed now—for so many things.

"This is the most important thing I've done," she went on, scraping the stir-fry onto two plates. "I know it has value. Just because you don't see it doesn't mean it's not real. It is real. It's good. It's right. It makes me happy. It helps people. I know it does."

He stepped to her and twined his fingers in her hair. She twisted her neck away from him. He rubbed her cheek with the back of his hand. She pulled away.

"I'm sorry," he said again.

"So am I," she said. Her tone made it clear she was sorry for him, not herself. But she let him wrap his arms around her shoulders, rest his cheek on the top of her head.

"I miss you," he whispered.

He wanted to tell her that he missed her not because she was gone so much, but he missed the her he'd once known. He missed the Miranda he'd watched blossom into a tentative young woman, the adult Miranda who wandered somewhat aimlessly in search of herself. He missed her softness and wide-eyed wonder. He tried tightening his embrace, hoping to find and release that internal gentleness that had been so abundant in her. Miranda held herself apart in his arms, stiff and unyielding. Dix also missed that, once upon a time, he'd been the source of her happiness. That their life together had been.

She did not give in to his embrace, so he let her go.

The next morning before he left for work, Dix brought Miranda, who was lingering in bed, a cup of coffee. She was sitting up, propped against the pillows, staring off into the middle distance. She did not turn when he came back into the bedroom or thank him for the fragrant mug he set down on the bedside table. He sat on the edge of the bed. He brushed her hair from her face.

"Miranda?"

She sighed lightly but did not answer.

"Miranda? I'll come. I'll see what you're up to out there."

She turned to him then, but her pale eyes did not warm when they took in his face.

"How about this afternoon? I can finish early and swing by before it gets dark?"

She smiled at that, just a slight turning up at the corners of her mouth. She thanked him for the coffee. She lifted his hand from the bed and kissed it.

There, he thought. *That makes it worth the effort.*

He left her holding the mug in both hands and blowing on it. By the time he got to his truck, he admitted to himself that the real reason he was going was not to appease her but to find out what was going on out there.

It was a cold, wet day. As Dix drove up the pitted drive, he noted that the plow had done a poor job against the early snows, and dangerous ice buildup was likely to follow for the rest of the winter unless they got an unexpected thaw and then started to do a better job. He told himself to alert Miranda to this. He hoped he'd not find too many other things to alert her to.

As he got out of his truck, freezing rain spit in sharp taps against his face. He waited for Miranda to appear. While looking around, his eyes involuntarily lit on the mistakes and the poorly executed, the out-of-level and the un-thought-through. The siding patches that were uneven and made with the wrong sort of wood. The lopsided concrete blocks under the trailer hitch that would sink in the first thaw and cause the camper to topple over. The porch supports set on flat rocks instead of Sonotubes. The half-done tree-house platform with the poorly secured blue-tarp roof that was snapping in the wind. The bicycle and lawn tractor left in the yard instead of under cover in the barn. Dix had expected a bit of a duct-tape-and-baling-wire approach, but not this degree of patched-together work. It looked like something a bunch of unskilled teenagers had done. He reminded himself that that was likely exactly what it was.

Miranda appeared, smiling widely, pulling a wool hat over her head as she came out of the farmhouse. She looked happy. It pained him to recognize this, but it was true. Then he wondered what sort of happiness it could be if she had found it out here, in this rough hollow, with this man he suspected was nothing more than a New Age charlatan peddling feel-good bromides. She ran down the steps, grabbed his hand, and led him from place to place like a child on visiting day at school. She showed him the henhouse that would not keep out a fox, the new garden plot planned for spring in an area bound to be far too wet, a couple of ornery goats in a stall that needed mucking out. She rattled on, excited about all the things he knew would never come to pass—the chicks would be eaten instead of growing into hens, the plants would mold instead of bearing fruit, the goats would get diseases in their feet. He kept quiet.

She took him into the school bus, the one they wanted to convert to a bunkhouse. Most of the seats had been torn out, and a few foam mattresses and sleeping bags had been tossed about. Miranda gestured here and there, talking about imaginary desks and curtains and double-decker bunk beds. Dix immediately noticed an offending odor. He sniffed. Miranda stopped talking and stared at him. Kerosene. He sought the source of the smell. An old heater with an open flame was tucked into the rear corner.

"Miranda," he said, warning in his voice.

"Don't start, Dix," she said, her hands up and her head shaking.

"Sweetie," he went on. "It's the heater. It's dangerous. Too close to the wall. Unprotected. And the fumes."

"Do you always have to immediately find what's wrong, Dix? Do you have to be so negative?"

Dix stared at her, uncomprehending. "It's not negative, Miranda. It's dangerous."

She rolled her eyes with an exaggerated motion. "Whatever," she said. "We're not going to be that stupid. We're not children out here."

Oh yes, you are, Dix thought. What he said was, "I thought you wanted my help."

"That's not help," Miranda insisted. "That's just bad vibes."

Dix stepped away from her, moved the heater away from the wall, and kicked at a piece of foam mattress that was in danger of melting.

"Forget it, Dix," Miranda said, annoyed. "Let me show you the house."

They crossed the muddy yard, Miranda no longer holding his hand but striding out in front of him, and went in the back door to the kitchen. It was a small space, already crowded with four women working at the stove and a tin-top table, pouring a bright-green, strange-smelling concoction from battered pots into mason jars. They wore skirts with leggings and heavy wool socks and kerchiefs over their roughly cut hair. Dix wondered what Miranda might look like dressed and shorn as they were. The thought made him shudder. Miranda didn't really introduce him but pointed at the women and ticked off words that must have been names, but which seemed to Dix more like nouns removed from their rightful object.

Sunshine and Violet, Luna and Willow.

These were words that belonged to bright and beautiful things, not to these young women who had dumbed down their looks and person-alities with drab clothes and sour expressions. Dix looked around for teenagers, the youth they were allegedly helping, but saw none. Miranda asked someone, Heather or Moonlight or something, where Darius was.

"He's unavailable," was the woman's blunt answer.

"Really?" Miranda was undaunted. "Are you sure? He was expecting us. He wanted to meet—"

The woman shook her head, averted her eyes, and placed a top on a pot with a clang.

Dix knew he was unwelcome. He began to wonder if Miranda was as well.

"Bummer," Miranda said, affecting a childish pout as she turned to Dix. "We'll have to come back again when he's here. He wanted to meet you! He wanted to ask you about some building stuff."

They stood awkwardly in the kitchen. The women moved slowly, silently, methodically, around them.

"What about Travis?" Miranda asked the room in general. "Is he here?"

The women shook their heads.

"He has an interest in carpentry," Miranda told Dix. "I wanted him to meet you."

Dix put his hand on Miranda's arm. The room was cold. He wanted to go. He wanted Miranda to come with him. She let herself be led from the room. They walked carefully over the slippery ground back to the truck.

"Are you going to follow me home?" Dix asked.

"Later," Miranda said. "I want to help them finish up." She closed the truck door on him. "Go ahead and eat. I'll probably be late."

Dix rolled up his window and watched her walk away. He started the truck and was just about to put it into gear when he had an unsettling feeling. Miranda was already at the front door. She closed it behind her. Light drifted through the window out into the darkening day. Dix kept looking. It took a few moments for his eyes to find what some other sense had known was there. A figure, a dark-haired man, came into view, a subtle silhouette against the dim glass of an upstairs window. Dix felt as if he were in a deer stand and a buck had slowly materialized in a patch of woods he'd already been staring into for some time. The man's body was turned to the side. Clearly, he was hoping to see without being seen. Dix's mouth opened, but no sound emerged. The other man let the curtain drop and disappeared.

Because she was rarely in the house, Sally absorbed what was happening at The Source through scattered clues and snippets of overheard conversation. One evening, she noticed that the garden had gone to weeds, and produce was being left on the vine where it was undoubtedly rotting in the unusually wet weather. Then, a few nights later, she tiptoed past a "community gathering" in the living room as she was on her way upstairs. She heard Darius's voice coming through her floorboards, patiently scolding the assembled women and teenagers for not "honoring the garden and its bounty" by caring for it properly. She listened as he told them that he was busy writing a book about their efforts and The Source's way of life, a book that would sustain them with its expected sales, so it was their job to keep the garden prolific. Within a few days, the kitchen calendar was updated with chores, as well as meals laid out by day and person.

Another time, she came across Sunshine or Moonbeam—she could never keep the names the women gave themselves straight—comforting Lily or Violet, who was crying in deep gulps because she'd let one of the goats, or maybe it was the cow, get loose. The animal had injured itself on some old barbed wire, which had apparently necessitated a costly visit from the vet after their home remedies and balms had failed and the wound began to ooze and stink. The vet stitched things back up and administered antibiotics, which the women feared would somehow contaminate the milk and cheese they were planning to make.

Then there was the night, as Sally smoked a cigarette in a dark corner of the porch and watched through a dirty, cracked-open window, she saw everyone gathered in the living room. One woman sat on a chair at the center of the group, and one by one, each person described her flaws and failings. Every complaint was punctuated by the eventual call and response, "I do this with love," to which the seated woman, her head hanging down and her face obscured by hair, responded, "I accept your correction with love." These "correction" sessions became standard practice. Darius would gather the women to impart some piece of instruction or wisdom Sally recognized he had filched from one of his self-help or pop-Buddhism books. Then he would end his little speech by calling out someone for "correction." She was struck with dumb awe at their clumsy efforts to improve one another. Yet she did not intervene. She knew anything she did would be received with hostility. And she didn't care enough about any of those people to step in. She saw the entire enterprise as some kind of comic and consensual adult camp for the spoiled and searching. For her, it had become entertainment.

In spite of Darius's claims to want to help teenagers, few delinquent youth came to The Source. Sally quickly sized up whatever issues the

occasional stragglers brought with them, and she saw only overly hormonal teens sick of fighting with their parents and bored with the very
few things that could occupy them in small towns tucked in the midst
of dense mountains. But the lack of anything with a screen on it at The
Source and the abundance of dirty vegetables and tasteless grains in the
refrigerator quickly dampened whatever enthusiasm they may have had
for getting away from home. They came and went with an unabated
listlessness.

That is, until Maverick and Cassandra showed up. When Sally
walked into the kitchen one cold, late October evening after work,
expecting to see the usual coven of women sitting around the table
straining curds or carding wool, she found just Darius and two teenagers. Sally started to sidle by, as she usually did, scurrying up to her room
to get out of the way, but Darius put his hand on her arm. His fingers
pressed into her flesh, suspending her movement.

"Sally, I'd like you to meet our two new guests, Maverick and
Cassandra," he said, his lips stretched back in a practiced smile as he
gestured with his free hand.

Sally looked at her arm where he held it. His grip was firm, and
the feel of his fingers made her insides tingle. She looked at his face.
Crazy handsome. A face from a fashion billboard. His gaze a caress. His
voice pitched to soothe and charm. Sally was embarrassed that it was all
working on her. Involuntarily. But still.

I should know better, she thought. *I do know better.* She wrenched
her arm free.

"Hey," Sally said to the new arrivals. "Welcome to the funny farm."

They hadn't had teenagers for a while. Darius must be happy to
have new recruits, she thought.

"They'll be staying out in the trailer," Darius said. "We're fixing
it up for them now. They've come all the way from Montreal to be
with us."

We. Sally tried not to scoff. She knew the women were fixing up the trailer. He did almost nothing around the place anymore. Huddled in the attic and worked on his manifesto.

"Hey, hi, how's it going? So nice to meet you," Maverick said, his words tumbling out in a nervous rush. He pushed some greasy hair off his sweaty forehead and grinned. Sally saw a flash of gray teeth and red gums. Cassandra was wearing a ball cap and sunglasses even though it was night and she was indoors. Sally watched the girl scratch her forearm with long, repetitive, mindless strokes of ragged fingernails. They were both scrawny. Just the type to appeal to Darius. Sally noted that the boy did not have a Montreal accent. She suspected the girl didn't, either. Undoubtedly the first lie of many they had told Darius. Or would tell him.

What does it matter? They'll be gone soon enough, she thought as she left the room.

But they didn't leave. In fact, they participated more enthusiastically than any other teens had before them. They sat, rapt, at the loving correction sessions, not yet allowed to participate but eagerly watching, waiting for their turn. Sally saw Maverick out on a chilly morning when the skies were dripping damp snowflakes, shirtless and sweating as he shoveled goat manure and turned it into the compost pile. Another day, while waiting for coffee to brew, Sally watched Cassandra methodically polish one glass after another, rubbing an old dish towel over and over nonexistent water spots. Sally took a step to retrieve a mug, positioned herself next to the girl, and inhaled deeply. An acrid, chemical smell hit her nostrils.

Of course, she thought. *Yes, of course.*

Later that night, when the house was dark and silent, Sally went to the window of her room. She had a view over the yard, past the garden, and directly to the trailer stationed at the end of a slushy path. Where the lights were on. From her perch of about fifty yards away, she watched two silhouettes move back and forth in the kitchen area.

Steam of some sort was coming out the back window. She shook her head in disgust and tiptoed from her room to the foot of the stairs that led to the attic space. Light seeped out from under the door. She knocked lightly. She listened to footfalls coming down the stairs. Darius yanked the door open, his face full of annoyance that quickly gave way to confusion. He was wearing a T-shirt grayed with wear. Sally noticed he'd lost weight. But his frame still filled the small doorway, blocking her view.

"What?"

"I need to talk to you," Sally said.

"That's obvious," Darius replied, his hand on the doorknob and his face drained of its habitual mask of forced cheer and solicitude he put on for everyone else at The Source. "Say what you need to say."

"It's about those two teenagers."

"What now, Sally? What negativity do you bring to me this time? We finally have two young people who are fully participating, and you're here to tell me what's wrong with them."

Sally glared at him. "Um, yeah, Darius. See, what's negative about them, what's wrong with them, is that they're fucking meth heads."

Darius crossed his arms. "Meth heads? Really, Sally? I think you watch far too much TV with your friends."

"Maybe, Darius, you should watch a little more. All the signs are there." She ticked them off her fingertips. "Talking too fast, sweating, weight loss, bad teeth—"

"You could be describing pretty much any teenager on the planet, Sally."

"Dilated pupils, obsessive activities, twitching eyes, chemical smell," she went on.

"And since when do you take such an interest in our charges, Sally?"

"Since I saw them trying to cook meth out in the trailer. Right now, in fact," she sneered. "Since I realized they could get us arrested as accessories, or even better, burn this whole fucking place down with one little chemical explosion."

Darius stared at her for a few moments, narrowed his eyes, pushed past her, and hurried down the hall and the stairs to the kitchen. She glanced up toward his attic lair and felt the temptation to go snoop. But there were more pressing concerns. She returned to her bedroom and watched as Darius's silhouette showed up in the trailer. His posture was pitched aggressively forward, and his hands waved in the air. Half an hour later, he was knocking at her door.

"That will be the end of that," he told her.

"Sure, it will," Sally said. "That's all any meth addict needs: a good, stern talking-to. That'll set them on the path to righteousness, pronto." She patted his chest, felt the ribs that were sheltered only by a thin layer of flesh and skin. He did not shrink from her touch. A memory of one of their hurried moments of sex flashed by, distant heat lightning. "Good for you, Darius," she continued. "But if it's all the same to you, I think I'll keep a close eye on them and that trailer myself. And don't think for a moment that I won't call the cops the minute I see any evidence of them cooking meth on my property."

Darius flinched at her expression of ownership.

"Nothing like a little time in juvie to dry them right out," she said.

Miranda wanted Dix to come back to The Source. She said Darius apologized for not being there. She said there was a new teenager, Maverick, who really wanted to meet him, to learn from him. Dix resisted as gently as he could.

"Sweetie, I spend my days fixing people's houses. There's a long list of things to do here. It's hard for me to get excited about working out there, too."

"Right. Of course," she said.

"Feel free to bring the boy over sometime. I could work with him on something here."

"Great idea! I'll do that."

Dix felt safe making the offer because he knew she'd never bring the kid over. Or anyone else, for that matter. She was less and less inclined to mix her Dix and Darius worlds. Instead, she followed him around on a few jobs. She peppered him with questions. In the evenings, over dinner, she interrogated him about how to jack up a barn, dry out a basement, trim goat hooves, build a sleeping platform, secure a chicken house, protect a heater, build a greenhouse with old windows. He gave her as much information as he could, but when he pressed her afterward about how this or that project had gone, she reluctantly admitted to dead chickens, melted sleeping bags, bloody goat feet. But even these sad tales she justified as important and necessary, if difficult, learning experiences.

Even more maddening to Dix, she cadged his tools. Which were both valuable and necessary for his work. When he asked if she'd borrowed his saw or backup screw gun, she would shake her head evasively, or bring back a different tool, or return his with dulled, broken, or missing parts. She also came home with bruised knuckles, ripped fingernails, and once a black eye from an angry goat. But she was unabashed, showing off her wounds with pride, as if they were evidence of a job well done, not stupid and clumsy errors. Dix had a deep sense of foreboding. It was only a matter of time, he knew, before she came home with something worse than a scrape.

It happened just before Thanksgiving. A holiday Miranda had recently informed him she would not be observing because she didn't think they should celebrate the exploitation of the original Americans by a conquering force. The house was empty when Dix arrived at the end of a long day of work. Many of his customers would be celebrating the coming holiday with large family gatherings at their mountain homes, and he had been busy laying in firewood, chasing away mice, and clearing driveways. He made himself a sandwich with leftover meatloaf and cracked a beer. The house was solemn and quiet. He checked the clock on the wall. Seven thirty. She had regularly missed dinners with him lately, but this was still later than usual for her. No point in checking his messages. Again. Her cell phone didn't work up there. Wasn't allowed anyway. She rarely took it with her anymore. When he'd asked her to call him from their house phone if she was going to be late, she'd said that phone was only for emergencies.

Dix made himself another sandwich, as much to fill time as his belly. The clock ticked past eight. He washed his plate, wrapped the leftovers, put away the bread, ketchup, and mayonnaise. As he surveyed the clean and empty kitchen, he was reminded of his years of bachelorhood. He hadn't felt lonely back then, had loved his solitude. Why did he feel so lonely now? He found himself wishing he had a dog, something, anything to greet him when he came home, to bring life into the house. He considered opening another beer but set the kettle on the stove instead. He stood at the window and stared into the dark outside, trying to ignore the dark inside. The kettle boiled away. He turned it off without making tea. Finally, a set of headlights made their slow way up the drive. It was almost nine. He refilled the kettle and turned on the heat beneath it. He turned on the outside lights and stood in the doorway, waiting for her. He watched as she got out of the car and came toward him slowly, tentatively, a dog who had turned over the trash. She did not look up or meet his eyes. He blocked the door.

"Are you going to let me in?"

He turned his body and she slid past him. She smelled like a campfire. He shut the door on the cold outside. She was in the mudroom, pushing her boots off her feet and shouldering off her coat. He reached over to help. She coughed—a harsh, grating sound of dry sticks rubbing together.

"What happened, Miranda?"

"Sorry I'm late," she said. "Got caught up in some stuff out there."

She ducked her head away from him, pulled free of her coat, and went into the kitchen where the teakettle was screaming. Dix followed her. She turned off the heat and grabbed two mugs from the shelf. Dix took her chin in his hand and turned her face to the light. Her eyebrows and eyelashes were singed. So was a line of hair along her forehead. The shoulder of her shirt was torn and smudged with black.

"Miranda? What happened?"

Dix tried to keep the alarm from his voice. Miranda pulled her head out of his hand and filled the mugs. He tried to recall if there had been sirens. It had been a quiet night.

"Nothing. It's nothing," she said quietly.

"It was the heater, wasn't it?" Dix said.

"It wasn't the damn heater, Dix," Miranda hissed, dunking teabags into the cups, splashing water over the sides. "Sorry, Dix, but you weren't right about that. For once, you weren't right. That fucking heater is broken. It doesn't even work anymore. We can't even light it at all. So stop with the heater shit."

Dix was shocked into silence. Miranda rarely swore. She dropped her face into her hands. He put his arm over her shoulder and guided her into the living room. She sat on the sofa. He put a blanket over her knees and went back for the mugs. He set hers on the table, held his in his palms, and waited for her. She didn't pick up her cup.

"It was a kitchen fire," she finally said, her voice not just exhausted but defeated. "They were in the trailer. It happened in the trailer. It was an . . . experiment. Maverick and Cassandra. Those teenagers I told you about."

An experiment. In his mind, Dix filled in what Miranda didn't, wouldn't say. Maverick. The kid who supposedly was interested in carpentry. Clearly not interested in building chicken coops, Dix thought.

"Miranda . . ." He could not keep the tone of rebuke from his voice.

"Don't start, Dix," she snapped at him. "I know what you're thinking. Drugs. Right. Of course. No surprise there. These are messed-up kids. That's why I asked for your help. They do drugs. They tried to cook meth. They probably learned how from their parents. I know how you feel. You're going to tell me this is a reason for me to stop going out there. But it's not. It's just the opposite. This shows how much these kids need us. You probably think we should kick these kids out. That's what everyone else has done. Even you wouldn't come back to help. They have no one. That's why they need us. Now more than ever."

Dix leaned back, away from Miranda and her onslaught of words. Away from her stunning rebukes. He heard Darius in her statements. He'd never met him, but Dix imagined him talking, as if in a scene from a movie he'd once seen—this charismatic, handsome man explaining why what was bad was actually good, what was wrong was actually right, and why they were in a unique position to see what no one else could. He must make the people around him feel unique and special, a tribe blessed with the burden of a special vision and purpose. Dix took a deep breath, composed himself, leaned forward, and touched Miranda's knees. She moved her legs. He did not pull away.

"I know how committed you are to these kids," Dix said, keeping his voice steady and quiet. "To the community. To trying to do the right thing, the good thing. I know you want what's best for them."

"But what, Dix? What's next? Go ahead, tell me how wrong I am. That's what you want to do, don't you? That's what you're going to do. You, who have all the answers. You, who always do everything right."

Dix pulled back again. He sat upright. Miranda had never tried to wound him before. This was something new. He told himself that she was just upset. That she didn't know what she was saying.

"Sweetheart. No. That's not it at all. Miranda."

She shook her head as if trying to rid herself of something. Dix tried again, his words full of caution. For her, but now for himself as well.

"I'm worried about you, Miranda. I just wonder if this kind of work isn't better left to professionals. Darius doesn't have credentials. You know that. And these kids are tough. They come from really rough backgrounds. I know. I went to school with lots of kids like this. I know their families. You haven't been exposed to these kinds of people before. They are so unpredictable. They have nothing—and nothing to lose. I worry. I worry about you, Miranda. I worry you'll get hurt. Like you have. This all could have been so much worse. So easily so much worse."

Miranda still said nothing.

"And. And I miss you, Miranda. I just miss you."

Dix hung his head, overcome with feelings made more acute by the act of saying them. Miranda stood up.

"You miss me, Dix? You?" she said, her voice shaking. "You miss me? Why don't you think how much these kids have missed, Dix? Think about that for a change of pace."

With that, she left the room, and Dix sat staring into the empty space where she had once been.

After the night of the fire, Dix and Miranda were tentative and polite with each other. Dix used a softer voice and kept a safe distance. Miranda adopted an aggressive cheerfulness and fluttering affection. They curled in on each other at night, handling each other gently. Miranda spent just as much time at The Source but now answered the question "How was your day?" with stories of cheese-making and garden planning instead of her usual evasiveness. She told him that the meth-making kids had run away from The Source the night of the fire. They were not replaced with others. It was apparently just Darius and a handful of women out there now, all engaged in relatively benign, back-to-the-earth activities. Miranda used the word *community* all the time when referring to the group. This was clearly something important to her. Something necessary. Dix found space within himself for a new kind of contentment that was informed more by her happiness than his own. They set aside time for a trip to Burlington, held hands as they walked the streets and wandered the shops filled with the residue of last season's tourists. He bought her some silver earrings, a pretty hat, some cashmere socks. She thanked him and immediately donned the gifts, yet never wore any of the items once they were home.

From this near distance, Dix watched Miranda. She knitted mittens and hats—she was now skilled with the needles, as someone at The Source had helped her—which she planned to give away to those in need at Christmas. She slept, her eyelids twitching from the depths of a dream she would not remember or would claim to not remember when he asked her about it in the morning. She swept the kitchen floor, murmuring some mantra over and over under her breath, swinging her hips, which he noticed had widened into a graceful curve spreading from her waist. She was no longer the skinny girl he had once watched puttering in the garden he had prepared for her mother at that huge log house. He saw she was growing more beautiful as the callowness of youth left her face and body.

In addition to this slow accretion of physical changes, Dix noticed that over the past few months, her nervous, self-doubting edges had been replaced by conviction and self-containment. He knew he should be happy about these things. But those qualities had been created in a space and time that was beyond and outside him. He didn't trust their genesis. He knew somewhere deep within himself, even as he told himself he should not judge, that there was something false and fragile in her newfound clarity.

Miranda was a puzzle to Sally. Although she seemed to be from the same privileged social class, she was unlike the other women Darius attracted. She was wounded in some less obvious, more subtle way, and needy in some more flagrant, less complex way. When Darius spoke, the other women listened, subdued, submissive, soaking in his words; Miranda leaned forward, took notes, was eager and attentive. Sally overheard Miranda asking Darius questions about how he thought celebrity worship subjugated women or how she could calm her thoughts during meditation practice. Miranda brought in tattered library books from the 1970s on the back-to-nature movement, offered ideas on natural refrigeration and more intensive farming practices, and suggested printing up pamphlets on what The Source had to offer and handing them out at the high school after hours to attract more teenagers.

Darius told her that people must "discover" The Source on their own.

Miranda was also the only woman who talked to Sally, apparently oblivious to or unconcerned about the general moratorium on making direct contact. Once she found out Sally was a social worker, she asked how much schooling she had, what the certification requirements were, if the work was gratifying.

That word, said with deep earnestness, gave Sally pause. "Gratifying?" she repeated.

Miranda nodded, smiling, practically squirming with delight at the expectation of the answer she hoped for. A dog waiting for a bone. It pained Sally in an unfamiliar way to know that she was going to disappoint her.

"Not as gratifying as you might expect," she replied, trying to soften the truth of her work.

They were sitting on the front porch. Sally had gone out into the cold to smoke. The one concession she made to the community was not smoking indoors. She was trying to quit anyway. Miranda, as she sometimes did on the rare occasions when they were both at The Source at the same time, had followed her. She remained undaunted by Sally's response.

"Really?" she asked. "Why not gratifying? Isn't it great to help these people improve their lives, get onto the right track? I mean, you must have such an impact on them! How can that not be gratifying?"

Sally finished her cigarette, doused it out in a mound of snow, and wished she had a joint. Something else she was trying to quit. She felt a sudden tenderness toward Miranda.

"Here's the thing," Sally said. "I know it's hard to imagine, but most of these kids don't really want to get off what we'd consider the wrong track. They're really pretty content with the track they're on. So are their families. So are their friends. The so-called right track would take them away from everything they know. Everything that's familiar to them. So mostly I just try to get them to do less damage to others, because they don't really care about the damage they do to themselves."

"But there must be some you can help," Miranda insisted. "Some you have helped."

Sally thought. There was the woman with kids whom Sally had gotten into a shelter just a day before her husband had set their trailer on fire and shot himself in the face. She now had a job as a health aide. There was the girl who had almost a dozen siblings, none of which had the exact same combination of mother and father because her father got women pregnant in between his bouts in jail for drug dealing, while her mother got pregnant every time her social-service checks were about to run out; that girl was now attending college on scholarship and planned to join the military upon graduation. There were those, yes. There were others, too. But these were the exceptions. The world was full of so many sorts of evil that Miranda, with all her upper-class, white-girl, emotional neglect could never imagine. Sally didn't want to be the one to tell her.

"There are a few cases that stand out," Sally cautiously said. "But honestly, Miranda, for those people who get out of the tough circumstances of their birth, they just have it in them. If they hadn't come across me, they'd have found someone else to help them."

"Yes," Miranda said, "but it was you. It is you. It isn't someone else. That must be so grand."

Grand? Hardly, Sally thought. *This girl is a soft person looking for a hard problem.*

She lit another cigarette. She gave up trying to school Miranda. Let her figure it out on her own. Let life be her teacher, bitch that it could be.

Miranda was also the only woman who was a "day camper," as Sally thought of her. Miranda spoke obliquely about her life outside of The Source, with offhand comments like, "I'll ask Dix. He'll know how to fix that." Or, "I'll bring something from home tomorrow to repair that—Dix won't mind if I borrow his stuff." Dix. Sally knew she'd never met him but wondered if they had ever crossed paths. Unlikely. They worked with very different clientele. As Sally listened to Miranda describe him, Dix seemed to attain almost mythic status—a kind, generous, competent, indulgent soul with an endless reserve of practical knowledge, as well as tools to implement his wisdom. Miranda did not, however, seem to speak of him as a romantic partner. They lived together, Sally knew, in a house that sounded stunning from even Miranda's generalized description. She suggested they were lovers, made passing reference to a desire for a baby. But there was something missing from Miranda's regard for the man, some passion or connection. Even so, Sally was surprised that Miranda would forgo what she surmised were the considerable comforts of life with this Dix person for ever-increasing hours and days with the grungy vagaries of life at The Source. Even if something or several things were absent from her life with Dix, it still had to be a lot better than this place.

In mid-December, the tentative calm of Miranda and Dix's quiet detente was disrupted. Dix heard the tittering of abruptly shut-down gossip one day when he went into the post office. He had become used to this—people in town knew Miranda was now associated with the "guru," so their whispering halted when Dix appeared—but this was something different. Now people were staring at him. He picked up a copy of the local paper and a cup of coffee on his way home. What he read, sitting in his truck in the gas station parking lot, left a stone in the pit of his stomach. When he got back to the house, he left the newspaper carefully folded on the kitchen counter so Miranda could not fail to see the headline when she came home. Then he sat in the gathering gloom and waited for her to arrive. He did not stir from his living room chair when he saw her car come up the driveway, when he heard the back door close, not even when she called his name. Lights went on behind him. There was a pause followed by the sound of the newspaper being shaken out. He waited a few moments, then stood and joined her in the kitchen where she was making tea. He cleared his throat.

"Did you eat already?" she asked pleasantly. "I hope you didn't wait for me. Had a heck of a time getting the chickens into the coop this evening. Mercury is still in retrograde, though. It's to be expected. Another week or two of that and then the planets and stars will realign—"

"Miranda."

The grim tone in his voice silenced her. He watched her back stiffen. She coughed into her hand.

"It didn't happen, Dix. That's all I have to say."

"Those are some pretty serious allegations," Dix replied.

"Yes, well, they are also untrue," Miranda said, turning to him and flashing a mocking smile.

"Don't try and tell me there's not plenty of crap going on out there, Miranda."

"Whatever you may think, there's nothing debauched going on out there, Dix. I know. I'm there. You're not."

Debauched. Dix rolled the word around in his mouth. A big word for the most common, the most low, of behaviors.

"She's a minor," he said.

"Yes, and as you have pointed out so many times, minors are not innocent, especially the ones we're trying to help. When evil has been done to you, you become capable of perpetrating more evil. The evil is in the allegations, because they are false, not in the action, because it did not happen."

"More riddles and platitudes," Dix said. "Not facts. Facts are that allegations of rape are rarely falsified."

"Whatever, Dix," Miranda sighed.

"Whatever?" Dix was shocked at her disregard. "That's all you have to say about this?"

"No matter what I say, you won't believe me. So why should I bother?" Miranda shot back.

"Seriously, Miranda, this is a place you choose to be associated with? There are so many ways to help. You don't need The Source or whatever they call themselves. First meth, now this?"

"These things are related, Dix. They came from the same person. These are things *she* did. Both of them. These are not things we did. I will not even speak her name. Gossip is not truth. Accusations are not deeds, Dix."

"Miranda, this is serious. This is a matter of law. Whether it's true or not, you could be charged. As an accessory. This could go on your record."

"On my record? That's what you're worried about? Some piece of paper in some bureaucrat's office? As if that kind of thing has any power over me. I can see you're worried about what people think of you, Dix. Thankfully, I am not. Not anymore."

"This has nothing to do with opinions, Miranda. This has the potential to destroy your future."

"Future? I'm not looking for a future, Dix," Miranda said, throwing her arms about. "I'm looking for a present, a way of life in the here and now. And I've found it. I have nothing to be afraid of. The truth will always win out. We may not be able to see the path it takes, but the truth always finds its way to the light, eventually."

"For Christ's sake, Miranda. The girl is pregnant!" Dix seethed.

"For your information, Dix—even though I am not supposed to discuss The Source or its rules with outsiders, with people like you, who are so full of preconceived notions and judgments, because what we do there is sacred and the world is a hostile place for the sacred—if you must know, in fact, sex is not allowed at The Source."

"What?" Dix said.

"Sex is a distraction from clarity of purpose," Miranda said with practiced serenity. "It clouds the mind with passions, desires, jealousy. It takes us inside our own desires and makes it harder to see what we should be doing to heal the larger world. It makes us pursue carnality instead of spirituality. Sex is not allowed among those who make The Source their home."

"No sex? Please," Dix said, giving full voice to a snide sarcasm he didn't know he was capable of. And also to a suspicion he had been harboring but was uncomfortable admitting. "A bunch of hormonal teenagers with not enough to do, hanging out in a trailer? One dude in a house full of young women? Who are you kidding? It's like a B-grade porn movie waiting to happen."

"My, haven't you gotten vulgar and degrading in your insults?" Miranda said dismissively.

They stared at each other, uncomprehending. Neither knew what to do with the distance that had grown between them. Neither knew what to do with the other. They stood on the opposite shores of a river of distrust that raged between them and saw the bridge they had tried to build for the rickety thing it truly was.

"I'm sorry, Miranda. I'm sorry for my tone," Dix finally said. "But none of this makes sense to me. The truth is, the bigger truth—the one that is more important to me than The Source, the kids, the meth, or these charges this teenager is bringing that Darius raped her—is, it's just that, I fear I've lost you. I have lost you. You're so rarely here anymore. And when you're here, you're not really here. Your thoughts are elsewhere. It feels like you'd rather be elsewhere. It feels like you're merely fulfilling some duty by spending time with me. I just want you back. I just want us back."

Miranda was quiet for a moment. Dix hoped she was reconsidering, softening. He hoped she would come nestle her head against his chest, wrap her arms around his waist. Instead, what she said next hit him like a wet towel slapped across his face.

"I am not yours, Dix," she said, her voice icy. "There is no me to get back. There is no us to get back. I am not an object to be kept and coddled and held onto. I have found my passion and my path and you don't approve. So be it. For me, there is no going back, coming back, whatever you want to call it. I ask you, Dix, do you really love me? Oh, I know you think you do, but it has become clear to me that it's much more likely you love some picture you have in your head of who you think I am. Which is who I have been. And not who I am anymore."

She turned and left the room. Dix listened, pinned into place by her completely unexpected and staggering pronouncement, as she moved down the hallway, then in and out of a few rooms and out the back door. He watched the red lights on her car recede down the driveway. He gasped into the empty, airless space she left behind and wondered how he had managed to drive her away when nothing could have been further from his intentions.

She did not come back that night. Or the next night. Or the one after that. Or after that. He would pick up the phone to call her and then remember that she'd left her cell phone behind. It wasn't allowed out there. Out there. It never occurred to him that she might have gone somewhere else. Where else would she go? He checked his own phone obsessively. Never a message or text. Days turned into a week. He considered driving over there, but he thought she needed time. He thought she needed to return to him when she was ready. He was also afraid she'd reject him again. He didn't want to force her hand.

Because he could not look forward, Dix looked back. He knew Miranda had been slipping away from him, bit by bit, for months, but still her departure was a shock. He wandered the echoing house and tried to find her in the things she had left behind. He stood in front of the bathroom cabinet and stared at her hairbrush, fingered the long strands that tangled themselves in its bristles. He picked up a half-finished mitten, still forlornly attached to a ball of yarn, and set it back in the knitting basket. He stood in front of her half of the closet. There was a large gap. He opened her drawers. Mostly empty. He realized both of her winter coats were missing from the hall closet. She hadn't taken time to pack when she left.

When did these other things disappear? he wondered. Had she been planning her departure, stockpiling items out at The Source? Had she come back to the house when he was out working and collected things then? Or did she just leave her things behind out there accidentally, as she had the tools?

He tried to give her the benefit of the doubt. He told himself that she'd always been absentminded. But his excuses for her could not stand up in the face of her absence. As the days passed and the stupor of his sadness lifted, it was replaced with a resentment that bordered on rage. He was angry at her for abandoning him and them as a couple, at Darius for seducing her with his smarmy platitudes, at the teenagers for seducing her with their raw-woundedness. And then at her again for being so easily taken in.

These were unfamiliar, uncomfortable feelings for Dix. Nothing in his life before had destroyed his innate equanimity. He tried to use work to distract himself from the twisted emotions Miranda had left behind. There was plenty of it, as the out-of-towners were full of need for him and his fixes and prepping their places for Christmas family gatherings. When he had finished with his customers' projects, he cleaned and sharpened his own tools. He took apart his tractor and put it back together again. He organized his shop. He beat back every bit of old dust and cobweb in the barn.

None of this brought her back. All of it reinforced his loneliness and vexation.

Dix tried to imagine Miranda out there at The Source. He pictured her in some kind of neurotically happy bubble, surrounded by those scruffy women, an ad hoc family so unlike the one she had grown up in. What a relief she must feel to be able to drop the elaborate and limited code of acceptable behaviors that were part of the playbook her class of people used. Yet, he knew and wished she could see that she had merely exchanged the old set of rules for a new set. Neither was hers. Both had been given to her by charismatic and controlling men. Dix knew he was neither of those things. Maybe that was the problem. Maybe that was how he'd failed her. Had he not given her enough space? Or too much? Had he been too soft? Too self-contained? As he searched for explanations, he missed the most obvious one: some people don't want to find their own way and are in fact searching for a path someone else has already made.

Christmas came and went. Dix spent the days when others were celebrating with hours of hiking the mountains alone in the knee-deep snow. After the holidays, he kept hiking. Then one day, soon after the first of the year, he opened the paper and saw that the rape charges had been dropped. He immediately had the jealousy-induced thought that of course Darius wasn't having sex with the teenagers, he was having it with Miranda. Probably had been all along. Why else would she be so taken with that foul place, that superficial man? Dix shook off his reeking, painful thoughts and focused on the news, reading and rereading the brief article several times. He was looking for something, anything, between the few lines of text. All it said was that the charges were dropped and the state would not be pursuing the case. End of story. He knew that dropping charges didn't mean the rape had not happened.

Maybe it was too hard to prove. Maybe she was scared. Maybe she was paid off. Maybe it really hadn't happened and the girl was just looking for attention. Or money. He told himself, over and over, that maybe it really hadn't happened. Maybe none of this was quite what it seemed.

After the fire, Sally noticed a new seriousness in Miranda's habitual expression. It wasn't just because of the lightly scorched hair of her brows and crown, sustained when she ran into the trailer on the erroneous assumption that Cassandra or Maverick was still in there, stuck on the wrong side of a small kitchen blaze, in danger of injury, when in fact they had almost blown up the trailer with their idiotic attempts to cook meth, bolted at the first sign of a flame, and kept running without warning a soul or trying to douse the conflagration they'd created themselves. No, it was that some light in Miranda had been absorbed by shadows. Then, after Cassandra brought the rape charges, Miranda's face had turned grim. Sally thought—hoped, really—that these changes were the beginning of her disillusionment with The Source. She had become fond of Miranda and hoped she would break free of Darius's spell and go back to her strong, silent, macho mountain man, Dix. Instead, Miranda arrived one night with a duffel bag. It was late. Darius came down from his attic lair. The other women were already tucked into their beds. Sally listened through a crack in the door as Miranda and Darius spoke in the kitchen at the bottom of the stairs.

"Miranda, my dear. What brings you back? You seem upset."

"No, Darius. I'm not upset. I'm ready. Ready to join. To stay for good."

There was quiet for a moment. As if Darius was taking this all in.

"Well," he said, "this is delightful news. Of course. Yes. We are thrilled to have you and all you bring with you."

Sally winced at his liberal use of the royal "we." He missed, either willfully or ignorantly, all the many signs of petty rivalries between the women, the significant looks that passed between them when he gave one or the other a compliment or praise. In spite of the communal vibe, there was a lot less camaraderie between the women than he thought there was.

"It's time," Miranda said. "I can't have my life split in two anymore. I need to choose. I can't . . . it's just . . ." She sighed. "I choose The Source."

"What a momentous decision," Darius said. "I admire your resolve. We will talk more in the morning. In the meantime, we will find you some space in the front bedroom."

"No. I mean, yes, thank you. But wait," Miranda said.

"What is it, Miranda?" Darius asked.

"I want you to cut my hair," Miranda said.

There was silence again.

"Now?" Darius asked, sounding uncharacteristically unsure of himself.

"Yes," Miranda demanded. "It will make my transition away from the egotistic concerns of the outside world complete. It will mark my commitment to The Source and our values. Please. Yes. Now. I want to be like the other women here."

Sally listened as a chair scraped, a drawer opened, silence descended. Moments passed quietly. Then the chair scraped again, and she heard two sets of footsteps approach the stairway. She closed the door to her room. She heard them enter the other bedroom, where there were a few whispered voices that quickly settled down. Then, Darius took the stairs to the attic. Sally returned to bed and slept fitfully, dozing and waking, startling easily from the middle of disturbing dreams where unseen pursuers chased her through dark alleys, over rickety fire escapes, across hallways that would not end. She finally rose from bed, wrapped herself in a robe, and tiptoed down the stairs to have a smoke on the back porch. It was cold, so she only smoked half of a cigarette, then came inside to douse it in the sink. She opened the cabinet to throw the butt into the garbage and gasped.

The discarded ends of Miranda's once-glorious mane filled the trash can. Even though Sally knew this was what Miranda had asked for, seeing the evidence of the drastic deed took her breath away. She was surprised at how affected she was by what she saw. It looked as if a long-haired animal were curled up atop the garbage heap, asleep. Some clot of emotion shifted deep inside of her. Sally found a bag and lifted Miranda's disembodied locks from where they lay, placed them gently in the cocoon of brown paper, and took them with her back to her room. She put the bag in the back of her closet. She didn't know why she saved Miranda's shorn hair. She simply felt that it must be saved, that something of Miranda must be saved.

Dix began to doubt himself. He was waiting for Miranda to do something, to give him a sign. But what if she was waiting for him? He was hoping she'd return. But what if she was hoping he would rescue her?

Eventually, he tired of wondering. He had nothing to lose. He had the one person he cared about in the world to gain. Even more important, to help. He decided to go on a Tuesday afternoon. There seemed to be a logic to this decision, something about the potential likelihood that it would be quiet out there, that Darius might not be around, but it was a rationale that existed only in Dix's imagination. Certainly the people at The Source did not recognize the flow of weekdays and weekends in the way that he or most others did. They lived and worked according to their own rhythms. But it soothed Dix to think that there was some reason to his choice of day and time that might lend his errand a better chance of success.

It was a bitter January day. The skies were heavy with snow that would not fall, so there was no fresh, white icing atop the dark and dirty piles of frozen accumulations that lined the roads. As he made his way up the pitted driveway, Dix's stomach lurched as much as his truck did. He pulled into the gravel area near the ratty farmhouse and sat, unsure what to do, hoping some person would appear and give him a reason to get out of the truck. He wanted to be drawn forth instead of having to step into the void of the empty yard, go up to the door, and knock—and suffer the indignity of having to ask for her.

Nothing happened to help him. So he stepped from the truck and slammed the door. A little too hard. Then the farmhouse front door slammed, as if in response. There was a woman on the porch. She was wrapped in an oversize coat, a man's coat. She had a baseball cap pulled low over her forehead, a rough fringe of hacked-off hair peeking out the back. She pushed the bill of the hat back with her wrist and crossed her arms over her chest. She was not smiling.

Dix was stunned to realize it was Miranda.

He felt the casualty of her missing mane like the loss of a once-close but long-estranged friend. She'd told him, in what felt like a prior lifetime, that the women here cut their hair for modesty. It was part of rejecting the celebrity-obsessed, culturally misogynistic, male-dominated, overly sexualized, capitalist-controlled outside world. Dix thought at the time that there was little enough excess here in these unforgiving and parsimonious mountains; cutting your hair to make a statement seemed to be an inverted, highly perverse form of vanity. Now here was Miranda with the same short hair, the same rough attire. He feared the gesture completed her estrangement not only from him but from the rest of the world.

"Miranda." Her name was a plea in his mouth.

"Dix." His name was a statement in hers.

He took a few steps toward her. Her posture tilted slightly, but she did not step back. "How are you?" he asked, catching a new, weathered roughness that had come into her face.

"I'm well," she said, her voice assiduously neutral.

"You look it," he replied, lying.

She cleared her throat and asked, "What brings you here?"

Dix saw a face move into and then quickly out of an upstairs window. "I . . . I . . ." He had no idea where to begin. The words finally fell from his mouth. "I miss you, Miranda."

She winced. Which caused him to do the same.

"I'm sorry," he said.

"There's nothing to be sorry for," she said, looking down and shifting her feet.

Dix knew this wasn't going well, but he didn't know what to do, how to fix that, so he blundered on, desperate to try any words that might reach her. "I'm sorry I upset you. I'm sorry we didn't fix things. I'm sorry you're not with me anymore. I'm sorry I don't know what to do about any of it. I'm worried about you. I love you. I want to make things better. I want to be a couple again. What can I do, Miranda? Tell me what to do."

She watched him quietly.

"I wish you'd come home," he said, now out of words.

Miranda cleared her throat, squared her shoulders, and said, "Dix, this is my home now."

His body drooped under the finality of her words. He turned his face from the sting of them. He closed his eyes against the pain. He had never imagined she could speak to him so coldly. Then he heard boots bang against porch steps. He felt his hands taken up, calluses and ragged nails against his palms. He opened his eyes on Miranda's upturned face, her eyes shadowed by the cap's brim.

"Dix," she pleaded with him, suddenly the soft, kind Miranda he once knew.

He tried to meet her eyes but found it difficult.

"I need some time," she said. "I think some time apart is important. I need to find out who I am. I need to find what's important to me."

He wanted to ask her why she couldn't do that with him, how she could possibly do that here. But he knew she had no answers to those questions. Perhaps no answers were even possible.

"Try, Dix. Try to be happy for me," she said.

He nodded, his face averted. He gently pulled his hands away from hers. She held on.

"Look at me," she implored him.

He turned to her.

"I love you, Dix. You've been nothing but good to me. You've done nothing but care for me and about me. I owe you everything. But I need this. I want this. The most loving thing you can do for me right now is to leave me be."

Dix leaned down and pressed his lips to her cheek. "I love you," he whispered, then removed his hands from hers, got into his truck, and drove away.

Miranda felt restless nausea slosh in her gut. Her diet had changed so much since she'd come to live at The Source full-time. This bloat and tiredness and stomach upset was just her body trying to rid itself of the toxins it had accumulated, she reminded herself. She told herself to lie still and breathe it all away. She remembered her meditation instruction, to send her breath deeper into her lower chakra. She tried to visualize the process of healthy digestion. She set her intention to allow her body to expel the fear and blood of all the meat she'd consumed in her life and, in its place, absorb and embrace the nutrients and nourishment from the new, natural, and lovingly raised foods she was eating at The Source. With each exhalation, she imagined dark vapors leaving her body. She listened to the breathing of the other women around her. Someone was snoring. Violet. They teased her about it. Luna had suggested a buckwheat pillow, but they were unsure of where or how to procure one made from organic materials. Miranda smiled at the sound, the comfort of being in this place, with these women.

No one was touching her where she lay on her thin futon, yet she felt embraced by the presence of several sleeping bodies nearby. She thought of the animal bodies nestled in straw out in the barn. The seeds dormant in the ground. The soil itself under its blanket of snow. She felt connected to it all. She remembered how she had felt separate, distant from everything around her, for so many years. No longer. Her stomach settled. The bile subsided. She listened in the predawn darkness to footsteps overhead. Darius was rising. Darius, who had brought all of this together, who had created this sanctuary. Darius who knew her brother, her parents, who was somehow the string that connected her past with her present and, she felt sure, her future.

How improbable it all was, Miranda thought, smiling to herself. How perfect. How magnificent the world was when you could tap into its inherent magic and ride its ancient and everlasting rhythms. It was time to rise and greet the miracle of a new day free of dread and anxiety. There was, after all, nothing to do other than that which presented itself. So easy in the end, that which had seemed so hard for her for so long. Darius had taught her all of this. Darius had shown her what she hadn't even realized she'd been seeking. Silently, she thanked him.

An undulation of queasiness hit her again. She began a check-in and assessment, starting at her toes and slowly working her way up her body, asking each part to relax, flow, connect with every other. She willed tension out of her ankles, from behind her knees, from deep within her hips. She spread her palms over the taut skin below her belly button. She whispered soothing words to her innards. She imagined them as calm seas. Her tummy did a flip under her hands. Her eyes shot open.

Wait, she told herself. *Could this be something other than simple nausea?*

She felt energy moving from the inside of her body outward, warming her palms. She felt what seemed to be movement.

My God, she thought. *Finally. It's happened.*

She dared not say the word, even to herself. She'd waited far too long to jinx her sudden certainty that a new life was at last growing within her. A vision of Dix flashed behind her eyes, his soft green eyes, his sheepish smile.

"Thank you," she whispered. "Thank you for giving this to me."

She heard footsteps. Darius coming downstairs, past her door. A picture of Darius supplanted the one of Dix, the green eyes turned bright blue, and the awkward grin became a confident smile.

Yes, Darius, she thought. *Thank you. This happened because of you.*

It had happened because she was finally doing the right thing with her life, and her body had become receptive to what she had wanted for so long. It was only because of Darius that she had been awakened in this way. This was a gift from Dix, but even more, an acknowledgment from the universe to her because of Darius, through Darius, because of the larger gifts he had bestowed upon her. She was sure of it.

Dix sat with a cup of tea going cold in his hands and watched the snow fall. He plowed, shoveled, scraped, and pushed it back. It came again. He returned to his truck and shovels. Then he'd drink tea and watch the paths he'd cleared refill with dense, white clouds of snow. Weeks drifted by. He didn't mark the days or notice the time. One early morning when the entire landscape looked like the color of old steel, the sound of gunshot in the distance reminded him that, somehow, he'd missed deer season this year. He'd never even cleaned his guns. That was a first. It was small-game season still. Maybe he could get a rabbit or two.

Possibly even a partridge. Unlikely. But he was growing restless. He'd been sitting too long. His body was starting to protest.

He cleaned his gun, loaded it onto his truck rack, got into his camo, and headed out. If he didn't hunt, at least he'd hike. But by the time he got going it was late morning, no time for hunting, and it was bitter cold, so the animals would be hunkered down. As he should be. He drove aimlessly. Or what seemed to be. Until he found himself on a particular dirt road near a certain driveway. He didn't hesitate, just turned in again without thinking. He didn't know why he had returned. He had no plan, no idea what to do once he got to the end of the drive. He simply stepped from the truck, slammed the door, and waited. He had nothing else to do, nothing else to lose. Once again, the front door answered him. But this time it was a man who stepped forth. He stood cross-armed on the porch.

"Dix," the man said, freighting the name full of disappointment. "Why are you here?"

Dix took a moment to assess the man in front of him. So this was Darius. The man at the center of The Source. Short, slender. Pretty.

Christ, Dix thought, *he could be a girl. So insubstantial. Hardly a worthy adversary.*

"I'm not sure," Dix answered. "Just kinda ended up here."

Dix watched Darius look him up and down, saw his eyes flick over to his truck, where his loaded gun rack stood in stark silhouette in the back window.

"We are a sanctuary, Dix," Darius said. "Your presence is disturbing."

Dix looked Darius up and down again as well. He was wearing roughed-up clothes that clearly had not earned their ragged edges honestly. Like those factory-aged jeans teenagers bought at the mall. He wondered what Miranda saw in this guy. Then it occurred to him how much alike they were. Soft, spoiled, fake. Trying to be unique by acquiring the tropes of individuality. His anger at Darius, at the both of them, was driven out for a moment by a wave of pity and disgust.

"Shut up, Darius," Dix said dismissively, as if he were talking to a barking but chained dog. "I want to see Miranda."

"I understand, Dix," Darius said, apparently ignoring the insult, his voice oily and cool. "But it's better for her not to see you. She was very upset the last time you came. It took her some time to recover her equilibrium. I know you want what's best for her. We all want what's best for her. What's best for her now is to be here. Where there is peace and where she is cared for within the structure of our supportive community."

In the face of this slick and sanctimonious stonewalling, Dix's anger returned, even stronger than before. It was an emotion he had blocked for Miranda, but he had no hesitation showing it to this man.

"You bastard," he growled. "You know nothing about Miranda, about what's best for her. You're a fucking charlatan." He took a few steps forward. Darius's face remained maddeningly still and expressionless. Dix pointed his finger toward the chest of the man in front of him. "Who do you think you are, anyway? You are a joke. You are a poser. A rich boy trying to find himself by playing games out here on this land. This place will take you down, Darius. Mark my words, these mountains will take you down."

The door behind Darius opened. A woman emerged, her pale skin set off by the bags under her red-rimmed eyes and the curtain of hair that hung limply alongside her caved-in cheeks. She wore a low-slung skirt and a long sweater that clung to her swollen breasts and protruding belly. Dix did not recognize her until she said his name.

"Dix. Please. You're scaring us. You're scaring me."

Miranda cradled her stomach with her palms in the subconscious and universal motion of pregnant women. Dix looked in desperation from Miranda to Darius and back again. Miranda shook her head slowly in an expression of weary dismissal. Her words came back to him in mockery. No sex at The Source. What a fool he had been for believing her, for working so hard to sweep away all his nagging doubts. Here was the damning evidence of what he had suspected but not wanted to admit all along: Darius had given her what Dix could not. She was not here out on some selfless, do-gooder impulse. She was here, had been here all along, because she was in love with this horrible blue-eyed devil of a man. She had lied to herself. She had lied to him. Dix was flooded with despair, regret, and shame—emotions he had never before experienced in even a small quantity and now felt in an engulfing wave. Miranda took a step forward. Darius held up his hand to her, and she obediently stalled where she was. Dix stumbled backward. He fell against his truck and banged his fist against the metal hood. He threw himself inside and sped away, spewing a wave of gravel behind him.

When Miranda had started to show, she had gained a new and different position in the community. Sally watched Darius single her out for one-on-one, whispered conversations, a coach conferring with his star athlete. She saw the other women begin to sidestep her, not as a pariah, but in deference. Sally searched for a moment when she could speak to Miranda privately. Back when Miranda was just a day camper, she would meet Sally's eyes, initiate conversation, and invite connection. But after she joined The Source full-time, there was an initial and short-lived bloom of enthusiasm and engagement with everything, and then Miranda's face grew increasingly somber and her energy turned inward, a tendency that increased when her pregnancy became clear. It was harder to talk to Miranda than it used to be. To even share a simple greeting. From what Sally could tell, it appeared that Miranda still participated in the orchestrated events and chores, but she spoke less and kept to herself more. Sally recalled Miranda telling her once, just before she moved to The Source, that she and Dix had been trying to get pregnant. She wondered if Dix knew they'd succeeded. Or if their estrangement was so complete that Miranda was keeping this all to herself. Sally watched her as closely as she could or dared, and caught the knowing glances Darius shot at Miranda. They seemed intended to nudge, instruct, perhaps remind her of something. Sally knew the asexual Darius was not the father, but he seemed to be trying to exert some sort of ownership over Miranda's pregnancy, as if he saw it as an opportunity. For what, Sally could not imagine. She knew the only way she could find out was to get Miranda alone.

The days were short and Sally was restless, often awake in the predawn hours, standing at her window, willing the day to come on, wondering why she was still at The Source. Saving money, watching the house, morbid curiosity—she mentally ticked off the reasons. She also felt as if she was waiting for something to happen; she just didn't know what or why. And now, there was also her concern for Miranda. Miranda was one of those people, Sally recognized, who incited worry in others. There was a delicacy and callowness to her that made one want to put away sharp objects, cover pointy corners, strew clean straw in her path. None of which Miranda was aware of. Which made the effort that much more compelling.

One clear, dark morning when the stars were bright pinpricks in the indigo sky, Sally stood at her window trying to talk herself not so much into leaving as out of staying. Then she noticed a dim light warming a window in the trailer. The structure had been abandoned, a chemical pariah, after the fire. But as she watched, a distinctive silhouette came into view through the busted-out window. Sally quickly pulled on boots and a coat and tiptoed out of the house, across the yard, and into the trailer. Miranda turned as Sally closed the door behind her. Her expression was troubled, her skin sallow. Sally wondered if she was ill. The thought scared her, as it came to her more as a premonition than a question. Some women glowed with vibrancy when pregnant. Miranda appeared as if the baby was draining the life from her as it grew.

"Miranda, honey," Sally said gently, as if she were approaching a spooked horse. "You shouldn't be out here. It's cold. This place is polluted."

"It's OK. The windows are open," Miranda said, her eyes drifting over the sharp shards that framed the opening above the stove.

Sally decided against explaining how little the open window would help clear the place from chemicals used to cook meth. "Miranda, are you OK?" she asked instead. "Is everything OK with you? With the baby?"

Miranda slowly bent over, righted a metal chair from where it was lying on the floor, and with exquisite exhaustion, sank into it. Her shoulders looked thin. The swelling in her womb seemed to be drawing sustenance from her other body parts. "Oh, the baby is fine." She patted her belly and a wan smile drifted onto and then off her face. "I'm not sleeping very well," she said. "That's all."

"Me neither," Sally replied.

"Guess I'm a little frustrated," Miranda said. "Seems we're never going to be a haven for wayward youth, after all. Kind of a disaster here. And now, apparently, word on the street is that this place is a big 'drag,'" she sighed, making air quotes with her fingers.

Sally was surprised and unsettled to hear this accurate but dismal assessment of the situation at The Source from Miranda, the truest of its true believers.

"Well, maybe there will be a new generation of teens who show up," Sally said tentatively.

"A new generation," Miranda said. "You sound like Darius."

"That's a little scary," Sally joked.

Miranda spread her hands over her extended midsection and stared at them.

"That's what Darius wants," she said. "To create a new generation, totally free from the distractions and seductions of modern life. With only Mother Nature as a teacher and guide."

"I don't know if you've noticed, but Mother Nature can be quite a bitch," Sally said. As Miranda described Darius's vision for her baby, Sally heard skepticism battling against belief. This was a first, coming from Miranda. Sally needed to find a way to take advantage of this, to steer Miranda further from Darius and back toward Dix. It was a delicate, risky moment.

"Miranda?" she said. The other woman did not look up. "Are you thinking about when you'll return with the baby to Dix?"

"Return?" Miranda said, her face still turned downward, confusion furrowing her brow. "Oh, I don't think that's possible. Darius wants me to stay. Wants us to stay. We'll fumigate and fix up the trailer for the two of us. We'll all raise the baby together. The baby will be free and innocent and become a model of what's possible in the world. He says he has realized that individuals get too damaged, in too many ways, too quickly, so repair and restoration become impossible. We need a 'tabula rasa,' he says." She'd made the air quotes again. "My baby came at just the right time, a gift from the universe, a gift we need to give back to the universe. That's what Darius thinks."

Miranda's tone was entirely unconvincing. Another rote retelling of someone else's vision. Sally felt prickles of sweat break out under her arms and on her lip and brow, even though the room was cold. "But, Miranda," she said.

"I agree with him, Sally."

"But."

"I know. I know," Miranda sighed. "The child is not mine alone."

"Exactly."

"Dix did want a baby. I think he did, anyway. Actually, I'm not so sure. It was always more my idea. I was the one who was pushing for it. He kept saying we had plenty of time. He was just indulging me. Like he always did. He didn't really care if we had a child or not. I realize that now."

"Still. He is the father," Sally said.

"I know. But these ideas of ownership," Miranda hurried on. "Of owning another person. She's mine. He's mine. That child is hers or his. That child needs to grow up to reflect my values, be an expression of me, the parent. Just like my car and address and job title are a reflection of me. That's not a baby—that's a doll you dress up. Wouldn't it be so much better to just let my child have many parents and guardians and teachers? To wander outdoors instead of being chained to a chair in a classroom? Isn't that the more natural way? A much better way? Darius says my baby could have a birth mother, a garden mother, a house mother, an instructional mother. That all seems so much better. And Dix would hate all of that. He'd never support me in the way I, the way *we* want to raise this baby."

Miranda seemed to be trying to talk herself into the words that were bubbling from her mouth.

No, no, no, Sally wanted to say. *That's just Darius-talk.*

But before she could reply, the door opened again and the man himself walked in. His eyes flitted from one woman to another, and a forced smile split his face in two.

"What's going on out here?" he asked with an obvious effort to keep his tone friendly. "Getting a head start on making this place your own?" Sally saw his obvious effort to ignore her. He inclined his head toward Miranda. "But you should be in bed, my dear," he went on, touching Miranda on the shoulder. "This place may still have some chemical vestiges that are not good for our baby."

"Our" baby? Sally thought, outrage heating her face. She wanted to smack Darius across his temple with the large wooden spoon lying close by on the counter. *I can't leave her here alone. I can't leave her and her baby undefended from this man.*

Darius ran the back of his hand along Miranda's arm a few times, then wrapped his fingers around her biceps and coaxed her, unresisting, from her chair. He nudged her toward the door. She crossed the small space in a few shuffling steps. Darius crossed his arms over his chest and watched her go.

Once Miranda was outdoors and on her way back to the house, he turned and hissed at Sally, "Stay the fuck out of this."

Then he was gone, leaving Sally in a miasma of garlic and manure, acetone and char, cold air and fear.

Things were not working out as Darius had planned. Not that there had been a plan. That would have been far too confining and restrictive. But there had been a vision. Lambs cavorting in a field, chickens scratching in the dirt, bushes laden with fruit, lush rows of green vegetables neatly tied to bamboo stakes, sweet smells emanating from the kitchen windows, a woman at a loom, another at a butter churn, the sun on the well-defined muscles of his sweating back as he showed a group of teenagers how to build a shelter from supplies found at hand in the woods.

What he had instead was a cold and muddy few acres, chickens that didn't lay eggs and were eaten by foxes, an ornery couple of goats, diseased produce, a bunch of scrapes, and pulled muscles. Darius wanted young people, cynical and worn-out already, whom he could scrub clean, return to their wide-eyed and open-hearted state, and then slowly refill with a new way of being in the world. He wanted the satisfaction of seeing their expectant faces and empty souls absorb his nutrient-dense diet of natural law and timeless truth. He wanted to watch as they went out and seeded the country around them with his ideas and insight. Instead, what he had was a gaggle of sullen, unskilled women with soft hands and needy egos continually looking for the indulgence of his kind word or warm look.

And he had Sally still hanging around. He had thought of her for some time as just an annoyance, a stray dog looking for scraps. He had figured she'd wander off eventually, bored, hungry, sick of being ignored. But she had stayed. She had become emboldened. Especially with Miranda. He felt she had developed a superior air, as if she was waiting and watching for him to screw up, so sure of her own prophecy of his inevitable demise, on the lookout for when she could pounce. He had tried to shoo her away. He had not been able to scare her off. He didn't know how hard he could push her. He felt that he was on her territory. She held the mortgage. She owned more of the house than he did. She was part of the "system" he despised. She knew cops and lawyers. He was concerned that her skeptical presence was making his flock of misfits more skittish than they otherwise might be. That she was keeping other, better specimens away.

Darius wanted to be sought out. He wanted to step out onto his porch and see people plodding up the path, asking for his succor and enlightenment. He envisioned himself up at a podium, heads in the audience nodding at his words, at a desk in a bookstore signing his manifesto, flipping through his busy calendar as he fielded requests that he speak at a conference or retreat. What he had instead were rape allegations, a burned-out trailer, and a few notebooks filled with a random collection of his own stubbornly disorganized thoughts and observations. He was growing frustrated and impatient.

He tried, in fits and starts, to instill discipline and structure into the few followers he had. A calendar in the kitchen with assignments—a technique cadged from grammar school—worked for a few weeks, but then the dishes, compost, and laundry began to pile up, the barn filled with manure, and the weeds took over the garden. The women blamed one another or whomever had recently left. He felt like a harried single mother with a passel of brats, not a man full of wisdom needed by a society that had lost its way. He began lecturing the women, taking cues on topics from his notebooks, and at first, their faces were rapt. But he always ran out of things to say and his sentences devolved into harangues and complaints that caused the women to bow their heads and to hide their eyes, which darted about in discomfort and embarrassment. Even

Miranda, his golden girl, his own personal Madonna, full of the child he recognized was not physically his but felt was spiritually his offspring, was growing morose and unresponsive.

He felt disgust with them all rise in his throat like heartburn. He could not punish the goats or the garden, the weather or the world, but he could punish them. He could school them and show them there were consequences to their weakness and self-indulgence. It was not mockery, he told them as he tied a piece of cardboard with the word *Slob* around the neck of a woman who had been slapdash in her dishwashing and kitchen-cleanup duties. It was instruction. It was not meanness, he insisted as he used a black marker to draw an anus around the mouth of a woman who had used profanity. It was a reminder. It was not punishment, he assured them as he stomped his boots onto a collection of hairbrushes and makeup he found in one woman's backpack. It was liberation.

And then, after the fire in the trailer, when he began his furtive forays into the women's bedroom when they were outdoors at chores, secretly inspecting pockets and purses, shoes and drawers, he discovered that Phoenix had smuggled in a cell phone, which she was keeping in a slit in her mattress. He read her texts. She apparently had found a spot on a small ridge behind the barn where she got just enough signal to send messages back and forth to Cassandra. He found her invitation to Cassandra and Maverick. They'd told Darius they'd heard great things about the place, and he'd assumed they meant from other teenagers. But no, it was Phoenix they'd heard from. She knew them, apparently through drug connections. She'd said, in her texts, that they'd be able to lay low here for a bit. She'd told them there was an empty trailer a convenient-yet-ample distance from the main house. She'd reminded them about what ingredients and equipment to bring, and where to find the unused feed barrel in the barn that they should use to hide everything. Darius read the messages that insisted they all pretend not to know one another and that described how they should behave to win Darius's trust. But what made his face turn red and his hands shake with anger were the texts that made fun of him. She wrote that he had "short-man syndrome," was a "eunuch" and a "wuss." She mocked his philosophy. She said The Source was a "dump." It was all too much. It could not be condoned. She would make an excellent example. He began to formulate something special for her. When the appointed evening arrived, he told the assembled community there was going to be a "cleanse."

Miranda was not there to see the cleanse. She had not been feeling well. Her pregnancy had been plagued with all kinds of digestive and sleeping upsets. She worried that something was wrong with her, that her body was not welcoming to her baby for some reason. The night that Darius had designated for the cleanse, she had taken a calming draught, gone to bed early, and fallen deeply asleep. She didn't know that Darius had ground some sleeping pills into her tea. He didn't want her there. He was afraid the presence of a pregnant woman would make the other women timid.

By the time Miranda awoke the next day, Phoenix had disappeared. Miranda began to inquire. Where had Phoenix gone? Why did no one seem to care that she'd disappeared? She'd heard a bit of a commotion in the night. What was that all about? The others dodged her questions. But she pieced things together through murmurs and whispers. It was a tale shared behind hands and with eyes averted. It became the stuff of myth. There was the time before the cleanse, when The Source was polluted with the likes of Phoenix, Cassandra, and Maverick, and the time after, when evil had been purged and purity restored. It was a pivotal experience the other women had shared with Darius, and Miranda had not.

Miranda was put out. She felt pouty. She thought that having missed the event, like her once-long hair, marked her as separate from the others. They'd all bonded over the test that Phoenix represented, and she'd been excluded from both the challenge and the victory. Miranda was also deeply disappointed in Phoenix. She hardly knew the other woman but felt sure she should have stayed on after the cleanse, contemplating the lessons the experience certainly had to teach and, having been scrubbed clean of her past and embedded notions, evolving her spirit in fresh and new ways.

I would not have left, Miranda thought. *I would have benefited deeply. I would have embraced the opportunity.*

Thoughts of the cleanse became an obsession for Miranda. She pressed the women for details, collected the whispered bits of information, and reassembled them into a fantasy mosaic. She imagined the excitement of so many hands circling her body at one time, the bittersweet taste of soap in her mouth, the cascades of cool water flowing over her face, breasts, and legs, the chills and shivers met by a bracing scrub with rough towels and then comforted away with a cocoon of warm blankets and bodies curled in on hers. She wondered what she could do wrong in order to be singled out by Darius for the treatment. She considered ways to provoke him and was strangely delighted by this fresh rebellious streak she found in herself. It was a new toy she wanted to play with. One evening she allowed a plate to slip through her hands as she dried it. She was looking forward to the resulting crash, the flash of anger in Darius's face as he turned to her, the feeling of the hard floor against her knees as she picked at the scattered, broken bits of crockery. But the dropped plate hit her foot, bounced, and merely wobbled in place a few times before coming to rest. The resulting sound was insufficient to arouse Darius from the conversation he was having with Violet about how to redistribute Phoenix's chores.

Miranda would set aside her dark fantasies and perverse longings for a time. She would tell herself to focus on the tasks at hand. She would discipline her thinking. She would succeed for a few days, but she invariably grew restless and agitated, full of physical and emotional discomfort. She became increasingly fearful that the baby growing within her was feeding from a vessel polluted with all the psychic toxins she had taken in throughout her life. She wanted to bring her child into the world with a purity of intention she felt unable to attain just by meditating and puzzling over passages in the Tao. She needed something that would shock her system and her senses into a new relationship with the world. She wanted a cleanse.

The image of Miranda so full of child and yet empty of beauty rattled endlessly in and out of Dix's head. He would be frying eggs for breakfast, and the smell of them burning untended in the pan would bring him back from his painful reverie. He'd find himself driving down the road, a mile past where he had intended to turn. Or still in bed, staring out the window, long after the sun had crept its way into the slow-to-warm spring sky. He wondered how far along she was. He wondered when she was due. He wondered how she had become pregnant so easily by Darius, and, if she had become pregnant by Dix, whether she would have stayed. If that would have been a good thing in the long run. If things weren't better this way. If it wasn't better that she left when she did, before their lives were even more entwined. He told himself to put her out of his mind just as she had put him out of her life.

One day, some two months after his last visit to The Source, he was out in the barn sharpening mower blades on his grinder. As he stared at the long blade, guiding it carefully along the spinning stone, watching as it ground away the dull metal and created a new, shiny, sharp surface, Miranda's silhouette clouded his vision, dulled his hearing, and pulled him down. Pain snapped his senses back to attention. He dropped the blade, and it landed with a thud against the top of his boots. He watched as drops of bright red blood began to decorate its surface. He changed his focus and looked at his hands. Both were bleeding, one from his knuckles where a bump into the hard stone had instantly scraped away soft flesh, the other from a precise incision where the blade had caressed it as it fell to the ground.

Enough, Dix thought. *She's taken enough of me already. I can't let her have my hands, too.*

He began to banish the thought of her when it came, shooing her away as if she were a buzzing insect. But still she persisted in her insistent, noisy need for his attention. So he began to go through the house, packing up reminders of her. Gradually, he filled a couple of boxes with her clothes, then another with her toiletries and jewelry, trinkets, and hairbrushes. He kept another box open and dropped things into it as he happened upon them: a pair of sunglasses from a drawer, a small bottle of lotion she kept by the sink, a favorite feminine coffee mug, a nail file on the side table, a framed snapshot of her with her brother, her knitting basket. Then finally, the small stuffed bear she had kept propped up in a rocker in the bedroom. Her father had given her that bear. It was the only sentimental thing she had kept from her family. Everything else from them—remarkably little once they had cleaned out the house and put everything up for auction—was in a small self-storage unit they had rented. As Dix taped up his boxes and carried them to the garage, he remembered Miranda murmuring the single word *someday* as she had lowered the door on the storage space and locked her past away.

Someday. A word full of hope and sadness.

Dix spent the next weeks refilling the empty spots she'd left in the house with his own things. He had no need for hair conditioner. A large container of bargain shampoo took the space where she'd once had two floral-labeled, scented bottles. The rocker where the bear had sat was now a place to toss his dirty work pants at the end of the day, until he took them up again the following morning. He adopted a cat. Her gray, furry form circled in on itself and slept in the spot that had held Miranda's basket of yarn. The house absorbed his footfalls when he came home in the evening, the cat curled herself against the small of his back at night, his coffee mug was front and center when he opened the cabinet in the mornings, but still the boxes neatly stacked against the garage wall mocked him every time he went to his truck.

Finally, one Saturday in May, when there was a chill in the air as the tentative spring tried to break through the vestiges of winter and the budding leaves seemed to shrink back against the tree branches, Dix pawed through the kitchen junk drawer until he found the key he was looking for buried under a pile of change. He loaded the boxes into the back of his truck and started toward the storage unit. As he drove, peevishness and resentment moved from a low simmer to a full boil in his gut. Here he was, once again, taking care of Miranda's stuff. This was what he'd done for years, first because she couldn't, then because she wouldn't.

And why? For what?

For the small pleasures of being able to run his fingers through her hair, seeing her face crinkle with shy gratitude when he helped her in the garden, sinking his teeth into a slice of her pie? And yet, to gain even those tiny victories, he'd had to spend countless hours trying to coax her out of her petulant, anxious mantle.

No. Enough already. He berated himself as he turned away from the direction of the self-storage place and instead onto a particular dirt road and then into a ratty driveway next to a listing mailbox. *Enough. Let her take care of her own crap for once.*

This was the third time he'd come up this drive but the first time he wanted to leave something behind instead of hoping to take something away. He stepped from his truck and surveyed the scene. Nothing had changed. The deadened stillness that hovered here seemed deeper, thicker, a fog no sun could burn away. He moved to the bed of his truck, grabbed a box, and carried it toward the porch. He didn't care if he saw Miranda. He just wanted to get rid of her stuff.

The door to the farmhouse opened. Dix tried to avoid looking up. A man's voice saying his name stopped his forward momentum.

"Dix."

The single note was a warning. Not of danger but of bad news. Delivered in a voice swelled with sanctimonious comfort.

There he was. Darius. The man who seemed to have given Miranda everything Dix was unable to provide. Dix met his eyes and waited for what was to come.

Darius's voice came at him like distant thunder that broke his sentences into truncated phrases: "sad news," "did all we could," "so very sorry," "it was not meant to be." Dix's eyes burned as he tried to make sense of what Darius was telling him.

Darius paused, bowed his head, and said, "She's gone, Dix. She is gone."

Gone? Gone where? Dix wondered, confused, unwilling to accept what he was hearing.

"Where is she?" he asked.

"We carried out her wishes," Darius said in answer to Dix's question. "At the end, when the fever broke and it seemed she might recover, she asked to be cremated. Here. She fell asleep then. She didn't wake up. We made a funeral pyre. As she requested. She wanted to stay here. She wanted her ashes to be spread here. Not by us. By the four winds. So she could stay with us forever."

Miranda? Cremated? Miranda? Dead? Dix murmured the words, testing them on his lips. "But the, the baby . . ." he stammered.

Darius just shook his head. "She's at peace on the other side, Dix."

Peace? No, Dix thought, *not at peace. Dead. Burned in this ugly, shitty, damp, cold place.*

Even in death she was torturing him by insisting on this ad hoc cremation. Miranda was gone. Forever. Grief came then, like a swarm of bees. Dix dropped the box where he stood as sorrow began its crawl all over his body, down his throat, into his ears, packing every orifice with its buzzing and stinging. His mind ran from this impossible news—Miranda, dead—the fact of it an insect horde raising a din in his head. His body took some moments to catch up to his thoughts, to come into motion, but his legs, leaden at first, gave way to what Darius had said.

Dix ran from the man, from his voice, his news, his words. He ran from the man with the eyes as blue and empty as a clear sky. He leaped into his truck and drove, spitting mud and gravel, down the drive. He steered along increasingly narrow and rough dirt roads, with no thought other than *Away, I must get away,* until he came to a dead end and could drive no more. He left his truck and continued to flee from what Darius had told him. He stumbled in the weeds and grasses, and his legs went haywire on the slippery leaves left over from the last year. He fell over himself as he hit the woods but scrambled forward even as he tripped over rocks and roots. Tree branches slapped at his face and still he blundered on, the hive of grief in hot, noisy pursuit. Away he went, and then up, up, up through the still-frozen mud, and then higher still, until he found the remnants of the winter just past, the season of his sorrow. Finally, he fell and had neither the will nor the strength to lift himself again, so he splayed out into the cold comfort of the snow, his fingers clawing at the punky flesh of the decayed tree he had crashed into, his howls of agony and loss absorbed by the dense immensity of the conifer limbs that waved their dark benediction above him.

DIX AND SALLY

The chill murk and damp cling of sadness became Dix's constant companion, the only company he wanted. Without consciousness, he indulged in the ancient rituals of mourning: he drew the curtains, stopped shaving, unplugged the phone, and sat for hours, staring at nothing other than the changing color of the sky. He let the weeds take over the lawn. Spring flowers bloomed and faded without him as witness; the garden went unplanted. He scrounged directly from the pantry or refrigerator, his hands his only utensils. He fell asleep on the sofa, allowed the mice to eat from the detritus he left in the kitchen, let the mail pile up, unplugged the phone. His customers could find someone else. There were plenty of capable men around who were more in need of work than he was. He watched with only the most impassive interest as the swallows returned to nest in the barn and a pair of fawns nibbled on the lettuce that had self-seeded in his compost pile. He became long-haired, bearded, and gaunt, a semiferal version of himself.

Sometimes he disappeared into the woods for days and days, living in rough shelters, foraging and fishing as needed. He dodged the tourists, not only because he didn't want to see their $350 hiking boots, $600 tents, and $1,200 backpacks he knew would get a few times of use before collecting dust in some attic in Westchester but also because he did not want to be seen himself. He knew they came because they wanted to view wild scenery, not wild men. In any case, he did not require the well-marked and mapped trails others used. He was guided by the angles of the summer sun and the terrain itself. His long, loping gait allowed him to easily step over downed trees, across rocks that dotted the small streams, and up and down hillsides strewn with ferns, decaying logs, red dogwood, witch hazel, sumac, and white birch. He saw nothing living other than the occasional squirrels and chipmunks scratching in the leaf litter.

One late spring day, as he was prowling the woods with nothing in his pack but a compass, some venison jerky, a bottle of water, and a pair of binoculars, he stopped in the middle of a deer track. Something unbidden had come to him, a sense that something familiar and portentous was nearby. He had not meant to come this way, but when he paused and realized where he was, a dark curiosity came over him. He looked around and then up into the trees, his hand shading his eyes from the brighter light overhead. He was like a wild animal testing the wind for a scent. After a few moments of scanning, he stepped over to a large beech tree, crouched, loaded his legs like springs, and leaped upward. He grabbed a branch with both hands and swung his feet up, overhead. Hand over hand, foot over foot, he climbed. When he had ascended into the very top of the ancient tree and was among the branches that could still reliably hold his weight, he hung his pack from a small snag, settled himself against the gray trunk that was, at this height, not much wider than his back, brought the binoculars to his face, and turned them northward.

He was a hunter without arms or the intent to kill. He was simply torturing himself by trying to lay his hungry eyes on a prey he could not figure out how to pursue. Miranda was gone. She had made her incomprehensible choices. He had mourned her when she left him, and then after she died. But nothing had allayed his hatred for the man who took her from him. Twice. Dix's head was beginning to clear. And into that emptiness a desire for retribution was beginning to stir.

That first day in his perch, he saw nothing of interest. He watched until the sun fell too low for his binoculars to be of use. He climbed down from the tree, made his bed in the leaf litter, used a decayed log for a pillow, and slept the deep, dreamless sleep that comes after long hours of intent focus and complete attention. He repeated his ascent in the morning. A rooster crowed, a dog barked, a cow lowed. A baby wailed and was soothed. All these sounds, made diffuse by distance, drifted to him from indistinct directions. Then the farmhouse door he had framed in his binoculars was flung open. Hard. A moment later, the slam came to his ears, the sound emptied of emotion by the ensuing distance. He watched as a woman stepped onto the porch, put a cigarette to her mouth, bent her head, and cupped her fingers around a match. She was neither tall nor feminine in bearing. Impatience infused her motions. The ember glowed. It took Dix a moment to register the disconnect.

Cigarettes? At The Source?

Before he could think the contradiction through, the dark head and slight frame that he knew belonged to Darius came out on the porch. The man's neck jutted forward from his shoulders like a running chicken's. His hands gesticulated in obvious anger, and he repeatedly poked an index finger toward the woman's chest. She began to mirror his motions. Finally, the woman stepped back, took the cigarette from her lips, placed it between her thumb and forefinger, and flicked it right in Darius's face. Then, as he stood gaping, she clumped off the porch.

Dix dropped the binoculars in amazement at what he had just witnessed. He smirked inside and silently cheered this unknown woman's brassy fortitude in the face of the man he hated. Then, he felt something unquiet in himself settle down. He felt less alone. He climbed down from the tree, free of any desire to return to his vigil. He sensed something was somehow being set right out there, that he had an unknown ally.

He wandered slowly back through the woods, meandering across slivers of trail few other humans would notice, much less take. There was no hurry anymore. There was no one waiting for him at home. He crossed a stream and stopped. A small noise in the quiet woods had caught his attention. He listened carefully and moved toward the weak whimpering. He had to push through a clump of underbrush to find the source. An animal, mottled gray and brown like everything on the ground around it, scrabbled and twisted at his approach and was then caught short. Its foot was in a trap attached by a chain to a stake in the ground.

It's not trapping season, Dix thought.

Then he got mad. This trap had either been left behind by someone who was too lazy or distracted to check all his gear or who just didn't care if an animal suffered a slow, agonizing death because he was less than scrupulous about keeping track of the traps he had set and left behind. Dix pushed aside his emotions. There was a job at hand. He lowered himself to the ground to appear less intimidating to the frightened animal. He moved forward bit by bit, at a crouch. The animal gave up in its efforts to flee and collapsed in a heap, eyes closed and sides heaving against visible ribs. Dix broke off a piece from the jerky in his pocket and tossed it to the animal. It was ignored. A serious sign of stress. Dix wished he had gloves. He knew that trying to release the coyote from the trap would put him at risk of getting badly bitten. Opening the old trap itself put him at risk of another sort of injury. Maybe the coyote was too weak to bite. Dix took off his shirt, wrapped it around a hand, and extended it toward the animal to test its response. It remained prone and merely opened its eyes in weary resignation. They were not yellow. Warm brown. No coyote. This was a dog.

Dix relaxed. He reached over and gently ran his hand over the dog's side, his fingers dropping over each rib. He poured water from his bottle into the dog's mouth and watched its tongue work gratefully over the liquid. He got a stout stick, pried the pan of the trap apart, held it open with his boot, and the dog pulled its foot free. Dix gently probed the paw with his fingers. The dog flinched, so he stopped. The skin was torn and broken; Dix hoped nothing else was. He slung his binoculars around his neck, shoved his water bottle into a pocket, cradled the exhausted dog in his arms, and slid her butt-first—because he'd seen it was indeed a female—into his pack and hoisted her onto his shoulders. She settled her weight into the pack and rested her forepaws and chin on his shoulder as he walked, darting her tongue out from time to time to lick his ear. When he got home, he took her to the barn and set her down in a long-empty stall. He was concerned she might be infested with fleas, ticks, worms. She made no effort to get free of the now-grounded backpack, merely let her head fall into a pile of straw and closed her eyes.

"I'll be right back," he said, backing out of the stall.

He quickly cooked up a batch of rice and ground venison. He also dialed the vet, made an appointment for the next day, and got some advice on how to care for her in the meantime. He brought a bowl to her, blowing on it as he crossed the yard to cool it down. The dog's nose twitched at the smell of the food. She wriggled out of his pack, ate delicately, and merely sighed when he took the bowl away.

"Not too much too soon," he told her, patting her head.

He wiped at her injured paw with some antibiotic ointment and wrapped it with gauze. She licked his hand as he worked. He left her once more and raced to the feed store, where he got a collar, leash, kibble, and flea treatment. As he was standing in the checkout, he picked up a bag of rawhides and a stuffed toy. He drove back home, gave her water, a little more food, and squeezed the small container of flea treatment between her shoulder blades. He tucked the stuffed duck between her paws. He was going to leave her then. He thought he'd let her rest. But as he backed away, she whimpered. When he started to close the door, she scrambled to get up.

"Easy, easy girl," he said as he reentered the stall and slid to the floor, his legs stretched out, his back against the boards.

She crawled over to him and rested her long jaw on his thigh. He stroked her head and she slept. The barn grew dark as the sun set. He did not move for more than an hour, and when he did, it was merely to stretch out alongside her in the straw and go to sleep himself.

The next day, the vet gave her an exam and told Dix he wanted to take X-rays. As the dog recovered, he popped the films into a viewer. Dix saw the outline of white bones and a strange scattering of white dots.

"What are those?"

"Birdshot."

"Someone shot her?"

"Yeah. Not uncommon for hunting dogs to get in the way from time to time, but she's not a hunting dog. Someone must have thought she was a coyote."

Dix shook his head.

"There's more," the vet said. "One of her back legs was broken and never set properly, so it healed crooked. There's some arthritis there, and in the other leg as a result. She's also mostly blind in one eye. Hard to say why. I suspect blunt-force trauma."

"You mean someone hit her. Hard."

The vet nodded. "Nothing to do about the shot," he said. "It just sits in the muscle tissue, mostly. She'll probably always limp. Might bump into things from time to time, especially as the vision continues to deteriorate. Good news is the trap actually didn't do much damage. Just surface wounds. Fortunately, she was sensible enough to not fight it and cause greater injury."

"Or maybe just too tired and weak," Dix said.

"That, too," the vet said. "Lucky for her that you were wandering by."

"Not much luck in her life so far, I'd say," Dix grumbled.

"No, but her luck's apparently just changed," the vet said as he filled out paperwork. "Got a name for her?"

"Seems like you just named her for me," Dix said.

"Lucky?"

"Yup."

"Well, it fits."

"She's so sweet and trusting," Dix said. "After all that abuse, how can she be such a nice dog?"

"Dogs don't hold on to the bad," the vet said. "They have no emotional attachment to the things that others do. They don't take things personally. They live in the present."

"Too bad more of us humans aren't like that."

"Take her home, feed her, love her, and she'll be your best friend for the rest of her life," the vet said as he closed the file.

Dix did just that.

Sally lay in her bed, swathed in blankets, listening to the sounds of the house waking up, something she herself did not want to do. The floors creaked and complained as the women rose and began to move about. The plumbing rattled the walls as the old pipes filled and emptied of water. It was impossible to hide in an old farmhouse. It telegraphed every movement. The sounds were fewer than they had been. Quieter, too. There were only three or four women living here anymore, by Sally's count, although she paid little attention to them. Even fewer than before. Restrained movement and hushed voices had entered the air since Miranda had died. Sally knew the other women hadn't liked Miranda much. She was too sweet, too guileless, too eager. Her pregnancy had made her too special to Darius. But still. Her death was a blow to everyone. There had been too many losses recently. The winter had been brutally cold. Spring had come and summer was starting to extend the days, but Sally could not warm herself to the season. Darius's mood was foul as well. He spent ever more time in his attic, and when he emerged, his eyes were hooded, his face grim, his expression glowering.

Sally had screamed and yelled and railed at him for days after Miranda's death. Weeks. How could they have done this? What had they been thinking? Why hadn't they called an ambulance?

They hadn't realized how serious it was, he'd insisted. She'd passed away in the middle of the night. They were all asleep and found her in the morning.

How could they have cremated her? Sally had demanded.

It's what she wanted, what she asked for, he'd hollered, pacing. She had no family, she had broken with Dix, there was no one to notify— The Source was all she had, all she wanted, he'd told Sally over and over.

In a crazy way, it made sense. It was all true, within its own twisted logic. Sally could easily imagine Miranda, ill, delirious, in what seemed to be about the last month of a pregnancy she had refused to share with real doctors and Western medicine, asking for cremation. Still, Sally had been insane with rage and agony over her death. And guilt that she might have prevented it. Now she was spent of feeling and emotion, a dirty dishrag, twisted and wrung out.

She turned her head toward the window. The gray sky, thick with clouds, was only a few shades lighter than it had been hours ago. The place had become intolerable to her, as emotionally polluted as the trailer the women continued to clean and tend and fuss over, as if it were a suppurating wound. She was rarely here anymore, creeping in at night after everyone had gone to their rooms, rushing away in the mornings before anyone was stirring. She no longer pondered why she stayed, just how and where and when to go. Still, she felt like a stagnant pond.

Today, she told herself. *Today, I will get the paper, look for apartments, find a way to walk away from this cursed place and not look back.*

She would rouse herself, go into town, sit at the Fishing Hole diner, circle items in the "For Rent" section, jot down phone numbers from notices stuck to the tackboard, go to the library, and get online. She'd start. Today.

She heard footsteps overhead. Darius. This was early for him. The sounds were of purposeful movement. Also unusual. Eventually footfalls on the stairs. Then down the next flight to the kitchen. A few words, lost as they drifted upward, filtered through the house. Dishes dropped into the sink. The back door opened and closed. The truck departed down the drive. Strange. When was the last time he'd left the house? How would she know? She was almost never here. Lying in bed like this, her body weighted down with weariness, was unusual for her. The back door opened and closed a few more times, and the house settled into quiet. Now would be a good time to get up, while everyone was out in the barn, the garden, trying to clean up the trailer. For what, they would not say. The whole place had become eerily quiet these last few weeks, a hush filled with secrets. Sally pulled on a faded terry-cloth robe and shuffled out of her room.

I need a long, scalding shower, she thought, hoping the hot-water tank had not been emptied by the others.

As she closed the door to her room, the small displacement of air caused another to crack open. The door to Darius's room. Always shut tight, an impenetrable barrier. She'd tested it before. Always locked. And yet here it was, left unlocked, unlatched. Again, strange. He must have been preoccupied. The dark, slender gap beckoned to Sally, an irresistible invitation.

She listened to the rare silence that surrounded her. No one else was in the house. She tiptoed through the doorway and up the dim stairway to the close attic space. The ceiling came down to the floor in sharp angles. A small, high, dirty window leaked in a little light. Sally stood at the top of the stairs, took shallow breaths of the fetid air, and looked around. There was a lumpy futon mattress with a faded quilt and flattened pillow. A stray sock on the rough wood floorboards. A small pile of dirty and discarded clothes. A mug with a dry, dark stain in the bottom and a chipped plate with a curled rind of cheese on the floor next to the bed. A dead plant, the soil cracked and desiccated. A pile of cheap spiral-bound notebooks and a plastic card file box on a small table next to an old schoolroom desk.

So grim, Sally thought. *So depressing.*

She listened again. No sounds came from the house. She squatted down and picked up a notebook. Many pages had been torn out, leaving serrated strips of paper stuck in the twisted coil. She opened the cover and flipped through the pages. Most were blank, but the first few were covered in dark blue ink. The writing was heavy and florid, the pen pressing down so hard in places it had torn through the paper. There were snatches of what seemed to be poetry, free-form verse attempting to articulate indistinct and incoherent ideas. Short paragraphs read like outbursts of thoughts that were thinly veiled counterfeits of well-worn bits of advice from his collection of self-help and back-to-nature books.

This was the manifesto he'd been working on? There was not even the hint of one original notion to be found.

There were a plethora of doodles along the margins of the pages. Geometric and hard-edged shapes had been scribbled everywhere as if, without anything substantive to record, Darius's restless pen had searched for some other outlet. Sally replaced the notebook and did not examine any of the others. She knew, without looking, that if she opened them she'd just find more of the same. She opened the file box and pulled out a card. There was a woman's name at the top, a real name, not one of the groovy names they took for themselves. *Anne Reynolds.* So plain. No one she recognized. There were a few notes. *Massachusetts. Father = banker. Not very bright. Outward Bound. Rehab for prescription pills. Credit cards = trust fund. Overweight. Said she ran away. Has car??? Bites fingernails.* Sally fanned through the cards. Each had similar notes about other women. Sally closed the box. She felt dirtied by what she had found. Darius was worse than she'd even imagined—dumber, less substantive, more petty. Like a bratty high school girl.

She stood and looked around. A shirt spilled from the open drawer of a small bureau. A stained towel hung limply from a bent nail in the wall. She didn't want to touch anything else. She moved to depart. As she turned, something in a far corner of the room caught her attention. It took her a moment to focus into the gloom. There, in the darkness under the eaves, was a pile of backpacks, purses, shoulder bags. The things the women had carried when they arrived here. Emptied and discarded. Sally wondered why were they here, why was he collecting them. She took a step closer to the pile. Everything in it looked deflated. She bumped into the desk. She looked at its empty surface. There were a few childish scratches there. A few doodles she recognized as Darius's. Some impulse caused her to lift the top. What she saw took her breath away. Scattered there in the well within were a dozen bank and credit cards. Several checkbooks. A handful of driver's licenses with photos of tidier, better-dressed versions of the women who had come, gone, or stayed at The Source.

Christ, Sally thought. *How did he get these cards and checks? How did he convince them to hand everything over? Did he make it a condition of their staying?*

Then, she realized that this was how he controlled them, kept them here, funded this place. She imagined his cloying, charming voice, speaking as if in confidence, telling an addled woman that it was necessary for her to break her ties with the evils of capitalistic society and, in order to show her commitment, give him all the tools that the bureaucratic, financial, and government institutions used to control her. Then, without those tools, they could hardly return to the world they had left. Darius hardly had to steal their money when they seemed so willing to abandon their common sense.

Sally lowered the desktop and left the attic.

That's it, I'm done, it's over, she told herself as she showered and dressed, her thoughts racing and pinging inside her head. *I've got to get out of here. I'll find a rental. I'll stay at a motel. Anything is better than this. I can't watch over this shit show anymore. I can't fix it. So what if he stops paying me? I can't take any more of his money, because it's not his money. It's never been his money. The first ten grand, his down payment, was his grandfather's, and now it's from these trust-fund hippies. And I'm complicit in his swindling these people. If I take stolen goods, I'm a goddamn accomplice. I won't do it anymore.*

She dragged a brush through her hair, spread balm over her lips.

Miranda's dead. She was the only thing keeping me here. I don't give a flying fuck about the rest of them. Let them rot out here. Kick them out. Get them evicted. How hard can that be? Fuck, I'll just give him the damn place. I'll sign it over to him and curse him as I do, she thought as she crossed the muddy yard to her truck. *Curse this whole godforsaken place.*

Her nervous fingers fumbled with her keys, they fell from her hand, and, as she bent to pick them up, the noisy rumblings in her own head were suddenly supplanted with a new sound. A cry. A muffled wail of raw, unadulterated confusion and discomfort. Sally tilted her head and listened. Maybe it was just a cat. Some feral things fighting or fucking each other. It was that time of year. She'd heard them howling a few times recently, their screams waking her suddenly but briefly in the dark of night. But then, through the damp air, it came again. Crying. She moved toward the sound. Without realizing it, she took several steps on the path to the trailer. Not a cat. A human sound. A baby sound. A baby was crying. In the trailer. The sound was now hushed. Someone was comforting—or maybe just silencing—a baby.

Fuck. Fuck. Fuck, Sally thought as she squatted in the mud. The trailer. The busy, secretive hustling and bustling out there. The snatches of conversation with Miranda about Darius's desires to raise her child.

It all came together.

The baby didn't die with her mother. The baby was here. Miranda's baby. They were hiding the baby right here.

Dix eased his way back into life. He started answering his calls, returning messages, getting back to work. Lucky limped along behind him in the house, a few steps from his heel, a constant trip hazard every time he turned around. She followed him into the bathroom, watched as he brushed his teeth, and sat outside the shower as he bathed. She moved from sleeping on the floor alongside his bed, where his bare feet had always found her first thing in the mornings, to sleeping in the bed with him and the cat, her cheeks huffing and her paws twitching against his back as she ran and ran inside her doggie dreams. If he pulled on his coat, she went to the front of the truck, her tail slowly wagging, so he was obliged to pick her up—her back legs were too stiff to jump in—and take her with him wherever he had to go. He found the feel of her chin on his thigh and her fur against the palm of his right hand as he drove soothing.

Dix also had a pile of paperwork and accumulated mail to sort through. Some of it was Miranda's. She felt so distant to him, he began to wonder if the closeness he had once felt with her had been some kind of mirage. He felt the loss of her less personally, as if it was something she had done to herself, not to him. Which he supposed was true. But she lingered in his life, detritus that had blown in on a bad storm and now needed to be cleaned up. He had to open envelopes, think about the storage unit, organize her finances, figure out what to do with her things, her stuff, the parts of her that were left in the world. He began with the most recent bank statements that had arrived over the last months and that he had left untouched. He was afraid to discover how much she'd given to Darius. He didn't want or need the money himself; he just didn't want Darius to have it. Whatever was left, he figured he'd give to a charity that served local, underprivileged youth. That's what she'd always wanted—to help that population. Her work with Darius had been useless in that regard. At least in her death, she could provide the service that had escaped her in life.

Dix sliced open an envelope. He was gratified to see at the top of the page that there was still a fairly substantial balance. He unfolded the statement. There had been three withdrawals: $500, $250, $750. He wondered what she might have needed those funds for. Then he looked at the dates. It was impossible. It didn't make sense. Until suddenly it did.

Dix did not require an appointment. When Warren Bessette's secretary knocked gently at his door and told him who was in the outer office, Warren stopped what he was doing and waved at her to show him in.

"Hello, Marshall," Warren said, unfurling himself from behind his cluttered desk as he stood to greet Dix.

Warren knew everyone called the man in front of him Dix, but after so many years of creating documents in the man's full, legal name—Marshall Dixon Macomb—he found it difficult to use the nickname. Warren had handled many transactions of both a business and personal nature for Dix—mostly sales, deeds, and lease arrangements. As well as the deaths and estates of his parents. Warren knew that Dix owned more land in various parts of the Adirondack Park than anyone suspected. It had come to him through the deaths of family members as well as through smart purchases, funded partially by shrewd lease arrangements, timely sales, and desirable rentals. Dix was a wealthy man who cared nothing for wealth but plenty for land. Which he wanted simply to protect. Warren understood that Dix did caretaking work not for the income but because he liked to take care of things—it was that simple. He was just a man bent on improving things.

Warren had heard people in town speculate that Dix had gravitated to Miranda for her money, and that she chose him in rebellion against her father. Warren knew, as no one else did, including Miranda, the multitude of ways this assumption was wrong. Warren was the only person in the world who understood the depth of Dix's resources. He also understood why a man like Dix, in a place like this, where most people's daily lives were defined by scarcity, would want to keep the details of his own abundance quiet.

Warren gestured to a seat, his large, long-fingered hand sweeping through the air between them. But Dix remained standing, so Warren did, too. Two tall men, one in canvas, the other in pinstripes, loomed, vulturelike, in the small office. They were quiet together. While Warren waited for Dix to start, he assessed the man's face. The crow's feet at the corners of his eyes looked raked in more deeply than he remembered, and the vague slump that had sometimes crept into his shoulders looked permanently sealed in place. Dix finally descended into a chair with a sigh. Warren lowered himself to his own seat and watched as Dix took six bank statements from the file folder in his hand and spread them out neatly on the desk, smoothing their folds. Dix's long index finger bobbed over the pages as he pointed to several numbers. Warren saw that each month contained one, two, or three withdrawals in amounts ranging from $100 to $800. There were no deposits, other than interest on the capital. Miranda's name was on every page.

Dix pointed to the date at the top of one of the statements. "Miranda moved out to that commune about a month before this," he said.

Warren nodded. He'd heard gossip about the situation. He didn't need any more information or speculation on the topic.

Dix pointed to the most recent statement and said, "Miranda died, Warren."

This was something Warren had not known. Miranda. Dead. It was impossible. And yet, totally believable at the same time. The final tragedy in a tragic family saga.

"Out there. In that shithole," Dix went on. "She was pregnant. She got sick, I guess. I don't know how or why. A fever, I think. She'd rejected technology, meat, Western medicine. Maybe she and the baby died in childbirth. There was no way for me to find out. She'd stopped talking to me. She was completely caught up in that place. In that man." Dix choked and then coughed down his emotions. "She . . . I guess she asked to be cremated out there. It's all so wrong. I tried—"

"I'm sorry, Marshall," Warren broke in. "You're saying they cremated her? Themselves?"

"She asked them to," Dix said. "It's all so wrong. But she'd changed so much, Warren. I tried to get her back. To talk sense into her. She wouldn't listen. Everything I said seemed to push her farther away. What could I do? What could anyone do? She was an adult. She had no family. No one had any claim on her. Not even me." Dix's words sputtered out.

Warren kept his eyes on the numbers on the statement in front of him. They began to swim. Miranda. Beautiful, sweet Miranda. Now dead. Like the rest of her forsaken family. He blinked back tears. The numbers came into focus again.

"She died at least six weeks ago, Warren," Dix said. "Maybe longer. I don't know. But that's when I found out she was gone."

Warren's eyes flicked over numbers on the statements, dates and amounts. He began to nod. The withdrawals on all the statements were similar. But several had taken place after Miranda died.

"The bastard is stealing her money," Dix said. "He's probably been doing it all along. Probably doing it to all the women out there. You know I don't care about the money. But now I have something on him. There was nothing I could do before. Now I have what I need to shut him down, don't I? For everything he's done to her. To who knows how many other people."

Warren nodded more vigorously. He looked up at Dix. The men locked eyes.

"We need to take him down," Dix said.

"Yes," Warren said. "Yes, we do."

Dix was in his backyard, trying to teach Lucky to fetch. She was so solemn, a creature both wise and world-weary. He was hoping she'd learn to play a little. A behavior he realized was as unfamiliar to him as it was to her. But Lucky remained uninterested in the ball. She'd watch it fly over her head and then turn her attention back to Dix, her tail slowly wagging. Dix fetched it himself.

He had his arm cocked back, about to throw the ball again, when he heard an unfamiliar sound. Tires on gravel. Strange. No one ever came up his driveway. Lucky's ears pricked up, she huffed once or twice, then barked. This was a first. Dix had heard her voice only when it was muffled in her doggie dreams. She padded away from him. Another first, her voluntarily leaving his side.

Strange day, he thought. *And now a visitor.* Probably just a lost person, hoping for directions, thinking he or she had turned down a small road instead of a private drive. He followed his dog, rounded the corner of the house, and there was Lucky, tail ticking back and forth in the summer sunshine, sniffing at a woman.

She was not old, not young, could be anywhere from her late twenties to midthirties, Dix thought. Not tall. Not short, either. Not unattractive, just not that interested in doing what it might take to be attractive. Bluntly cut, medium-length, medium-brown hair. White T-shirt of the kind that came in a three-pack. Well-worn Levis, lightweight lace-up boots of the kind that came from a store that sold guns and ammo along with clothes. She was squatting on her heels in front of a small truck with a lot of rust on it, petting his dog.

His dog. He had a dog. It seemed a long time since he'd had anything he cared about.

"'Lo," he said, not quite ready to close the distance between him and this other person, not wanting to intrude on what was happening between her and Lucky. "Can I help you?"

The woman stood. Lucky returned to Dix and sat on his feet. The woman looked at them both, her gaze full of frank assessment.

"Nice dog," she said, not answering his question.

"Thanks. Found her in the woods." Dix rarely offered information unsolicited. Something in this woman's matter-of-fact stare invited him to share more than he normally would.

"Good place to get a dog," she replied. "Certainly good for her, anyway, I imagine."

Dix waited. There was something very vaguely familiar about this person, a face seen maybe once, from a distance, in an unfamiliar context.

"You Dix?" she said.

It was more a statement than a question. He didn't respond. She didn't seem to need affirmation.

"Not quite what I expected, from what Miranda told me," she continued, crossing her arms over her chest.

Dix stiffened.

"Relax," the woman in front of him said. "I'm Sally. And I'm on your side. I'm on her side."

Dix was suddenly displaced from his own yard. He was back in a tree, binoculars to his face, watching as this woman flicked a cigarette into Darius's face. He tried to stop a smile that was forcing its way to the corner of his lips. Sally noticed.

"What?" she asked.

"Nothing," he said.

The woman in his driveway stood silently, watching him, waiting for him. It was not an unpleasant experience. He knew, instinctively, that her judgment would be as fair as it would be accurate.

"I saw you once," he finally said. "From a distance. You flicked a cigarette in the face of someone I don't like much."

She squinted at him. "Well, I don't like him much, either."

"That was apparent."

"Where were you?"

"Up a tree."

"Of course you were. Tree stand?"

"None available in that particular tree. For the view I was seeking."

Sally scuffed her toe in the drive. Then she lifted her face and looked around. Dix followed her gaze as it skimmed over the property and house, lingered on the garden beds with the bamboo teepee trellises filling with pea vines and the heat-retaining cages around his tomato plants, passed his mud-spattered truck, moved through the open doors of the garage and barn where his tools and equipment were neatly arranged, and then over to the cat emerging from the shrubs under the tree line. She looked at his mutt dog again, and then her eyes settled back on him. "No offense, but Miranda didn't really get you, did she?" she said.

The question stung, not because she asked it, but because it was true in a way he had never considered before.

"No," he said. "I don't suppose she did."

"We have something to discuss," Sally said.

"I have no plans for today that can't wait," Dix said, gesturing toward the house.

"You may be adjusting an awful lot of plans by the time we're done," Sally said as she walked toward him.

By the time the coffee had dripped through and Dix had filled their mugs for a second time, Sally had given him a quick accounting of herself and sketched in a summary of how she came to be involved with Darius and The Source.

"Miranda mentioned you once, I think," he said. "Told me that Darius said you were his cousin. Renting a room out there."

Sally gave him a dramatic eye roll. "Yeah, that makes sense," she said. "At least around here where cousins sleep together often enough, too. Makes for more intimate family gatherings."

Dix was too agitated, waiting for what was to come, to laugh at her joke. He gave her a quick, polite grin of acknowledgment. It was the best he could do. He was preoccupied with a dark foreboding. He wondered what ax this woman had to grind, what she wanted from him. Maybe she needed his help getting the guy and his followers off her property. As much as he hated Darius, he wasn't sure he'd want to get involved. He had his own mess—well, Miranda's mess, yet another Miranda mess—to clean up. Maybe for once he'd say no to fixing someone else's problem. Why this woman would have put up with Darius's bullshit for as long as she had, he did not understand. But then again, he didn't understand much of what people did, why they complicated their lives in ways that seemed so obviously unnecessary and avoidable to him. He never could figure out why smart people did such stupid things. And the woman in front of him was obviously smart. Sharp and street-savvy, too, no doubt. She'd have to be to survive as a social worker around here. Just didn't apply the same logic to her own life as she did to others', apparently.

Sally took a sip of the hot coffee. "How much do you know of what went on out there, Dix?" she asked.

"Miranda was always pretty vague," he said. "Protective of the place. Said everything was secret because it was sacred. Silly stuff like that. I was out there a few times. But just briefly. Didn't see much. Pretty rag-tag for a supposed slice of heaven."

Sally stared at him. Hard. As though she were trying to figure out how to tell him what she had come to say. He shifted in his seat. There was something he wanted to know.

"Look," Dix said, "I don't know why you're here or what you have to tell me. But can I ask you something first? How the hell did Miranda die? Darius said something about a fever. Not that you can trust anything that asshole says. Did something go wrong with the pregnancy? I've always wondered. But there was never anyone to ask."

Sally's face darkened. "I don't know for sure," she said carefully. "But I'll tell you everything I can."

The previous winter had been long and brutal. Sally was cranky and frustrated with the weather, The Source, her job, her own inability to find a change she wanted to make. But she kept coming back because she had nowhere else to go. One frigid night, as she drove up to the farmhouse, her headlights illuminated what appeared to be the entire community gathered in the yard. This was something she'd never seen before. She parked the truck and cut her lights. It took her eyes a moment to adjust to the sudden darkness. First she became aware of the women as ghostly shapes in the dim illumination from the porch light and the full moon, high in the sky, and then the scene in front of her came into focus. The women appeared to be speeding up, hurrying their movements. Scrambling to finish. Because she was there, watching? Four or five of them moved in a strange circular motion around something she couldn't see. They darted in and out of the group. In between the moving bodies, Sally caught glimpses of a chair. Then, a person sitting in a chair. The other women's hands moved in circles. They were rubbing the seated person with something. Darius stood off to the side. His head was bent and his mouth was moving. He started waving his arms, encouraging the women to move faster.

What the hell?

A woman bent over and picked up a bucket. The others stepped back. She tossed its contents over the seated woman. The wave of water as it moved through the air glistened in the light from the porch and the moon.

"What the fuck?" Sally said out loud to herself.

Other women, one by one, picked up buckets or bowls or whatever they had filled with water and threw the contents at the seated woman. White rivulets cascaded from her hair and down her body. Just outside the group, Darius began to clap, slowly, methodically applauding their work.

This is insane, Sally thought as she opened the door to her truck.

A blast of freezing air clutched at her face. She threw the door closed behind her and moved toward the group. They twitched their heads toward her and went quickly back to throwing water on the seated person.

This is killing cold, Sally thought. *And whoever is in that chair is now soaking wet. This has to stop.*

She trotted into the scene, cursing at the women, shoving them aside and sending them slipping and sprawling on the ice rink they'd created. Her boots held, she stayed upright, and got to the woman at the center of the group. Phoenix. Tied to a chair. Blindfolded. Covered in soap foam. Dripping wet. Shivering and chattering her teeth.

"You people are fucking crazy," Sally hollered as she grappled with the strips of sheet that held Phoenix by the ankles, wrists, and chest to the chair. Her hands shook, but she managed to unbind the knots. "What the fuck is wrong with you?"

No one answered and no one intervened. They disentangled themselves from the frozen ground and stepped back. Darius lifted his chin and then raised his arm over his head.

"The cleanse is complete," he announced. "Sally may assist Phoenix with her recovery. Our work here is done."

Sally shouldered Phoenix to her feet, guided her into the house, and got her into a hot bath. Neither woman spoke for some time. They were both trembling from shock and the cold. Sally listened as the other women returned to the house and went to their shared bedroom. When her shivering subsided, Phoenix told Sally, in brief and whispered fits and starts, about the cell phone Darius had found, the mocking texts, how he had descended upon her at what had started out as a normal evening gathering, blindfolded and bound her, and exhorted the other women to participate in the cleanse. She said they were hesitant at first. Then he read the texts. They became eager.

"You've got to get out of here," Sally told her. Phoenix gave her a number to call. Sally went to the phone in the kitchen, tapped in the numbers, and gave the person who answered directions to the bottom of the drive.

"You need to get out of here, too," Phoenix said as she dressed in the layers of warm clothing Sally handed her from her own closet.

"I know, I know," Sally said. "I will. I will. I'll get out of here."

She clamped a hat on Phoenix's head, wrapped a scarf around her neck, and sent her out the back door.

I do need to leave, she thought as Phoenix's departing figure made its careful way across the yard, turned down the drive, and disappeared into the dark. But the image of Miranda, swollen with child, sleeping soundly in the other room, thankfully missing out on the evening's escapade, came to mind. Sally knew she wouldn't leave. Couldn't leave. Not yet.

Dix listened closely to Sally's story about the cleanse. Even after all he knew about the place, this behavior shocked him into a strange stillness. Dix thought about telling Sally what he'd found on Miranda's bank statements. But he held back. He wasn't ready. He shifted his weight and looked at this stranger at his table, wishing she'd get on with it. Explain what the bizarre ritual she'd described had to do with Miranda.

Sally sighed deeply. "Dix," she finally said, her face filled with weary regret, "Miranda got it into her head that she wanted a cleanse, too."

"What?" Dix said, appalled. "A cleanse? Like that? Why?"

"She had some crazy idea that she needed it, needed to be cleansed of the past before the baby came. So the baby could come into the world 'pure and unburdened,' she said." Sally shook her head. "She wasn't well. It was like that baby was sucking the life out of her. She wouldn't go to a regular doctor, just relied on the advice of a woman there who claimed she'd been a midwife. I tried and tried and tried to get her to go to a doctor. Then I tried and tried to talk her out of the cleanse." Sally's voice pled for forgiveness. "I warned Darius over and over not to do it. I threatened the other women if they participated." Sally dropped her face into her hands. When she looked up, her eyes were red but dry. "I thought it was over. I thought she gave it up. She told me she wasn't going to do it. I was wrong. They all just placated me and did the cleanse when I was out of town at a conference. They were afraid I'd call the cops or an ambulance. Which I would have. I don't even know how they knew I'd be gone. I had no idea how they were spying and snooping on me. On each other. I was gone ten days. That's all it took to go from cleanse to sepsis to . . . Oh, Dix. I'm so sorry, Dix. I'm so sorry."

Dix wanted to slap her, to back up to the start of his day before she came up his drive. He wanted everything to be her fault so he had someone to punish. He wanted to bang his head on the table and smash his fist into the wall. Lucky lifted her head from her paws, looked at him with concern, and slunk out of the room. Dix turned his face to the window. There were robins on the lawn, probing for worms. Miranda used to love to watch the robins. He decided he would waste no energy on fruitless displays of rage. He would save that for dealing with Darius.

Dix turned his attention back to the woman sitting rigidly at his table. "Why are you here?" he asked her. "You didn't come here to tell me how Miranda died. You came here to tell me something else. What is it?"

Sally rolled her shoulders and straightened her back in her chair. "I came to tell you about the baby," she said.

"What baby?" Dix asked, stalling on this new, unexpected topic as confusion and alarm swirled in his mind.

"Miranda's baby," Sally said.

Dix stared at her. As if he didn't know, as if there could be any other baby.

"I thought the baby died with her," Sally explained. "I thought the baby may have even caused her death. Both their deaths."

"Right," Dix said. "That's what Darius told me." Wasn't it? He remembered clearly the look on Darius's face, the sad, slow shaking of his head when Dix had asked about the baby. He couldn't remember all the details of what Darius had said. But he could remember the feelings. Feelings he didn't want to recall.

"The baby didn't die," Sally said. "They have her. They're hiding her. They're hiding Miranda's baby so they can raise her according to all his whacked-out principles."

"Why are you telling me this?" Dix asked, frustrated, growing angry that this woman was dragging out all these things he'd packed up, put away, gotten over. She was making a mess of all the emotions he'd so carefully organized. "What does Darius and Miranda's baby have to do with me? Why does Darius have to hide his own baby?"

Sally stared at Dix. "Darius and Miranda?" she asked, confused. "Darius's baby?"

Dix returned her look, challenging her to explain.

"You thought . . ." Sally couldn't complete her sentence. She dropped her head to her chest. "Dix. The baby. Not Darius's," she stammered. She lifted her face and met his eyes. "It's *your* baby, Dix. Yours. That's why I'm here."

My baby? My daughter?

Sally shook her head in dismay.

Dix remembered Miranda similarly shaking her head at him. As Darius had done when he'd asked about the baby. They'd deliberately misled him. Deceived him. He could not fathom that degree of falsehood. The heat of betrayal filled his body. He began to tremble. He wanted to vomit.

Miranda had become pregnant by him. Not Darius. Flashes of her, of the two of them in bed together, cluttered his head. The feel of her hair. The smell of her skin. The release of his climax within her. He'd made her pregnant. He had a baby. Alive. His baby. Out there. Without him. He dropped his face to his hands. Then he looked directly at Sally.

"That bitch," he said. "She stole my baby."

"Do you want to go get a cup of coffee?"

They were standing outside the back door to Warren's office. The three of them had just spent two hours together, sharing information and coordinating plans.

"Probably a bad idea." Dix answered his own question before Sally did. "Can't be seen together."

"Right," Sally said.

"You going to be OK going back out there?"

Sally shrugged. "Just like Warren said. We have to keep things as normal as possible until we can get a warrant and social services all lined up."

Dix stared off into a tree, where a squirrel was scolding them. "You sure they'll tell you in advance when they're coming in so you can get out of there?"

"Believe me, the last place I want to be when the state shows up with a warrant and a baby seat is anywhere near Darius. Let them deliver the eviction notice. Let them fill up their banker's boxes with evidence. I'll make sure they tell me when it's going to happen and when it's done."

It was a hot day, even in the shaded parking lot. Dix lifted his ball cap and wiped his brow with his forearm.

"Don't worry, Dix," Sally said. "It'll be OK. They'll move fast because of the baby. They'll get her safe and into foster care quickly. Then it's just a DNA test, home visit, paperwork, and she'll be with you."

Dix wanted to cry. Dix never wanted to cry. But he had grown unaccustomed to kindness. He was unused to receiving help. He had never needed it before. He was also scared about becoming a father. And just as scared he'd never have the chance.

Sally crossed her arms over her chest. "I do wish I could be there to see his face when they arrive, though," she said. "Wipe that smug grin off his pretty little mouth."

"Yup," Dix said. "And to watch him realize we are the ones who snuffed out his little world."

She nodded. "Too dangerous, though," she said. "It's bad enough he'll know it was me. I'm going to be watching my back for a long time after this."

Dix expelled a breath. He shifted his weight from foot to foot.

"What?" she asked.

"I have an idea," he said.

Sally's colleagues told her when they were going in. The night before it was to happen, she got back to The Source in the diffuse dark of a summer night. She ran into no one as she ascended the steps to her room. She heard footfalls above. Darius was in the attic. The lights were still on in the trailer. She stood at her window and watched as two of the women returned to the farmhouse.

For the last time, Sally thought as the lights went out across the yard. *This is the last night you will spend in my house.*

Dix wanted Sally at his place two hours before dawn. She was afraid to go to bed, afraid to sleep. As if staying awake, on guard, could guarantee success. She listened to the floorboards creak as Darius dropped his weight onto the thin mattress overhead. A toilet flushed and a door closed across the hall. Silence descended. Sally stood by the window, watching the sky darken, waiting for everyone to fall into a deep sleep, then tiptoed around her room, packing a bag with a few essentials, a couple of changes of clothes. She hadn't made any preparations for what was about to happen. She hadn't wanted anyone to discover she was making plans of any kind. She'd stay in a motel for a few weeks, or however long it took to evict them. However long it took her to recover some equilibrium. Then she could come back. Then she'd figure out the next step.

Her bag packed, there was nothing to do but wait. She pulled up a chair and watched the moon rise, the stars prick the black curtain of sky.

Hours passed. She'd never sat this still for this long. Her mind emptied. There was nothing for her to do. This was a new feeling. She checked her watch. Soon it would be time to go, to slink down the stairs to her truck and drive away. After this morning was over, nothing would be the same again.

A muffled cry spilled into the dark. Sally listened as it was hushed.

Don't worry, little baby, she thought, making the words a singsong in her head. *Don't you worry. Soon, this will all be over. Soon, your real life will begin.*

Mine, too, it occurred to her. *Mine, too.*

An hour later, she was making her way up Dix's driveway. He met her with a steaming mug of coffee, which she gulped gratefully.

"I'm not exactly an outdoorsy person," she said. "More a Stewart's doughnuts-and-pizza type. Just so you know."

Dix smiled and said nothing. Their breath sent vapor up between them in the cool predawn air. She handed him the mug when it was empty. He took it indoors and came back with a small pack. He patted the side, indicating a slender metal thermos.

"There's plenty more coffee in here."

He handed her a headlamp and then helped her stretch it over the ball cap on her head and switched it on for her.

"Ready?"

She nodded. "Just remember that my legs are, like, half as long as yours, and I'm completely out of shape. Just quit smoking. Sort of."

They broke into the woods at a spot where Sally would never have even noticed a trail. She kept her head bent so the headlamp illuminated the small track that wound through the dense trees. She lifted her face from time to time and was reassured by Dix's broad back only a few steps in front of her. They trudged on in silence. In the dark, Sally had no sense of time. Her thoughts were hazed with sleep deprivation and anticipation. Her feet moved forward in mindless repetition broken only by the occasional stumble over a clod of dirt or a downed sapling.

Dampness seeped into her shoes and through her socks. Movement kept her toes from getting chilled. Eventually, her lungs began to burn with exertion.

I've got to quit smoking for real, she thought. *I've got to eat better. I need to start taking care of myself. Today is a fresh start. Today, everything changes.*

She was too stubborn to stop or ask for a rest. But her body was about to give up on her. She heard birdsong. Silhouettes of individual trees crept out of the dawn. Small breaks of sky overhead were just becoming visible through the canopy. Her legs were heavy, her muscles spent. She slogged forward and bumped into something. Dix. He'd stopped in the track.

"Sorry."

He was looking upward. "Tired?" he asked, peering down at her.

"Didn't sleep well last night," she said.

"Me neither."

"At all, honestly."

"Me neither." Dix removed her headlamp and then his own, stuffed them into the backpack. "We're here."

Sally looked in the direction of his gaze and saw an enormous tree with a smooth gray trunk and stout, horizontal limbs. It reminded her of an elephant. The ground around it was littered with bristled nut casings. Dix motioned her forward, interlaced his long fingers into a stirrup, and held it out for her to step into.

"Are you fucking kidding me?" she said.

"C'mon," he said. "Up we go. Don't want to miss the show."

Dix helped her climb from one limb to the other, alternately supporting her from below or lending her a hand from above, until they were settled on a branch high enough up that Sally dared not look down. Dix took a wide piece of webbing from his pack, wrapped it around her waist and the tree trunk, and then ratcheted it snugly closed. Supported in this way, Sally began to relax. Dix then draped a pair of binoculars around her neck, put a granola bar in her pocket, and handed her a cup of coffee from the thermos. His movements were so fluid and understated, it took Sally some moments to register how well he was caring for her. Only he wasn't, really. He was just doing what needed to be done. Just being Dix. Even knowing him as little as she did, she could see that.

Through the dissipating mists, the increasing light, and a gap in the layers of tree branches, Sally could see the lopsided roofline, sagging porch, scrappy yard, and, farther in the distance, a corner of the trailer at The Source. The whole place looked uninhabited. Long uninhabited. It was hard to believe she had left there only a few hours ago.

Dix shifted on his branch and Sally gestured at him with the thermos. He shook his head and brought his binoculars to his face. They didn't talk. They just stared and waited. Sally felt light-headed. Her hands trembled slightly. No sleep, no breakfast, this absurd errand, and this crazy perch. But still, she was glad she was here. She wanted to see this. She took a few bites from the granola bar. Another gulp of coffee. Then Dix leaned forward and Sally looked in the direction his binoculars were pointed. Red and blue lights were coming toward them, up the driveway. Sally reached for her binoculars and, in the process, dropped both the coffee and the bar. She didn't look after them, just listened to the metal cup ping off a few branches, echoing in the morning stillness.

By the time she got her binoculars focused, there were three cars blocking the drive: a beige late-model, state-issued sedan, which she knew was driven by a social worker; a black unmarked police car; and a police cruiser with its lights spinning in the early-morning air. She figured there was another cruiser positioned down by the road. Doors slammed in quick succession as the cars emptied. She watched two officers, one plainclothes and the other uniformed, step up to the farmhouse. The cop rapped his knuckles on the door, but the sound didn't carry to her perch. Another cop and the social worker went to the trailer and did the same. The farmhouse door opened. The trailer's did not. The cop took Darius by the arm and cuffed his hands behind his back before walking him to the cruiser and pushing him into the backseat. Then they pushed their way into the trailer, and the social worker emerged a few minutes later with a blanketed bundle over her shoulder. The cop and beige car drove away. The two men left went into the farmhouse. They'd be in there awhile, Sally knew. Looking around. Collecting evidence. Telling the women to leave. The scene returned to empty silence.

Sally stared into the void. She felt Dix, on the other side of the trunk, doing the same. It seemed there should have been more. She didn't know what sort of more she wanted, but something. The whole scene had transpired in minutes. Darius didn't resist. The baby didn't even cry. And yet, everything was suddenly, dramatically different. She let her binoculars fall to her chest. Dix did the same.

"She's safe now?" he whispered.

"Yes, Dix. Yes, she is."

He cried then. Sally could feel it—the regular, gentle vibration as the tree shook in solidarity with his sobs. It didn't last long. One sustained spasm of grief and relief. Once he had composed himself, they climbed down. Dix helped Sally through the awkward process, showing her where to grab hold, taking her foot and placing it on a branch, supporting her with a palm on her back. When they were on solid ground again, he retrieved the cup she had dropped and left behind the granola bar for the squirrels but took the wrapper. They found the trail and started back, now walking slowly in the filtered light and warm breeze of a bright summer's morning. There was no hurry, nowhere either of them needed to be. They were unburdened. They had set everything in motion, and now other people were taking care of all that had been weighing on them.

They walked as if in a daze. All the stress and anticipation had left them both, a rush of water down a drain. The amped-up emotions would return, they both knew. The world of lawyers and court cases was waiting for them. But for now, for this brief interlude, they were simply two people on a walk in the woods. Sally watched as Dix stopped and squatted from time to time to examine something near or in the trail. He picked apart bear scat and owl pellets. He pointed out faint deer tracks and ginseng patches. He named the trees and mushrooms, the birds that flittered past and the ones that beat their bills against a tree.

"Guess dealers pay good money for these wild things now," he said. "Mushrooms. Ginseng. Sell them to restaurants."

"Foraged," Sally said. "That's what they call it now, right?"

Dix nodded.

"Another one of those words from away," she said. "We always just called it picking berries."

"Yep. If those downstate diners knew some redneck collected this stuff in a dirty old basket, the chefs couldn't charge extra for it. *Foraged* sounds so much more romantic, you know?" Dix said. "Kind of like using the word *cabin* for some three-thousand-square-foot, totally decked-out second home with every modern convenience."

"Right. No single-room shack in the woods held together with roofing nails, filled with beer cans and cigarette butts, smelling of sweat, wood smoke, and animal blood."

"You're a local, then?" Dix asked, recognizing how much was already, natively understood between them.

Sally said the name of a town that was also that of a prison.

"Guard?"

She nodded, answering his question of what her father did for a living. As if there was anything else her father might have done in that place.

"Disability now. For a long time," she added.

Dix sighed, and in that exhalation she heard sympathy—for her and also for all those people in this part of the world who relied on "the system" to stay alive.

They walked on. The light slanted through the dark branches and green leaves. Sally took in the layers of mature evergreens and deciduous trees, the smaller shrubs and young, spindly saplings reaching toward the intermittent patches of sun. She inhaled the damp, tangy smell of decay. She listened to some animal chattering up in the canopy. She heard a long, plaintive bird call. She realized that the bulk of her life had been spent experiencing the woods from the road and the inside of her car. She had seen them as little more than a wall of trees that hemmed her in on her way to somewhere else and occasionally jettisoned a frantic squirrel or startled deer into her path. She had never tried to experience, much less enjoy, the mountains that surrounded her as a park, a place of beauty and recreation. That was all for rich visitors and tourists. To the people she knew, the woods were a place to hunt, trap, fish, snowmobile, or avoid. She did none of the former, so instead she did the latter. Maybe this was something else she could change. Maybe, these woods could be something she could take some time to enjoy. Like Dix did. Dix, who was clearly as comfortable in the mountains as in his own backyard, was stopped in the path up ahead, adjusting his boot laces.

Waiting for me, Sally thought. *Giving me a rest. A polite man. A nice man. What a concept.*

"You from around here?" she asked when she caught up.

"Yup," Dix replied. "Dad's side's been here for generations. Mom was from away. They met in architecture school."

"Architects." Sally tested the word. "I've never met an architect. Where'd you go to school?"

Dix looked mildly amused at Sally's question. She figured most people he encountered assumed he hadn't gone to college. At least most people from away.

"Started at Paul Smith's. In forestry. Finished at St. Lawrence in environmental studies. You?"

"Plattsburgh State."

Sally knew she and Dix were filling in worlds of information about each other. She, blue collar, state school, state job. He, professional parents, private college, self-employed. But they were both locals, shaped by the land and the weather, the people and their pervasive view that life was pretty much just a long, hard slog.

They began to trade stories that had recently been in the news—or just in the air. There was the man who had allegedly offered a woman he befriended at a bar his life insurance policy if she helped him commit suicide by driving over him in his car. Which she did, and got jail time instead of an inheritance. The contractor hired to do some grading work at the cemetery who got drunk, climbed in the tractor in the dark, and pushed several dozen headstones over a cliff and into the river before rolling the machine over on himself, crawling out, falling asleep in the grass, and waking up with no injuries save a bad hangover. The young man who beat his wife to death and was pulled over for a broken taillight by police who found her corpse, three young children, and a litter of puppies in the car. The café owner who drank all night from her own bar. The pancake breakfast fund-raiser that raised $2,500 for the local girl without health insurance who got internal injuries and a leg broken in several places when she crashed her ATV, and how small a dent that would make in her six-figure hospital bills. The need for volunteer firefighters and medics. The closing of the post office.

All the talk of local tragedies seemed to remind Dix of something.

"What about those rape charges against Darius?" he asked Sally. "Do you know anything about that?"

"Yeah. That was Cassandra, the meth head," Sally said. "Turns out, sadly, I know that girl. And her entire fucked-up family. Of course her name isn't really Cassandra. I hadn't seen her for a long time. She'd changed a lot. Aged a lot. Meth will do that to you. It was her daddy who got her pregnant. Mother denied it, said the girl was making it all up, and Dad acted like it was no big deal. Said his daddy had done the same to his sister. That's why they dropped the charges. After the story came out, the father disappeared. The rest of them—alcoholic mother, junkie brother, and mentally challenged baby—moved up to Plattsburgh. Living in some old motel converted to Section 8 housing. All part of the system, now."

Dix sucked his teeth. "American Dream," he said.

"White-trash version."

They popped out of the woods and into Dix's yard. They stood blinking in the high midday light.

"Sally," Dix said, his voice quiet, "once you get the all-clear, once the police tape comes down, can I come out there with you? I'd like to see it again. See where—"

Sally stopped him by putting a hand on his arm.

"I'll call you. I promise. First thing."

They nodded at each other. It was time to go. It was time to get ready for whatever was coming next.

Dix stood in the doorway to the room his mother had always referred to as the guest room. The walls were painted a soft green, the underside of a leaf. Plaid curtains in subtle shades of lichen and pumpkin hung in the windows. There were twin beds covered with laundered-soft chenille spreads. There were pillows in the same fabric as the curtains. An antique desk with a needlepointed chair. A closet with only a few empty hangers. His mother loved the sight of those twin beds, he remembered. They always brought a smile to her face. They must have seemed full of hope to her. Hope for good company. And, it occurred to him, probably for grandchildren.

He thought of Miranda. She seemed so far away, as though their time together had been a decade ago. He was surprised by how few actual memories he had of her. She was more of an idea than a person. Already. And yet. They had a daughter.

Dix had never changed a diaper or held an infant. He'd never soothed a crying baby. He'd never bandaged a scraped knee or helped a kid with homework. The previous night, after dinner, in those dark hours when insomnia kept him awake, when other men might be furtively turning on their computers to look at porn, he hunted the Internet for information about babies' developmental stages and key parenting tasks. He fretted over car seats and Montessori education, vaccinations and bullying, summer camps and cloth versus disposable. He finally went to sleep and dreamed that the dog lying next to him was instead a wild, woods-reared and fur-covered child who didn't understand a word he said. He woke up frightened that before he even got a chance to try being a father, he was going to fuck it all up. He was scared that he already had.

He wished his mother was there to help him. It crossed his mind that Sally, with all her rough pragmatism and coarse good humor, would be good counsel and company for this chore. He noted, without sadness or remorse, that he was not wishing Miranda was there. Then he'd have her to take care of, as well as all this. It was a harsh, cold thought, but it was also true. She should be there. He recognized that. But he had grieved for her as much as was possible. That job was done. He had other jobs to do now.

He was reluctant to disturb the room. Doing so would disturb his mother's memory but also disturb fate. What if, in spite of everything, this room was never filled with a crying or laughing or sleeping child?

Platitudes filled his head. Get your house in order. Be in a position to succeed. You'll rise to the occasion.

He'd rather clean out two decades of compacted manure from an old barn than do this. Cleaning out a barn was something he knew how to do.

He stepped over the threshold. He began by taking down the curtains—they seemed too adult and tailored for a little girl's room. He rubbed a cloth over the sills and removed the fine dust of disuse. He wiped the glass with vinegar and water. The light that came through the sparkling windows was a soft caress. There was nothing to hide from in here. Maybe he didn't need curtains at all. He calculated where he'd put a changing table, small dresser, and crib once the beds were moved out. For now he'd put them in the back bedroom, his old room, where he used to sleep with his feet sticking out from under the blankets; that room was now empty of everything but camping gear. There was space in there. Maybe his daughter would like the twin beds. Someday. When she was old enough. When she wanted to have a friend over to spend the night. As impossible and improbable as that seemed now. Dix pulled back the bedspreads, folded them, placed them in the linen closet. He stripped each bed of its musty, unlaundered-for-years sheets and threw them in a pile next to the washing machine. He then picked up a pillow but immediately dropped it back onto the bare bed, as if he'd been burned.

He watched for what he had felt inside the stuffing, and eventually the pillow began to move of its own accord, throbbing and pulsating. He placed his hand gently on its taut surface and felt the life squirming within. He went to the kitchen, found a scissors and a small basket, returned to the guest room—the baby's room, his daughter's room— and gently split open the skin of the pillow. The white stuffing, released from its container, spilled apart, revealing at its center a gray field mouse with a cluster of pink pups at her teats. Dix used both hands to gently scoop all of them and a generous amount of pillow filling into the basket. Then he took the whole family to a protected corner of his wood shop and tucked them on a shelf behind a box of spare tractor parts and a bucket that held his tree-climbing harness. He grabbed a palm full of birdseed from the can where he kept it locked up from the raccoons and spread it out near the basket.

This is ridiculous, he thought. *Most of the time I'm filling gaps, sealing holes, and setting traps for these guys.*

This time was different. He covered the furry mouse and her naked pups with a layer of pillow stuffing, tiptoed backward out of the shop, and just before closing the door, turned the heat up by a few degrees.

Dix had a fantasy that his first visit with his daughter would take place in a park where they could dash about on the green grass in the sunshine. He wanted to see her move and play, watch the wind riffle her hair, which he imagined hung down to her shoulders in blonde streaks. He wanted to take her for an ice cream cone and wipe the melted drips from her chin.

But instead, she was just a baby, and he was being summoned by the State of New York to some bureaucratic office building where he had to find a room designated by just a number and a letter.

The day came on stormy, the skies gray and angry, the air thick with late-August humidity. Dix drove along wet, black streets to an imposing brick building with white pillars out in front. He bypassed the grand front entrance and pulled around the back, where he had been directed. He had been too eager, so worried about all the things that might have caused him to be late—bad weather, slow farm equipment, getting turned around—that he was now twenty minutes ahead of schedule. He sat in his truck and stared out the window. It had started to rain again. Heavy drops flung themselves from the sky and pinged their damp desperation onto his windshield. He didn't bother turning on the wipers, just let the water run in rivulets that obscured his view. With nowhere else to go, his eyes wandered around the cab of his truck. His toolbox, big enough to occupy the entire foot well on the passenger-side floor, was surrounded by several coffee-stained paper cups. A grease-marked coat and pair of beat-up boots were against the far door. He ran his callused, scarred hands over the gimpy, coyote-looking dog curled up at his side. He raked his hands through his recently cut hair and over his cheeks, still stinging slightly from the close shave he'd given them that morning. He was wearing a pair of flat-front khaki pants he'd bought for the occasion, a button-down shirt he'd freed from a several-year-old dry cleaning bag in the back of his closet, and a pair of plain brown loafers he had taken from a box on a shelf, which had sprouted a thin layer of mold he had to polish away before levering his feet into them. He was wearing his newest, cleanest Carhartt jacket, but still, there was a tear on a pocket and a stain on the sleeve.

He didn't feel much like father material. He also didn't have a clue how to turn himself into father material.

Nonetheless, it was time to go in.

He was met by a squat woman. She looked like a larger woman who had been inadvertently shrunken in a dryer. She was also young and aggressively unadorned, wearing a stiff, matronly, beige pantsuit, and her hair was pulled back tight into a black rubber band. A spray of acne dotted her forehead. She held out her hand.

"Aline Beaudin."

Dix shook her hand but forgot to say his own name.

"We need to establish a few ground rules for this first visit," she said primly, looking at a clipboard.

A clipboard. A strange accoutrement for a visit with a baby.

"The rules are merely to protect the child until paternity and custody are established by the court."

The child. The child without a name. The child he wanted to name. But didn't dare. He was told not to touch her. Not to call himself "Daddy" or "Papa" or anything that denoted himself as her father. Not to be affectionate, emotional, or demonstrative. He would be supervised. The meeting could be terminated at any time. He had thirty minutes. He was to be relaxed and act natural. Dix fought the urge to scoff at that notion.

He was brought to a room as beige and nondescript as Aline's pantsuit. A low table at the center. Brightly colored plastic toys scattered across it. A woman, an older version of Aline, Dix thought, sat in a chair that was too small for her, talking in a low voice to something he could not see. Aline stepped away from him and settled herself in a chair in the corner of the room with clear sight lines to the table. The other woman stood, motioned to Dix to come forward, and left the room. Dix hesitated. He'd never fit in that chair. His knees would be banging against his chin. He took a step forward. Now he could see to the other side of the table. There was a baby in a small seat, on a blanket on the floor. She was holding a stuffed toy in front of her face. She was talking to herself. Babbling. Dix took another step forward. One more and he'd be at her side, looking down at her. His heart hammered in his chest. The baby flung the toy away and looked directly at him.

Dix took in a sudden inhalation. In that first moment, when his daughter turned and met his eyes, all he saw was Miranda. The sharply angled cheekbones still swathed in baby fat were Miranda's. The frank and puzzled expression was Miranda's. The broad brow was Miranda's. He blinked at the heat that had risen in his eyes. Slowly, the vision of Miranda dissipated, and in its place, he was left looking at a pretty baby with sandy-blonde hair and gray eyes who was staring back at him. Her eyes opened slightly in alarm. He was a stranger. Not her father. Just a stranger. Dix took the final step he needed to reach his daughter's side. He folded himself like an old-fashioned wooden yardstick until he was in a kneeling position. His knees clicked in protest.

"Hi," he said. His daughter was already about four months old. With all Sally had told him, he had figured that Miranda probably got pregnant the previous fall. She probably didn't realize for a few months—her periods were always erratic, and she wouldn't have started to show until she was about twelve weeks along. She had moved to The Source in mid-December. The baby had been born in early May. She may have been a few weeks premature, delivery brought on by the stress of the cleanse. Fortunately, she'd had several days with Miranda, nursing, bonding, before the sepsis took over. She was healthy. She was here. That was all that mattered.

The girl continued looking at him, gurgled, and stuck her fist into her mouth.

"Whatcha doing?" he tried.

She tossed her head back and forth a few times. Dix was terrified she'd start crying. Then what would he do? But she just scrunched up her nose. She seemed colossally unimpressed with the strange and so-far-useless adult next to her. Which was exactly how Dix felt about himself. Whatever swell of emotion had risen in him when he first saw her quickly ebbed and left him feeling washed out and empty as a deserted beach. He had no idea what to say or do. None of his online reading had prepared him for how small and not-yet-verbal she would be. Dix stretched his legs out in front of him like two felled trees and picked up the toy she had cast aside. It was a stuffed giraffe. He danced it a few inches from her face. She reached forward and grabbed it from him. He let her have it. She tossed it away again. They repeated this routine a few more times.

She's already trained me to fetch, he thought. *Something I still can't get Lucky to do.*

Then she stuffed it in her mouth. Dix was worried about germs—the thing had been on the floor—but he couldn't remove it without touching her, which he'd been told not to do. And he didn't want to make her cry. So he just looked at her. He silently counted her fingers and toes. He looked at the chubby folds of flesh at her elbows and knees. Her skin reminded him of bread dough. Her gray eyes stared at him, unblinking, even as she mouthed the stuffed animal. Dix wanted to do something with his overgrown hands. He picked up a picture book from the table. He held it up so she could see it and turned the pages, pointing to the animals and naming them *cow, dog, cat, chicken.* She slapped at the book. He turned a few more pages. *Pig. Donkey. Rooster.* He went slowly. He went back to the beginning. He didn't want the book, the visit, to end. But inevitably, Aline eventually stood and looked at her watch.

"That's enough playtime now. Time to go home," she said.

Home. The word made Dix flinch. Aline approached. The little girl, his daughter, ignored her and tried to grab at another toy. This pleased Dix. He showed her how to turn the knob on the toy so it made noise. Aline stood there for a few moments. The baby squealed in delight. Dix turned the knob again. Aline took another step forward. The baby gripped the toy. Aline removed it from her hands and lifted her from the seat. Now the baby squealed in frustration. Aline ignored her cries, patted her on the back a little too hard for Dix's taste, then carried her across the room and out the door. They left Dix, marooned, alone, in the middle of the room.

Dix picked up Sally at the motel. It was a low-slung building with twelve evenly spaced doors surrounding a parking area of broken asphalt. The Dew Drop Inn. She was waiting in a plastic chair outside the door marked with a seven. She climbed into the cab and they sat, just looking at each other, taking each other in, for several moments.

"Are you ready for this?" he asked.

"Are you?"

He shifted his gaze out the windshield. "Going to be strange to go back. See the place all empty this time."

"Just ghosts," Sally said.

They spoke little as he drove. Sally asked how his meeting with his daughter went, and Dix said it sucked. She told him not to expect much until he had her home. Dix asked if she knew what her own next step was; she shook her head. Dix suggested she take her time. He stopped the truck before turning into the driveway. A torn piece of yellow police tape flapped from a fence post in the hot, humid summer air, the words *Do Not Cross* tangling as they twisted in on themselves in the restless breezes. He made his way slowly and silently up the drive.

"I feel like I'm going to a funeral," he said as he turned off the truck.

"You are," Sally said as she pushed her door open and stepped into the yard.

Dix followed her into the stifling, stagnant day. No animal sounds came from the barn—they had all been sent to rescues. No human sounds came from the house—everyone had been evicted. The trailer was still swathed in yellow warning tape, with a notice that included a prominent skull and crossbones glued over the door. Dix and Sally stood there, heads swiveling, as they took in the sad sense of desolation that hung over the hollow. Dix had hoped to find whatever remained of Miranda's pyre. Sally had told him she had no hopes whatsoever.

"Creepy," she finally said.

"Whatever I thought I'd find out here," Dix said, "I won't."

"Me neither. Let me get my stuff, and let's put this place in the rearview mirror."

But still, they stood as if at a graveside. A curtain in one of the farmhouse windows luffed. Then, Dix felt the hair on his arms stand up. The breeze had stilled. And the window was closed. Something had moved the curtain from within. His eyes scanned the windows. A silhouette made indistinct by the dirt covering the glass flitted by.

"Dix . . ." Sally's voice was a whispered warning.

"Get into the barn," Dix said as the handle on the front door of the farmhouse began to move. "Run."

Sally did as she was told. Just as she slipped into the darkness of the barn, the farmhouse door opened. Darius stepped onto the porch, blue eyes blazing and white teeth sparkling.

"Well, well. Dix."

The men stared at each other.

"Darius, you're not supposed to be here. You need to leave."

"What, Dix, did you think I'd still be in jail? For all your petty accusations?"

Dix knew Darius had made bail. He wondered if he'd used Miranda's money to do so. "I don't care where you are, Darius," he said, "as long as it's not here."

"I was there. In jail. Where you put me."

Dix shook his head slowly back and forth. Saliva pooled in the back of his throat. "You put yourself there," he said.

"She gave me that money, Dix," Darius said simply, as if he were describing the weather. "She wanted me to have it. She wanted to invest in this place, in what we were doing here." He spread his arms wide. "She wanted to invest in me." He poked his thumb aggressively toward his chest. "In me, Dix. In me!"

Dix remained silent.

"We had plans, she and I," Darius continued. "Such plans. Things you'd never understand." He began pacing back and forth on the porch. "We were going to start a whole new way of life. A whole new generation. A new way for humans to interact with the natural world."

Darius stopped moving. He stared at Dix.

"You're going to ruin that child, Dix," Darius said. "You almost ruined Miranda, but you failed there. Thankfully she had the life she wanted for a while, at least, before Mother Nature reclaimed her. Now you'll have another shot at ruining a life—her baby's."

Dix ignored the insults, refused to take the bait. "Time to go, Darius," he said. "This is no longer your house."

"Your house. My house," Darius said with a dismissive wave of his hand. "You and your conventional notions of ownership. None of us owns anything, Dix. Everything's merely on loan to us. Even our own lives." Darius stared down at him from his perch on the porch. "Why are you here, Dix? It's not your house, either. It's Sally's house again, right? Where is she, anyway? Where'd she run off to? Did you two come here looking for some piece of Miranda? Trying to find forgiveness for what you did, for your part in the mess you made? For ravaging her life? For ruining mine?"

Dix hung his head and shook it slowly back and forth in disgust. When he looked up, Darius was holding a brown paper grocery bag.

"I have a surprise for you, Dix," Darius said. "I found this in Sally's room. Who knew that sour bitch could be so sentimental?" He reached into the bag and came up with a fistful of golden corn silk. He tossed it high overhead. Dix looked at the strands quivering in the air as they caught the long rays of afternoon sunlight. Not corn silk, no. Hair. Human hair. Miranda's hair, freed from her head. Golden strands drifted down toward Dix, settled across his shoulders, mingled with his own hair, tickled the tops of his cheeks. Darius threw more into the space between them.

"Here she is, Dix. Here she is!" he sang out.

There was so much of it. Such beautiful hair.

"This is all that's left of her," Darius taunted him. "Take it, Dix. You've taken everything else! Her life is over. So is mine. There's nothing left for you to destroy, you bastard. You bastard!"

Dix closed his eyes. This was the hair he had run his fingers through when he tried to comfort Miranda, the hair he had felt thrown over his bare back when she curled against him in the night. This was the hair he had twisted in his palm when he had penetrated her, trying to make the baby that he'd waited for and who was now waiting for him in a foster home. The hair was dead. Miranda was dead. Dix felt fully free of her. A whole new life, an actual life, the life contained in his daughter, was waiting for him.

When he opened his eyes again, Darius was there on the porch, legs braced in a wide *V*, staring at him. It was an expression Dix had never seen before, empty of everything other than conviction. The brown bag had been tossed aside. There was something different in Darius's hand now, something small and dark.

Of course there was. Darius was all about the grand gesture. He'd want to go out in a big way. Dix crouched, ready to duck or dive away. But Darius didn't point the small, dark thing at him. Darius's arm went up, up, and then bent as he pointed the gun in his hand to his own temple.

Dix bolted then, his boots pushing and slipping against the gravel, Miranda's hair swirling in his face. He ran not away from Darius but toward him. He pumped his arms and flung himself across the porch steps just as an explosion of sound deafened him. He crashed to the porch, his limbs entangled with those of the man beneath him.

The impact blackened Dix's world. Sound came back as the first sensation, but all he heard was an intense ringing in his ears. He wondered how long he'd been out. Feeling returned more slowly, a severe stinging in his arm, and a warm, wet puddle between his fingers where they were jammed against the floorboards, pinned beneath something heavy. There was hair in his mouth and eyes. Not his own. Not Miranda's. Dix looked past the dark brown ropes stuffed in his face. He saw brown, aged wood. The porch. He heard a groan. Not his own. The body beneath him began to squirm. He heard his name spoken in a familiar voice. Then, the sound of a car barreling and bouncing up the drive. Skidding to a stop. He turned his face toward the swirl of pulsating red-and-blue lights. A booted foot landed near his head. Muffled, hurried voices. A hand on his arm.

It's over, he thought. *It's over.*

Sally visited Dix in the hospital every day. At first, they told her she wasn't allowed. Family only. She told them he didn't have any. She brought paperwork on the case and told them she was his social worker. They shook their heads at her. She came back with Warren. They let her in.

Dix was sedated. She watched him sleep. She watched the steady blips on the machines. The doctors told her he was going to be fine, but he'd lost a lot of blood. The bullet had gone through his arm, and there was a chance he'd lose some of its function. She sat and waited for Dix to wake up and felt something she'd never felt before. Fear. Fear she'd done the wrong thing somehow, that she could have, should have, handled this whole thing differently, that she had caused him irreparable damage. Irrational fear that he'd blame her, hate her for the whole mess. Fear she'd lose him. Fear over the many different forms that loss could take.

Then, on the fourth day, she walked in and he was sitting up in bed, talking to Warren. He looked at her. He smiled. He patted the edge of his bed, motioning her to sit. She gratefully lowered herself to his mattress. They talked about the baby. She was doing fine in foster care. They'd take care of her for as long as he needed to recover, Sally assured him. They didn't mention Darius. Dix asked Sally how she'd called the cops that day out there at her grandmother's farmhouse. She reminded him of the small spot of cell-phone reception Phoenix had found. Dix thanked her for saving his life, his daughter's life. Sally shrugged and looked away, thinking of Miranda, wishing she could have saved her, too. Dix sighed. She asked if he was tired. He nodded. She'd said she'd come visit again. He thanked her for coming, not knowing how many days and hours she'd already spent there at his bedside. She squeezed his hand and left him to sleep and heal. Then, out in the sterile and desolate hallway, she did something else unusual for her. She cried. She cried and cried, releasing the pent-up tears of a long-held worry finally relieved.

It was a crisp fall day, the green leaves changed almost fully to red, orange, yellow, and brown, the air tinged with the taste of winter's chill, as Dix stood at his back door, waiting. A late-model sedan came slowly up the drive. Aline stepped from the car and handed Dix a small bag holding the very few things his daughter was bringing with her. Dix set the bag on the porch. Aline freed the child from the constraints of her car seat and carried her to Dix. Aline tried to transfer the baby to him, but the moment proved awkward. His arm was still weak and his daughter was shy. She held on to Aline, buried her face in her shoulder. Dix was nothing to her. He knew this. He knew it would take time. But he was not above wishing for a miracle of filial recognition.

Dix and Aline waited. The baby did not budge. Dix held up a finger, silently asking Aline to wait a moment, then walked back to the house and let Lucky outdoors. When Aline peeled the little girl from her shoulder and directed her attention to the dog, she squealed with delight and wriggled to get free. Aline set her down on the lawn. Lucky sniffed at the new creature and then gave her hand a few tentative licks. The girl giggled and patted the dog, who immediately flopped down next to her and rolled over to show the baby her belly. Aline waved at Dix and scuttled away, leaving Dix looking at the child at his feet and feeling a wave of nausea and loneliness. He swallowed it down.

"Lucky," he said, kneeling next to her in the grass.

Dix's daughter looked at him, her eyes suspicious and inquisitive. They were Miranda's in shape and color but deeper, darker in expression. Already.

"Lucky," he said again, passing his hand over the dog.

The girl tried to say something, some garbled sound that was a complete mangling of the dog's name. And yet, an effort to copy him. He hoped, anyway.

"Yes," Dix said. "Yes, that's it. Lucky."

And he thought, *Yes, lucky indeed. Lucky we have been, and lucky we'll need to be.*

Activity helped Dix get through that first afternoon and evening. There were toys to play with and exploring the house and yard and feedings and bath and then, thankfully, bedtime. He laid his baby in her new crib, among her new sheets, and she was asleep before he had time to arrange the blankets. He backed out of her room.

Now he had no idea what to do with himself. Fears and worries pursued him through the house. He wished he'd gotten a nanny. He berated himself for trying to do this alone. He was also deeply relieved no one was there to see him struggle.

What if she got sick? What if she's already sick, some nasty disease swirling in her bloodstream?

He paced and paced and then he heard a whine and stopped pacing. It had come from Lucky. She was lying across the threshold to the baby's room. Dix joined her there. He stood in the doorway for a few moments and listened to his daughter's small, puffing breaths. Then he stepped into her room and watched her sleep. He looked at the fawn lashes where they rested on her cheeks, the curlicue of cartilage that was her ear, the line where her flesh turned deep pink and became her lips. She was beautiful. She was real, alive, healthy. Here. He wanted to touch her, but she seemed suddenly a forbidden museum piece.

The phone rang then. The sound, breaking into the evening quiet, shocked him. He stumbled over the dog as he ran to try and stop the sound more than to actually discover who was calling. The harsh noise stopped. The baby didn't cry. Dix sighed hello into the phone. It was Sally, checking in. Wanted to know how Day One had gone. The depth of his relief at the sound of her familiar voice was so complete, he almost collapsed under the release of it all.

"She's here. She's sleeping," he whispered.

They spoke a little, he told her about how strange and wonderful and awkward it had all been, and then they sat together in silence, listening to each other breathe into the phone.

"I know you said you didn't want to name her until she was home," Sally said. "Have you chosen something?"

"Colden."

"After the mountain."

"And the lake. One of the prettiest of the High Peaks."

"Colden Macomb. It's perfect. I'm happy for you," Sally said. "I'm sure you'll take her there someday."

"Couldn't have done it without you," Dix said.

They said quiet good-byes. Promised to stay in touch. Dix slid to the floor, his back against a kitchen cabinet. His ribs ached. His arm throbbed. He was afraid to go to sleep. Afraid he'd wake the next morning and Colden would be gone, disappeared as miraculously as she'd arrived. He wished Sally was there. No, he wanted to be alone. He wished everything had turned out differently. No, it was perfect for him to do this on his own. He was angry at how everything had turned out. He was grateful it had turned out at all. He gave in to the emotions pinging in his chest and allowed tears to drip like heavy dew from his eyelashes.

He heard movement from Colden's room. He ran the back of his hand over his eyes, scrambled to his feet, and went to her bedside. Her soft, sweet face was twisted and red, her hands balled into tiny fists. She turned her head back and forth on her chubby neck and whimpered. *She's having a bad dream,* Dix thought. He feared it was about him. She quieted down for a moment. Then her face flamed again and her mouth stretched open in a silent cry. Dix reached into the crib, his hands splayed above his baby like gnarled roots. He waited, hoping she'd settle herself. Instead, she started crying the frustrated sobs of disturbed sleep and strange visions that will not resolve themselves to wakefulness. Dix dropped his hands, wrapped them around her body, and lifted her from the crib. She squirmed like a cat that did not want to be held. He held on, spread his fingers against her back, tucked her in the crook of his good arm, and coaxed her head against his shoulder. Lucky paced and whimpered at his feet. Dix felt Colden twist back and forth until her hand found her mouth. He felt her breath heave once or twice in her chest. Then her full weight slowly descended against his body. She pushed against his sore ribs. His bent arm protested in pain. He ignored his body's complaints and walked back and forth in the room, just three steps for his long legs each way. Colden's small tears came through his T-shirt, warm, wet spots against his skin.

"You're OK," he said. "You're OK."

She sighed once, her breath settled into a steady rhythm, and then she stopped crying.

"We're OK," Dix said. "Shush, shush, shush."

She sighed again, chewed on her knuckles, squirmed herself into a deeper spot within his arms, and fell asleep.

"We're OK," he said again. "It's all going to be OK."

He felt the delicate pressure of his daughter in his arms, the rise and fall of her birdcage ribs against his chest, the puffs of her moist breath against his collarbone. Something moved inside him, a warm ether. He felt suffused with the feelings of steadiness, protectiveness, and responsibility. His body seemed to hum with the sensation. He smiled, bent his head to his daughter's, and breathed her in.

Dix had been out of the hospital for almost two months before he saw Sally again. They'd spoken on the phone a few times, but Sally was hard to reach and Dix was usually interrupted midsentence by Colden pulling something off a shelf or disappearing under a piece of furniture or simply screaming at the top of her lungs for what seemed to be the mere joy of it. Finally, one evening when Colden was asleep, Dix made a cup of tea and dialed Sally's number.

"Come visit," he said, without introduction, surprising himself. "Come meet her. Come see what you set in motion."

The appointed day dawned with the soft, warm glow of gentle late-fall light. As he shaved that morning, he looked not just at the stubble he was shearing away but at his face itself. He looked at himself as someone else might. It was not a handsome man that stared back at him from the mirror, certainly not in any conventional sense. Certainly not like Darius. He saw a craggy face with deep-set eyes, prominent brows and cheekbones, a somewhat jutting chin. The last year had aged him. There were new creases around his eyes and mouth that came from worry, not weather. His home had changed, too. It was now an obstacle course of toys and baby gates. He wondered if Sally would find him absurd.

When she drove up, Dix stood in the doorway of the house. He wanted to see her from a safe distance. It had been a while. He felt unsure of himself. He needed to be reminded who she was. She got out of her car and stood there. Though she, too, seemed unwilling or unready to close the gap between them, Lucky felt no such inhibition. The dog squeezed between Dix's legs and raced to Sally's side. He watched the dog and woman greet each other with an exuberance he was afraid to display. Sally looked well. She was not a beautiful woman—a bit too square in her body and face, with eyes that played hide-and-seek in the depths behind her cheekbones and brow—but there was a raw frankness to her face that Dix found trustworthy. She was much more appealing and without the sense of danger that often emanated from a woman more accustomed to using her looks to gain attention.

Sally glanced up from the dog and smiled at Dix. She fluttered her fingers at him and started to cross the drive, Lucky dancing in between her feet. *She has a lovely mouth,* Dix thought. Her skin looked brighter, smoother. He wondered if she'd finally quit smoking for real. She looked trim. He wondered if she'd given up doughnuts and frozen dinners. She looked happy. He wondered if she was in love with someone.

He stayed where he was and let her come to him. Sally pressed by him in the doorway, still smiling, without a greeting, and went directly to Colden, where she was babbling on the kitchen floor. Sally squatted and produced a small toy puzzle of many bright plastic pieces that elicited an instant gurgle of approval from the baby. Lucky joined them, and the dog, woman, and child splayed out together. Dix gathered plates and glasses. Sally asked if he needed help. He shook his head.

He took the coffeepot and a bowl of salad out to the deck. Came back for dishes and cutlery, some applesauce and cubes of tofu for Colden, then took a quiche from the oven and a large bone from the pantry and brought them outdoors. The day had bloomed into clear sunshine, with a light breeze. Indian summer. Cold was coming. But not yet. Not today. He arranged everything on the table, put the bone on the deck for the dog.

"Hey."

Sally had appeared in the back doorway, Colden on her hip, Lucky at her heel. Colden had her fingers in her mouth, her head on Sally's shoulder. The breeze riffled the soft strands of her hair. Dix's chest filled with warmth at the sight.

"Quite the spread," Sally said, settling Colden and herself into their seats.

Dix served himself and Sally, fed Colden some applesauce, and dropped a handful of tofu cubes on her tray. He and Sally spoke quietly about the beautiful day, the dry summer, a woodpecker hammering at a tree, Colden's enthusiasm for her tofu, how he'd made the quiche, how happy the baby seemed, how pretty and thoughtful she was. They allowed long, empty spaces to gather between their sentences. They watched Colden play with her food. They watched Lucky chew her bone.

"So, how's fatherhood?" Sally finally asked.

Dix chewed on his lip, considering how to answer. "It's, it's . . ." He threw up his hands. "It's amazing and wonderful and terrifying and exhausting. It's a cliché, but I'm overwhelmed. By the love and also the work. And I feel bad sometimes that all Colden has is me, a rangy old bachelor."

Sally tilted her head at Dix and slipped a crust of quiche to Lucky. "Don't be so hard on yourself," she said. "You're a far better father than most of us get. And we've both seen what so-called good upbringings can produce."

Dix looked away, uncomfortable with the compliment—and the memories. "Any word on Darius?" he asked.

"Well, you gave him quite the concussion when you pounded him onto the porch. But, sadly," she said, grinning, "he recovered from that. Guess they've sent him home to his parents. They're supposed to keep him under control. Rehabilitate him. Pay off his debts. He got probation and a fuck-ton of community service. Blah, blah. Slap on his rich-boy wrist."

"Just so long as he's away," Dix said. "Just so long as he's back over the blue line."

"Next thing we hear from him, he'll probably be running for public office."

"Undoubtedly on some right-wing platform," Dix said, smiling. "What about you?" he asked. "What are you doing?"

"Found an apartment. Working. Thinking about law school. Studying for the LSATs."

"Law school? All these shenanigans inspire you?" Dix asked.

"Sort of," Sally answered. "But really, Warren kind of inspired me."

Dix raised his eyebrows.

"We had a couple of great talks in the hospital. During visiting hours. Waiting for you to wake up, those first few days."

"Thank you," Dix said. Warren had told him how much time she'd spent there. By herself. Even after visiting hours. Drove the staff nuts. "Thank you for being there for me."

Sally waved her hand dismissively. "Me and those machines. Listening to you snore."

Dix laughed. "I don't snore!"

Sally grinned at him. Dix imagined her watching him sleep, watching the lines blip on the monitors while he lay there, his body healing. It was an intimate vision. An intimacy he'd experienced without even knowing it. He wanted to thank her again, thank her more. He didn't know where to begin. And, once begun, where he would stop.

He asked her about the farmhouse. "What will you do with it now?"

"Post a few 'No Trespassing' signs and just let it rot into the ground," she said. "Too much bad juju out there. Let Mother Nature sort it out."

They both watched Colden inexpertly work a puzzle, attempting to position different-shaped blocks into inappropriate places. Even Lucky had sidled over as if to offer assistance. Dix wanted to ask Sally so many things. But his thoughts were all jumbled together and in the wrong places, just like Colden's toy. He conjured a distant memory of that odd collection of patched-together buildings, sinking into the mud. The place where his daughter was born and her mother died and was cremated. He imagined what the place might look like a few years from now, a decade from now, thirty years from now. A time-lapse video of the encroaching forest, tiptoeing deer, feral cats, a foraging bear breaking into the kitchen played in his mind.

"Hey," he said. "You want to take a little drive? There's something I want to show you."

"Sure. Sounds intriguing." Sally stood and began to collect the plates.

"Leave it," Dix said. "Let's just go. The ravens and chipmunks can have what's left."

Sally stepped away from the table, swooped down with a dramatic gesture of her arms, scooped Colden up, and swung her in the air.

She is so natural with her, Dix thought. And then, *So much more natural than I am.*

Sally loaded Colden in the car seat in Dix's truck. Lucky jumped into the foot well, and she climbed in after. She watched the familiar scenery tick by outside the window, the fallen leaves opening up the scenery. She breathed in the crisp, dry air and realized she felt happy. It had been a long time since she felt that way.

A few miles out of town, Dix turned into a once-wide but now-overgrown gravel drive. They drove past several **No Trespassing** signs. Sally started to remark on this, to ask why they were heading onto posted land, but instead she kept her mouth shut and waited to see where Dix was taking her. It could be his land; he could have posted it for all she knew. They drove up a gently curving slope for a half mile, then suddenly, the dense trees gave way. Sally furrowed her brow in question at the view that opened up in front of her. In the midst of an overgrown acre of what had clearly once been lawn, there stood an imposing log home with a broad front porch. Her eyes flicked over a large garage, barn, shop. Dix stopped the truck near what was left of a half-dead tree with a ripped and jagged snag where a full crown of branches had once been.

They both stared out the windshield in silence. The home had a sad air of desertion, of something once grand and now long forgotten. A sapling pushed up through the front porch. Weeds sprouted from the gutters. Empty planters hung from wrought-iron hooks. Lucky stood up between Sally's legs. Colden had fallen asleep. Sally listened to her light snores as she waited for Dix to explain.

"This," he finally said, his voice a whispered breath. "This is Miranda's house."

Sally surveyed the spread in front of her and imagined it in its more well-cared-for days. "They really were fucking rich, weren't they?"

"Rich in dollars. Poor in spirit," Dix said.

"White-people problems," Sally said. "First World problems."

"Yeah, but problems nonetheless," Dix said. "I guess I always thought of Miranda as having a kind of psychological limp. Healed crooked from whatever hurt her. Like my dog."

They both quietly opened their doors and slipped from the truck. Sally took several steps into the yard, toward the house. A squirrel chattered at them from where it clung to a gutter. One of the boards covering a window had fallen free. It swayed back and forth in a fitful gust of wind, held in place by a single screw. A tattered velvet curtain hung outside a broken pane.

"Who owns this place now?" Sally asked.

"I do," Dix said, his voice flat and quiet.

Sally blew air between her lips. "Miranda never knew you bought it, did she?"

Dix shook his head.

"Let her save money and save face."

Dix shrugged.

"And now you're giving it back to nature, aren't you?'

Dix nodded. "Some things can't be fixed," he said. "Some things just need to be let go."

Sally turned her head over her shoulder and looked at Dix where he stood near the open-doored truck. This was a good man. A very good man who had no idea how good he was. It took his eyes some moments to stop their wandering surveillance and come to rest on hers. She held his gaze for a long time. No joking now. No smart-ass or snark. She wanted him to know how dear he was to her. How much she admired and respected him. That she adored him. She made herself feel it, all of it all at once, because she wanted him to feel it, to know it so deep in his bones that the speaking of it became unnecessary. When she was sure he got it, that he had registered her feelings, understood and accepted them, she dropped her eyes.

There, she thought. *Let him chew on that for a moment.*

A moment was all it took. Two strides later, he was behind her, his long arms clasped around her shoulders, his chin resting on the part in her hair. She reached up and wrapped her fingers around his hand. She let her cheek drop until it rested on his forearm. Lucky trotted up and lay down at their feet. Colden, still asleep in the truck, murmured from deep inside a baby dream. Sally felt Dix snug his arms tighter around her. She smiled and closed her eyes. It felt like he was never letting go.

ACKNOWLEDGMENTS

With deepest thanks to:

The team at Lake Union Publishing, who make my literary life not only deeply pleasurable but possible.

All the individuals and organizations who preserve, protect, and maintain the Adirondack Park, where I have spent many—although not nearly enough—sweaty, muddy, bug-slapping, contented, contemplative hours.

Ned, for climbing so many mountains with me.

ABOUT THE AUTHOR

Photo © 2013 Brooke McConnell

Laurel Saville is an award-winning author of numerous books, articles, essays, and short fiction. Her work has appeared in the *LA Times Magazine*, the *Bark*, NYTimes.com, and other publications. She holds an MFA from the Bennington Writing Seminars and lives and writes near Seattle. She is also a corporate communications consultant and has taught and spoken at a variety of colleges and writing conferences.

Her memoir, *Unraveling Anne*, won the memoir category of the 2011 Indie Book Awards and was a runner-up to the grand prize winner at the Hollywood Book Festival. Her first novel, *Henry and Rachel*, a fictionalized account of her great-grandparents' lives, was a finalist for a Nancy Pearl Award from the Pacific Northwest Writers Association. Connect with Laurel at www.LaurelSaville.com.